CANARIES

CANARIES

ALEX MAKEPEACE

Elsewhen Press

CANARIES

First published in Great Britain by Elsewhen Press, 2025
An imprint of Alnpete Limited

Copyright © Alex Makepeace, 2025.
All rights reserved

The right of Alex Makepeace to be identified as the author of this work has been asserted in accordance with sections 77 and 78 of the Copyright, Designs and Patents Act 1988. No part of this publication may be reproduced, scanned, stored in a retrieval system or transmitted in any form, or by any means (electronic, mechanical, telepathic, magical, or otherwise) without the prior written permission of the copyright owner. No part of this book may be used or reproduced in any manner for the purpose of training artificial intelligence technologies or systems. In accordance with Article 4(3) of the Digital Single Market Directive 2019/790, Elsewhen Press expressly reserves this work from the text and data mining exception.

Psalm 39 quotation taken from The Holy Bible, New International Version® NIV® Copyright © 1973, 1978, 1984, 2011 by Biblica, Inc. Used with permission. All rights reserved worldwide.

Elsewhen Press, PO Box 757, Dartford, Kent DA2 7TQ
www.elsewhen.press

British Library Cataloguing in Publication Data.
A catalogue record for this book is available from the British Library.

ISBN 978-1-915304-87-2 Print edition
ISBN 978-1-915304-97-1 eBook edition

Condition of Sale

This book is sold subject to the condition that it shall not, by way of trade or otherwise, be lent, re-sold, hired out or otherwise circulated in any form of binding or cover other than that in which it is published and without a similar condition including this condition being imposed on the subsequent purchaser.

This book is copyright under the Berne Convention.
Elsewhen Press & Planet-Clock Design are trademarks of Alnpete Limited

Designed and formatted by Elsewhen Press

This book is a work of fiction. All names, characters, places, governments, political parties, media organisations and events are either a product of the author's fertile imagination or are used fictitiously. Any resemblance to actual events, organisations, activists, states, places or people (living, dead, or morally corrupt) is purely coincidental.

BBC, Newsnight, Question Time, Radio 2 are trademarks of The British Broadcasting Corporation; Bluewater is a trademark of Blueco Limited; Boots the Chemists is a trademark of The Boots Company PLC; Burger King is a trademark of Burger King Company LLC; Capital Radio is a trademark of Global Media Group Services Limited; Channel 4 is a trademark of Channel Four Television Corporation; Chelsea FC is a trademark of Chelsea Football Club Limited; Conservative is a trademark of C & UCO Services Limited; Duke of Edinburgh Award is a trademark of The Duke of Edinburgh's Award; Eurostar is a trademark of Eurostar International Limited; Ford is a trademark of Ford Motor Company Limited; Gay Times is a trademark of Gay Times Limited; GB News is a trademark of All Perspectives Ltd; Guinness is a trademark of Diageo Great Britain Limited; Harrods is a trademark of Harrods Corporate Management Limited; Harry Potter is a trademark of Warner Bros. Entertainment Inc.; Labour is a trademark of The Labour Party; London Eye is a trademark of Merlin Attractions Operations Limited; Marks & Spencer is a trademark of Marks and Spencer Plc; McDonald's is a trademark of McDonald's International Property Company, Ltd; Mondeo is a trademark of Ford-Werke GmbH; NHS is a trademark of The Secretary of State for Health and Social Care; Notting Hill Carnival is a trademark of Notting Hill Carnival Limited; Peroni is a trademark of Asahi Europe & International Ltd; Playstation is a trademark of Sony Interactive Entertainment Inc.; Prius is a trademark of Toyota Motor Corporation; Sky News is a trademark of Sky Limited; Spotify is a trademark of Spotify AB; St Pancras is a trademark of HS1 Limited; Star Trek is a trademark of CBS Studios Inc.; Steiner School is a trademark of Steiner Waldorf Schools Fellowship Limited; Stella is a trademark of Anheuser-Busch InBev S.A.; The Guardian is a trademark of Guardian News & Media Limited; The Spectator is a trademark of The Spectator (1828) Limited; Twitter is a trademark of X Corp.; Uber is a trademark of Uber Technologies, Inc.; Warcraft is a trademark of Blizzard Entertainment, Inc.; Wetherspoon is a trademark of J D Wetherspoon plc; WH Smith is a trademark of WH Smith Group Limited; Wizard of Oz is a trademark of Turner Entertainment Co.; WTO is a trademark of World Trade Organization; Xbox is a trademark of Microsoft Corporation; YouTube is a trademark of Google LLC; Zoom is a trademark of Zoom Communications, Inc. Use of trademarks has not been authorised, sponsored, or otherwise approved by the trademark owners.

*To Prue Crane,
who would let us in*

I dwell with you as a foreigner,
    a stranger, as all my ancestors were.
Look away from me, that I may enjoy life again
    before I depart and am no more.

                                                            Psalm 39

1

How could he just sleep like that, thought Bryan as Phillip snored gently beside him, his legs tucked up, back turned away. How could he sleep at all? It was not precisely a revelation – Bryan had always known and loved Phillip for his resilience, but still: tomorrow was their Somme and this bed was their trench.

Their friends might have seen Bryan as the steady breadwinner and Phillip the homemaker, but it was actually Bryan who revolved around Phillip's sun – as it always had been, ever since that first evening in Manchester.

'Are you going to stand there all night?' It was not the most original pick-up line, but who needed originality? You just had to say *something*.

'I was planning to, yeah.' Bryan glanced sheepishly across the foam of his pint at this small, lean man.

'And what's your name, you big lunk.'

'That's not very nice,' said Bryan. He added quickly: 'Bryan. It's Bryan.'

'I like big lunks, you big lunk,' Phillip tugged on his belt, causing Bryan to spill his pint in alarm.

'Oh, I'm sorry! Sorry!'

Phillip chuckled. 'You're not from around here, Bryan.'

'Conference,' he said. 'Housing.'

'Ooh,' Phillip stroked his arm. 'Sexy.'

Bryan laughed. 'And what do you do?'

'What *don't* I do, chuck…'

A blur of drinking, dancing. Bryan was no smalltown boy, but neither was he on the scene. He tended to find it boring and only ended up in Manchester's Gay Village after the others in his group – almost exclusively women – had headed off for an early night. He hadn't wanted company, exactly, but neither had he wanted to be alone. He certainly hadn't expected to be picked up, though, to be dancing until two in the morning with this chatty,

1

sharp-faced but pretty man who now took hold of his belt again and led him, wordlessly, off the dance floor and downstairs to the coats.

Bryan let it happen – for once, he let it happen. Yes, he was drunk. Yes, it was late – he imagined his colleagues sleeping the sleep of the just – yes it was a reckless thing for a 38-year-old Senior Housing Supervisor to be doing the night before his workshop (his workshop! Sobriety washed over him, then ebbed just as swiftly as he grabbed his jacket and bumbled out behind Phillip) but hell, you were only young once, and if there was one thing Bryan knew for sure, he was getting older.

They were out, walking arm-in-arm along the canals. Bryan had no idea where they were going, and was happy not to ask. He was a stranger to these parts and the unfamiliarity – the unfamiliarity of it *all* – was refreshing.

It was a drizzly Wednesday night – or Thursday morning to be precise – and the Village was relatively quiet, the great bustle having drifted off or still packed inside the bars and clubs that lined Canal Street.

Phillip stopped, reached up, kissed him. Drawing back, this street-smart, shrewd-looking fellow's face had softened, and in the lamplight Bryan saw another side to him – tenderness, compassion. He shivered, perhaps with the shock of it. Or even recognition: a signal sent from the future that this was his husband-to-be.

'Sparks fly, eh?' said Phillip. 'So, big lunk, your place or mine?'

'Whichever's nearer?'

'In a hurry, huh? Well, I'm about ten minutes away on foot, if you can wait that long?'

'I'm not in any hurry, really,' Bryan didn't want to sound desperate. 'Honestly…' Phillip laughed, pressed a finger to his lips.

They would have been half way there – at least, it was five minutes later – when it happened. They were cutting down a lane between a pair of old warehouses when Bryan heard running. He looked around just in time to see the youth launch himself, feet first – he remembered seeing the rubber soles of his trainers just before their impact, at maximum velocity, against his ribs (he would have hit Bryan full in the back if he hadn't turned at the last moment) and there was an audible, wood-like crack as he was propelled onto the cobbles, the youth bouncing off his body as if it was a mattress and letting out a whoop.

Then they were on them – sportswear-clad young men, rubber soles stomping, kicking.

'Queers! Fucking Queers!'

'Arse bandits!'

'Kill the fuckers!'

Bryan tried to rise but was bashed back down by the hardness of closed fists, ringed knuckles.

Again he tried, again he was clobbered. Punches landed like cudgels. A foot stomped on the back of his head, smashing his face against the cobbles. Pain shot through his nose. He roared like a beast assailed by jackals, managed to seize hold of a flying trainer before it made contact, twist the foot inside. A satisfying yelp as the youth spun to the ground.

Another knuckleduster blow to the head. Bryan zinged with pain, lashed out, might have been lucky as there was an *oof* – he had hit something soft. But just as he was trying to get to his feet, another rubber sole contacted with his back, propelling him forward...

There are too many, he remembered thinking. Then:

I might die here. Then:

I don't want to die like this. Then, the one that would haunt him over the weeks, the months, the years:

Death does not care what I want.

The dull smack of metal against a body. Was it *his* body? Would he soon be looking down on this rain-glistened alley watching some feral youth beating the final wisps of life out of him? Bryan saw his mother. He saw his sister, the pair of them arm-in-arm at some bleak crematorium. He had left no instructions, he realised. He realised: it didn't matter.

Steady, targeted *whumps* accompanied by a squeal, a squeak. But they weren't *his* noises, he began to realise, they weren't coming from *his* throat. They sounded like squashed rats, like vermin.

'Fuck it!'

'Fucking psycho!'

Bryan, still laid upon his front, managed to rise upon his elbows and, squinting through the hazy, amber lit gloom, and the blood, it would turn out – his face was streaked raspberry not only from the nose but a head wound – he saw this spindly figure, this avenging angel, Saint Michael, he would think in the delirium of a Catholic education, holding his sword aloft.

Only it was Saint Phillip, wielding an iron railing he had wrestled from one of the youths before dealing them out some of their own medicine.

'Go on, then.' He kicked one in the behind. 'Bog off.'

The sound of more rubber soles pounding the cobbles. Bryan let out a sob. Another wave? Even armed as Phillip was, only truly divine intervention would save them now.

'Christ! Are you all right? What happened?'

It was their own people. They were saved.

'Bryan. Are you okay?' That tender face, that tender man. 'Jesus, look at you! Are you sure you should move? Don't move…'

'Hello?' One of the gathering crowd. 'We need an ambulance…'

Bryan sat up, his legs splayed out in front of him. Someone handed him a clump of tissues. Bryan tried to press the paper to his forehead but his hands were trembling too much. Phillip took it and held it there.

His teeth were chattering, too, the adrenaline probably. Or death's chill touch. 'Are they… gone?'

'Don't worry about them, chuck.' Sirens approaching. 'They only come out at night.' Phillip lifted up the paper to check the wound and winced, pressing it back. 'They're just ghosts is what they are,' he muttered, 'their time has passed.'

And put like that, as the bars and clubs finally spilled out and a great crowd of concerned men and women collected around them, Bryan could almost believe him.

2

A decade later, a year before – Bryan looked up from his computer.

'Hello Meena. Everything okay? You're looking a bit peaky.'

'Peaky, Bry?'

'Pale.'

'I'm fine.' She hung up her coat and adjusted her headscarf. 'Lovely morning.'

'Polls aren't looking sunny, though,' said Bryan. 'We're still trailing the Tories. Short of a miracle it looks like they're going to get in *again* – another five years! Things seem to go from bad to worse …' He gave her a fatherly look. 'Voted?'

''course.'

Bryan and Meena had been sharing the office for four years – Bryan was now Head of Housing and Meena's boss. She loved working for Bryan, who understood housing inside out. He always encouraged her and had her back when clients challenged one of her decisions or lodged a complaint – not an uncommon occurrence in their business. Bryan always told her: the technical stuff could be learned, but the indispensable qualities of a good housing officer were to be compassionate, collegial, and street-smart – qualities Bryan had in spades, thought Meena.

Bryan and Phillip lived with their two teenage children in a town house on the other side of the borough. 'I know it's a bit of a journey,' said Bryan, 'but you would all be more than welcome tonight for our election party, even if it might end up being more of a wake.'

Meena smiled. 'Love to, but Aisha's got swimming in the morning, a seven o'clock start. I don't think Sanjay would thank me!'

'Well,' said Bryan. 'You're welcome, anyway. But you'll be coming to the barbecue?'

''course!'

'People don't come for our scorched veggie burgers, you know, it's your famous beef behari.'

Meena smiled modestly and switched on her computer.

Nathan, the new boy, made a loud entrance, still fully kitted out in his cycling gear. 'Sorry!' he said. 'Voting!'

Meena didn't think she could criticise, as she had only just got in herself, although that was an exception. With Nathan Drake, the team's trainee, it was rather more the rule. She glanced over at Bryan, who was apparently engrossed in something on his computer. He had been quite clear to Meena that she was Nathan's line manager and that he wanted her to get the experience. 'Did you manage to complete the case file on the Madleys?' she asked. Nathan had been working on it all day yesterday, when it should have only taken him an hour or so.

'Almost!' he said. 'I'll get it over this morning.' He suddenly looked very serious and marched out with his sports bag. The door closed.

'After his shower,' said Bryan, not looking up.

'After his cup of tea and flirt with Sasha,' said Meena. Clearly a confrontation with Nathan was coming, and in a sense she appreciated Bryan's apparent recognition of the issue. Trouble was, even though she didn't like to admit it, perhaps not even to herself, she found the young man a bit intimidating. It was not his physical size as such (everyone was large to Meena, who was barely over five feet tall) but the whole 'package' – one that, be it the whimsical handlebar moustache or his ease at chatting about anything from obscure French philosophers to premier league soccer, spoke of adamantine self-confidence.

And there was that time Meena had passed him in the kitchen with Sasha and some of the other youngsters and heard him say 'chav'. The others laughed. Meena stopped in the corridor, had actually turned around and was about to stick her head in and tell Nathan that that kind of language was not acceptable, particularly when she suspected he had been referring to one of their clients. But then she pictured their faces – their young, uncomprehending faces – and something stopped her. To her shame, Meena had continued down the corridor.

'Who have you got coming then, this evening?' she asked.

'Oh, you know,' said Bryan. 'The usual suspects.'

3

Besides the 'usual suspects', Bryan and Phillip were also expecting the Turners at their election night party. They had just moved in next door and had somewhat surprised Phillip by accepting their invitation.

'I hope they know what they're letting themselves in for,' he said as he and Bryan got the kitchen ready.

'What do you mean?'

'Well I only mentioned it to them because I was a bit worried about the noise. They don't strike me as exactly PLU.'

'PLU?'

'People like us.'

'Gay you mean?'

'Not gay, obviously,' he said. 'But ... they seem somewhat ... conventional, let's say. Have you seen their car? They're not short of a few bob. And I saw a priest!'

'A priest?' Bryan paused.

'All dressed up at their door, pointy hat and everything, shortly after they moved in. And they leave bright and early every Sunday morning.'

'You've been watching them?' Bryan looked amused.

'I've just ... noticed, that's all,' said Phillip.

The doorbell rang. 'Kids,' called Bryan. 'Action stations!'

It was Emma and Rory, who Bryan had known since university. 'We managed to bribe Maria with an extra night off next week,' said Emma.

'How's she settling in?' said Phillip.

'All right, I think,' said Emma. 'The poor girl barely speaks a word of English, but that's what we wanted – she's doing wonders for Hamish and Isla's Spanish. Come e va il tuo Spangolo?' she asked Ben, Bryan and Phillip's thirteen-year-old.

'All right,' said Ben, 'but isn't that Italian?' He looked at Phillip. 'Where do I put these?' He meant Rory and Emma's coats.

'In our bedroom,' said Phillip. 'Good boy.'

'He's grown, hasn't he,' said Emma. 'And so sharp.'

'Too sharp sometimes,' said Bryan.

'You must be so proud.' Bryan and Phillip exchanged a look. They were.

They had adopted the kids when Ben and his younger sister Hallie were four and three respectively. Bryan had come across them through work. He had been standing in a bare living room, avoiding sitting down for fear of catching something, while the kids festered in their own mess on the floor and a pair of pitbulls roamed the hallway. The smell had almost made him gag when he had first stepped into the maisonette, but experience had taught him to be patient, and it had become bearable in time, bearable enough for him to tune in to the dreary lament of their mother.

Something about the benefits not coming through, a pay day loan that had not been paid, bailiffs forcing entry and taking her TV – they couldn't do that, could they? Wasn't it a human right? – and ... stop that Benji, shush now can't you see I'm trying to speak to the nice man.

'Maybe he needs changing?' said Bryan.

Out of the depths of this pallid, bruise-eyed teenager came a look of sheer venom.

'What would *you* know?' she said.

Two weeks later Bryan received a call from social services. The property at 27 Amber Court was now unoccupied and in need of an industrial clean.

'What happened?' asked Bryan.

'The tenant was murdered,' said the social worker, 'domestic. Ex-partner, stabbed fourteen times.'

'I was there only recently,' said Bryan. 'And the kids?'

'Oh they're in care,' she said. 'Poor loves.'

That evening Bryan discussed it with Phillip and a few days later they began the process that resulted in adoption.

Soon after Emma and Rory, arrived Juno and Diane, a lesbian couple with a pair of children around the same age as Ben and Hallie. The kids promptly disappeared upstairs with barely a 'hello'. The adults smiled indulgently.

'When we were their age,' said Diane, 'there would have been a constant battle to keep the sound down. Now,' she said, 'listen … nothing.'

'I'm not sure what's more frightening,' said Phillip.

'Definitely now,' said Diane.

'You never know what they're up to on their phones,' muttered Rory.

'It's actually quite terrifying,' said Diane. The others nodded glumly. 'Our parents didn't realise, but they had it easy.'

Juno let out a laugh mid-way through pouring a glass of wine. 'I'm not sure your mum and dad would agree with that,' she said. 'Have you seen what she was wearing when she was a teenager?'

'I work with a lot of youngsters,' said Emma. 'They seem a lot more conservative and hard-working than we were.'

'Is that actually a good thing?' asked Phillip. 'If they don't challenge authority at their age, when will they ever?'

'Careful what you wish for,' said Rory. Everyone laughed.

'It's almost time,' said Bryan.

For once, there seemed something like real excitement in the eyes of the TV anchor as the panel discussed the exit poll, which, thanks to the new proportional representation system forced through by the Liberal Democrats during the previous minority-Conservative government, visually resembled a kaleidoscope rather than the three-party tricolour of old.

'My God, does that mean we've won?' said Juno, already pissed, Bryan noted.

'What do you mean?' said Diane.

'They're our colours, aren't they?' It was true – the

breakdown of the vote did rather resemble the Rainbow Flag.

'And the terrible thing is,' said Phillip, 'I can't tell if she's joking.'

'Looking like a Pyrrhic victory, if it is the case,' said Rory, leaning closer to the TV. 'Look at that,' he shook his head. 'The Patriots are surging.' He meant The Patriots Party, which had inherited the mantle of the UK's leading nationalist party following the Tory split.

Emma turned to Bryan. 'You know, we still can't get rid of mum's place in France – the market's flooded, especially since the government slapped all those extra taxes on second homes.'

'It could be worse,' said Bryan. 'You could be an Arab.' Emma looked at him as if she hadn't understood. 'Those ferries the French are herding them on to,' he said. 'To Algeria. Most aren't even from there.'

'Oh,' she said. 'Yes, terrible.'

'The Tories are down,' said Rory. 'That's something.'

'Ah, but you see who's up,' said Bryan. 'Our England. And look at that: Shared Values.'

'I see the Socialist Party have passed the threshold,' interjected Diane. 'That's got to mean a few seats.'

'Shared Values,' said Juno. 'That's that nasty woman who's always on the radio telling people off. Horrible, homophobic bitch. If anybody needed a good seeing to with a twelve inch strap-on …'

'Juno!'

There was the sound of the doorbell. Bryan got up. It was Bill, a recently-separated friend of Phillip and Rory's who had gone on to have a regular politics column with the *Herald* online.

'I come bearing good cheer.' He held up a bottle of bubbly. 'We may need it.'

'The polls are looking grim,' Bryan agreed, taking his coat. 'As you predicted, I believe.'

'Oh, you actually read it? Glad someone did.' He pulled out his phone again to check if there were any messages. He had been hoping for a last-minute slot on the telly – having noted there was a nasty flu bug in progress – but still no interest. He was not young enough, he had concluded glumly, or sexy enough. He hadn't even received an invitation from one of YouTube's politics shows, which were naturally all streaming, but he was going to be damned if he asked. What with his wife giving him the heave-ho, he wasn't sure he could handle any more rejection. He found a spot beside Rory as the polls flashed up again, this time as a pie chart with projected seats.

'The axis of evil,' said Rory. 'The Patriots with bugger Berlin, bring back hanging and all that bullshit. Shared Values, the sour-faced "moral majority" – minority, more like – and the Our England boot boys, black shirts in all but name. Axis,' he repeated, as Bill didn't appear to have registered and Rory rather fancied seeing his phrase published, 'of evil.'

'Presuming they get into government,' Bill asked him, 'how do you think the Civil Service will respond?'

'Off-the-record?' Rory asked. Bill gave him a condescending look.

'I'll make you an "unnamed source", mate.'

'Politicians talk big, but the devil's in the detail, and the detail's our job.' Rory had just joined the most junior branch of the Senior Civil Service at the Department of Transport, although if you listened to Emma, Phillip had remarked, you'd think he was about to enter the House of Lords.

'Sir Humphrey lives, then?'

Rory smiled smugly. 'He never died, although countless governments have tried to kill him off. But the reality is, if they want to get things done, they need civil servants. Even if they say they want to cut red tape…'

'As they all do.'

'Then who do they need? More officials to cut it. My point is, no matter what they say, the doing's another matter, and the rubbish this lot spout will soon become watered down when it come into contact with reality.'

'You think so, do you?'

'You don't think so?'

'I think history teaches us that clever people like you think you can control nasty people like them, and it doesn't necessarily work out that way.'

'But this is England,' said Rory.

'Britain,' said Bill.

'You know what I mean. We've got a different tradition, checks and balances, a culture of tolerance.'

'I've never liked that word – *tolerance*. I tolerate your farts, but it doesn't mean I like them.'

'*Gross*,' said Emma.

'That's absurd,' said Rory.

'Apparently, Penny tolerated me,' Bill said, meaning his wife. 'Right up to the point she kicked me out.'

Phillip gave him an affectionate squeeze of the leg. 'You should have controlled your wind,' he said. 'I don't know how many times I warned you.'

The door went again and Bryan flitted out. From the hallway came the sound of greetings and a booming voice: 'Has Sunderland declared yet?'

A space was made for the Turners.

Bryan immediately understood what Phillip was talking about. The Turners were *certainly not* PLU, although Bryan had not entirely understood his meaning until now. Perhaps he had spent too long in the metropolitan bubble, with his clients at one end of the spectrum and everybody else at the other. It was only now Bryan remembered 'everybody else' did not necessarily mean everybody else was like him and his friends.

Not that there was anything screamingly different about the Turners at first glance: they had probably sprung from a similar background to him and Phillip – the lower-middle or middle classes grown affluent thanks to a confluence of career opportunities and house prices. They would have gone to the same kind of schools and had the same kind of parents. But where their paths diverged, Bryan realised as he went to fix them drinks (a lager for

John, Prosecco for Patricia) was that while he and his friends would have probably been the outsiders at school, for whatever reasons – sexuality, creative leanings, politics – John and Patricia would have been insiders, members of the majority that had variously mocked, tormented or ignored the likes of him and his kind. Bryan had fled the suburbs to get away from people like this. Only now, it seemed, they had followed him here.

But returning to the room, Bryan thought everything seemed okay, at least on the surface. Patricia Turner was discussing the French house with Emma. Rory and Diane were trying to decide if the Socialists would go into coalition with Labour. Then he realised Juno was engaging John Turner in her version of small talk.

'So who did you vote for then?' she asked. John grinned. He and his wife seemed remarkably relaxed, Bryan thought, if not oblivious, to the social dissonance.

'Thanks, Bryan.' He took his drink. 'Well, this might come as a bit of a surprise to you, Ju-*no*, is it?' Juno nodded civilly. 'But my model politician has always been Margaret Thatcher.'

The conversation in the room stalled at the sound of that cursed name, then continued in a perfunctory fashion, as if the interlocutors were half-listening in. Only Juno seemed unperturbed, but as a performance artist who had paid her way by taking part in porn films before meeting Diane, Bryan reflected she was probably less shockable than most.

'And now?' said Juno, draining her glass of wine and looking at Bryan expectantly. But Bryan wasn't budging, not just yet.

'Oh, I still think they're the best of the bunch,' said John. 'The Tories, I mean, although I don't suppose that's a popular opinion in these parts?' He gave her a mischievous smile.

'Not really,' said Juno. 'We're all Marxists and queers here. How do you feel about that, Patricia?' she asked.

'Me?' John's wife looked startled. Emma let out an exasperated sigh.

'I noticed your cross.' Juno raised her glass again, pointedly, toward Bryan, who ignored her equally pointedly. 'Phillip was saying you're Christians.'

'Don't bring me into this!' said Phillip. 'I'm sorry – it's just that I saw the priest.'

John and Patricia looked puzzled. 'Oh,' said John, 'you must mean Father Gordon. He came around to bless the house when we moved in.'

'A blessing,' said Bryan, 'how nice!' He looked wildly around the room. 'Look,' he said. 'You were right, John – Sunderland *is* declaring first.'

Sunderland, to few people's surprise, went big for The Patriots, with rowdy celebrations thereafter.

'Fools,' said Bill, absent-mindedly. He checked his phone again. Still no messages.

'I met one of them today,' said Emma.

'A fool?' Bill looked amused. 'There's no shortage.'

'I mean, one of *them*, from the North East.'

'That must have been a shock.' Bill had never liked Emma, but as Rory seemed to – having married her – he had decided he might as well make the best of it.

'He wouldn't shut up. Kept asking me personal questions, like where I came from, what I did…'

'He was probably just trying to be friendly,' said Bill. 'Northerners can be like that.'

'And then he complained about having to come down south for work, but he didn't seem to have any sense politics had something to do with it. "The way of the world", he said, as if it was something to do with the weather. I asked him if he voted, he said he never bothered because it never changed anything!'

'This bloke … who was he?' said John Turner. Emma looked surprised.

'My Uber.'

'They're still being driven?' said Bill. 'I thought they'd all gone automatic.'

'This one was,' said Emma.

'You can hardly blame this Uber driver of yours,' said John, 'for the economic situation "oop north".'

'She can, and she will,' said Bill. Emma gave him the vague smile she employed when she couldn't be sure if someone was agreeing with her or taking the piss, but wanted them to think that either way she was in on the joke.

'The Government can only do so much,' said John.

'For workers,' said Bill. 'They can't seem to do enough for their banker pals.'

'Ah,' said John, 'but we all need banks.'

'And we don't need workers?'

'Isn't it all AI these days?'

'And what are people supposed to do? Crawl away and die under a rock?'

John took a sip of his lager. 'I'm sorry,' he said. 'What is it you...'

'I'm a journalist.'

'Don't journalists occupy the same place as bankers in the popularity stakes?'

'Look...'

'Ooh, here comes another one,' said Phillip. He turned the TV up.

This was from Luton. 'Solid Labour,' said Rory.

'Strong showing from the Patriots under first-past-the-post, though,' said Bill, turning away from John. 'The Labour vote tended to come from Asian households, while the white working class was divided between Tory and Patriot.'

'Racists,' said Rory automatically. Bryan noticed John and Patricia exchange a smile.

The returning officer was standing at the lectern, saying: '... do hereby declare and give notice that the total number of votes cast for each party was as follows. Our England, two thousand one hundred and ninety. Labour, eight thousand, three hundred and thirty-four ...'

Rory leaned forward to say something to Bill, but he waved him down.

'... The Liberal Democratic Party, two hundred and

thirty. The Shared Values Alliance, two thousand four hundred and thirty-three. The Patriots Party, twelve thousand four hundred and seventy ...'

'There we go,' Bill sat back, satisfied. The others looked at him. *'Didn't anybody else read my bloody column?'*

4

Stuart saw them coming across the green and winked his lights. A couple of tough-looking white blokes. He would have usually packed it in by now but he'd wanted to make up for the two stars the posh woman had given him that morning. His previous fare, a nurse, lovely lass, had lived in a block around the corner. He'd picked her up after delivering a doctor to the hospital for his shift, and arrived at his place in Swiss Cottage after taking a banker lady home from a bar in the City, so he'd done almost a full circle, or a sort of lasso, around central London. He thought he would find cabbing boring when he first got into it, but what he hadn't counted on was the ... could you call them stories? Not everyone liked to chat, and you'd occasionally get some right ones like that cow today, but in any case, every person, like every destination, was different. And that kept him interested.

These two, though. They looked like trouble, even though, in truth, they also looked like any pair of blokes from Hetton. In fact, they looked like Stuart. Short hair, polo shirts, jeans, trainers. Like a pair of off-duty squaddies. They'd fit right in back home. They stood right out, down here.

They got in.

'Wood Green, all right?' said Stuart.

One of the men laughed. He smelled of whisky and cigarettes.

'Doesn't that cap it all,' he said. 'A Geordie!'

'A sign,' said the other. 'It's got to be a sign.'

'What's a Geordie lad doing down here?' The first man leaned over the front passenger seat. Stuart glanced across at him. Despite his jet black hair and gym-toned biceps he was older than he'd first thought. Older than Stuart, any road. Mid-Forties? He relaxed a bit.

'Mackem,' he said. 'Technically.'

'Fuck me, we wouldn't want to get that wrong.' The

man had an Essex accent. 'It'd be like serving a Mozzie pork fritters. So you're from Sunderland?'

'Aye.'

'Still mid-table in the Championship?'

'Right side of mid-table,' said Stuart. 'We're in with a chance.'

'What are you doing down here, then?'

'In this dump,' said the other.

'Well,' said Stuart. 'Working …'

'I don't mean literally, mate,' said the first man.

'Do you mind if I smoke?' said the second.

'I'd rather you didn't,' said Stuart. He watched him shrug and put his cigarette back in the carton.

'What I meant,' said the first, 'is why. Why did you come down here? Isn't it better up there?'

'You're not the first to ask me that today,' said Stuart. He thought about those two stars from 'Emma' – you never knew with Londoners – but this pair seemed different. Cut from a different cloth, a different class. 'There's not the work,' he said.

'What work do you do?' said the man. 'Other than driving I mean.'

'Warehouseman,' he said.

'See?' said the first man to the second. 'Warehouseman. And have you still got family up there. Sorry.' He checked his phone. 'Stuart.'

'Stu.'

'Stu. I'm Vince.' He reached across and gave his hand a brief shake. 'And this reprobate is Mike. So,' he said. 'Family?'

Just hearing the word made Stuart unconsciously stroke his chest as if tracing the line of a scar. 'Ex-wife,' he said. 'Two kids.'

'You're paying for,' said the man. Stuart nodded.

'There's no warehousing work here?' said Mike.

Stuart sighed. 'Not for someone my age.'

'And colour,' said Mike. Stuart looked in the rear view mirror and remembered his original suspicions.

'That,' said Vince. 'Is the sort of language that can get

us into trouble. He's pissed. Been a big night for us. And he doesn't mean it anyway, do you, you racist bastard.' Stuart saw Mike shrug.

'If you don't mind me asking,' said Vince. 'You're ... what? Early-thirties?' Stuart nodded. 'It's not got any better, has it. Up there. I mean, you being here, I can guess. It's the same for all of us, the indigenous. The natives. Say *that*, and they'll say you're being racist, so we don't say it, do we, Mike.'

'We don't, Vince.'

'Also,' Vince shook his head. 'Because it's not the whole story. You can't *blame* the migrants – they're like everybody else, just want to escape from whatever shithole they came from. It's them that let them in.'

'The elites,' said Mike.

'Elites,' echoed Vince. 'And most of them are white, right? Whether it's your Tories or your Labour or whatever – they're all against *us*.' He shook his head. 'And they've been at it since fucking 1066.'

Stuart wasn't sure he got that last bit, but let it go. He was thinking of packing it in for the night – he didn't live far from the destination address, and it had been a long, long day.

'So how did you vote, then?' A voice from the back – Mike.

'Now, now,' said Vince. 'You don't ask a gentleman that.'

Stuart thought about it, about what to say. It hadn't gone down too well with that 'Emma'. To hell with it, he thought. 'I didn't,' he said. 'Too much on my plate.'

'And if you had?' said Mike.

'Dunno ...' He glanced in the rear mirror. 'Patriots, I suppose?' Mike chuckled. Vince said:

'How about Our England?' Stuart shrugged.

'Don't know them,' he said. 'English independence, is it?'

Vince smiled. 'Something like that ... Anyway, I think we've arrived.' They were at the beginning of an industrial estate. Seemed an odd place to drop them, but

Stuart had learned not to ask questions. 'You can pull up anywhere.'

Mike got out without a word and immediately lit up. Before Vince opened the door, he reached over to shake Stuart's hand. 'Good luck Stu,' he said. He gave him a card. 'And if you're ever in need of advice, or would just like to help out – we're always on the look out for sound blokes. We pay too.'

Stuart thanked him and pulled out. Decided he *would* call it a day – a little short of fourteen hours – and drove from the industrial estate to the council estate where he lived with Auntie.

Before opening the door, he turned on the light and inspected the card. *Vincent Cave*, it read. *Welfare Organiser, Our England.*

*

It did turn out to be a long night at Bryan and Phillip's, at least for some. John and Patricia Turner left amicably, and more or less unnoticed, around one in the morning, Diane, Juno and the kids shortly thereafter, although Juno had been passed out in her chair for half an hour. Emma and Phillip repaired to the kitchen for a gossip, while Bryan stayed with Rory and Bill in the living room as the night unfolded.

By about four o'clock, when Emma came in and announced she could wait no longer, the complexion of the results was clear. The Labour vote had shrunk to what could best be described as a metropolitan middle-class rump, accounting for between fifteen and twenty per cent. But the Tories had done little better, with twenty to twenty-five per cent across the country. This was the poll lead that had worried Bryan, who had actually been fibbing about reading Bill's article.

The rest of the vote had gone to parties that formerly wouldn't have had a look in – in short, the 'Axis of Evil', although Bill still hadn't appeared to have registered Rory's repeated references. According to current predictions, the night's big surprise was that almost thirty-five per cent of the vote had gone to The Patriots Party, while a further six had gone to Our England. Meanwhile the Shared Values Alliance and the Socialist Party had both scraped across the four per cent threshold. The jury was out on the Liberal Democrats who were teetering on the margin that would win them seats in Parliament.

'To be honest,' said Bill, as they pulled on their coats. 'It's worse than even I predicted.'

'A disaster,' agreed Rory. 'The Patriots and Our England together is over forty per cent!'

'Labour, Socialists, Scottish, Welsh and Irish Nationalists ... '

'The Irish Nats refuse to sit in parliament, remember.'

'That's thirty-five, then,' said Bill.

'Tories and the Patriots? It's got to be. The Patriots hate Our England.'

'A nightmare,' said Bill.

'Nightmare.'

Phillip guided them to the door. 'So glad you had a great evening,' he closed it behind them, shook his head. 'Never again.'

'It's become a bit of a tradition,' said Bryan.

'They used to say that about burning witches,' said Phillip.

5

Sanjay had the radio tuned to a news channel as they drove to the barbecue. He had always been a bit of a political junky and had been a Labour councillor before Aisha was born. He would certainly have come to Bryan and Phillip's election night bash had he known he was invited, but Meena had artfully side-stepped that: she didn't like the idea of him spending the whole night away from home, especially with all that booze flowing … he didn't drink these days, but he hadn't always been that way, she knew, and if *he'd* stayed up all night, so would have *she* – waiting for him to come home. All right, so in the end he *had* stayed up all night in the living room, but at least he had been away from temptation and she had been able to get some sleep.

They drove in silence, listening to a radio talk show. As had been evident on election night, no clear winner had emerged from the polls and the subsequent weeks had been occupied by furious political horse-trading. For the first few days it had indeed seemed about to turn out as Rory had predicted with a Tory–Patriots alliance, but in the end talks had broken down. The Patriots leadership had refused to 'play second fiddle', as they had put it, to the Tories, especially given their higher vote. 'We are the masters now,' their leader had proclaimed outside Tory Central Office, and few could disagree.

Then a new possible coalition had emerged, one in which the Patriots would indeed be masters.

There had been a series of bombshells. Miraculously, despite their 'one nation' stance, the Patriots had made peace with Our England, promising to stage an English independence referendum in their first term. Next, the staunchly Protestant Ulster Democrats, who had traditionally been allied to the Tories, came into the Patriots' camp following the promise of a rumoured multi-billion pound 'investment' in Northern Ireland. Then the Patriots called a press conference.

Here was the Patriots leader, along with a set of new MPs from the Shared Values Alliance, including Juno's 'horrible woman from the radio'.

'There's no arguing,' he said, 'we clearly do share many of the same values: a respect for the traditional family, hard work, justice and patriotism. We want our nation's borders to be respected and to see an end to the economic misery caused by the failure of successive governments to stand up to the WTO. There is far, far more that unites than divides us.'

Sanjay let out a long sigh. 'God help us,' he said.

'Sanjay,' said Meena, who didn't like him to blaspheme in front of Aisha, although she was happily absorbed with a toy in the back.

'It's finally happened then. You know what this is, Meen'?' he said. 'A disaster.'

'But they still haven't got a majority, have they? Isn't that only forty-nine per cent?'

'They'll be by far the largest coalition,' he said. 'That will give them first dibs on forming a government. And there's still the question of the Lib Dems. If they lose the court case then their votes will be distributed – four per cent across the other parties, and you know what that equals, don't you?'

'What?'

'For the parties in the Patriots' camp – an absolute majority.'

They drove on in silence. Finally Meena said: 'Maybe it won't be so bad.'

Sanjay pulled up behind a bus. 'Are you serious? The Patriots want to make every mosque sign a loyalty pledge. From there it's a just few small steps to what's happening in France. What?' He knew that look on his wife's face.

'I wish you wouldn't exaggerate.'

'Who's exaggerating?'

She shook her head. 'Nothing like that is going to happen here, Sanj.'

'What's the difference?

'There's a world of difference. The French have always been racist.'

'And the British haven't?'

More silence. Then Meena said: 'Well, the Tories and the Patriots would be just as bad.' Sanjay shook his head.

'As much as I may hate the Tories, darling, even I have to admit they wouldn't be as bad as this bunch of fascists and headbangers. The Tories ... I can't quite believe I'm saying this, but at least the Tories would have been a restraining influence. With this lot of loonies, well, there's nothing stopping them.'

Meena looked back at Aisha. *'But we're British.* Nothing's going to happen to us.'

Sanjay let out a long sigh. 'You're old enough to remember Brexit, Meena.'

'Vaguely.' She had been ten.

'I remember – the hate. It's always there, just beneath the surface – and, let's face it, they were only going after white Europeans because they couldn't get away with blacks and Muslims. Our England are even worse than the Patriots: proper ethnonationalists, or do you think they're including us with their talk about "English Rights"?

'As for "Shared Values", for all their "moral majority" talk, what they really mean is the four per cent of Christian fundamentalist nutters that voted for them, and – literally – to hell with the rest of us.'

They drove further on. Sanjay glanced across at his wife, who was looking queasy. 'I'm sorry, love,' he shook his head. 'You know me – mister drama. I'm probably exaggerating. They'll soon break up squabbling then sanity, even if it's the Tory kind, will return.'

'Is that where we've got to, Sanj?' asked Meena. 'Hoping for the Tories?'

'Auntie Meena!' Twelve-year-old Hallie opened the door and eyed the tubs of food she was carrying. 'Aisha!' she darted past her and picked up their four-year-old, who cooed with pleasure.

'Saved the day!' said Phillip, standing in the hallway. 'Come through guys.' He led them to the kitchen. 'Bryan's just started burning the veggie burgers. Sanjay – have you heard the news?'

'I was just saying to Meena. Disaster.'

'It goes from bad to worse,' said Phillip. 'Let me get that, Auntie Meena,' he took the tubs. 'Okay guys, I've prepared something extra special for you.' He opened the fridge and removed a jug with mint leaves poking from the top. 'A variation on your usual cocktail, but I think it will hit the spot.' He poured them two glasses.

'Can I have one?' said Hallie, coming back into the kitchen, still holding Aisha.

'When you're old enough, chick,' said Phillip.

'There's no *alcohol* in it, Dad,' said Hallie.

'It's for the refined, grown-up palette,' said Phillip. 'We've got plenty of tooth-rotting pop for you and your friends. Stick to the hard stuff.' Hallie turned around and marched Aisha back into the garden.

'Such a sweetie,' said Meena. 'Aisha adores her.'

'Sanjay,' Rory had come in, holding a bottle of Peroni. They clinked their drinks together.

'They are the masters now,' said Sanjay solemnly.

'I bet it's times like this,' Rory smiled rather awkwardly at Meena, 'you wish you could get pissed.'

'You can drink enough for the both of us, mate,' said Sanjay.

'What's there to stay sober for?' said Rory.

'Emma driving, is she?' said Meena.

'Oh, she's driving, all right.' He looked into the garden where his wife was chatting to Diane and Juno. Then across at their au pair who was having a seemingly intense conversation with Bill while Rory's seven-year-old, Hamish, stood behind her poking a stick into the pond. 'She's just a kid,' he muttered 'Too young for Bill.' He began to move off. 'I'd better keep an eye on Hamish.'

'Have you ever thought about getting an au pair?' Sanjay asked Phillip.

'You mean an attractive young Spanish man to help me with the dusting?'

The pair watched as Rory jovially inserted himself between the au pair and Bill while his son continued to prod around the pond.

'I'm not sure how well that would go down with the fella paying the bills.'

6

Stuart was with his auntie when he got the message. It had turned out lovely so he had taken her – wheeled her, to be exact, because she needed a chair for journeys that involved more than shuffling around the flat on her frame – to sit outside The Oak, the main pub serving the estate. Auntie was parked at the end of the bench, her respirator on her lap, a small Guinness and pack of Cheese and Onion open in front of her, Stuart across ways with his pint of Stella and Ready Salted.

'This is the life, eh, lad?' Auntie gave him a wide smile, showing off the new dentures he had got for her. 'What's so funny?'

Stuart shook his head. 'I was just thinking, Auntie, how you managed down here all these years with your accent. You never lost it, did you.'

'You're saying I've got an accent? Get away!' She grinned.

'Didn't people say something? I get it all the time: *where are you from?* Like I'm from Africa or something.'

Auntie laughed. 'They used to think I was from Wales. Or Scotland. Or even worse: Newcastle!'

'But you're glad you came? You don't miss home?'

She shook her head. 'No, lad. Not for a minute. We came – your uncle and me – to escape the poverty. Coming here, to London. Well, it was our New York. We *were* like immigrants from Africa!'

Stuart looked around. There were only other white people on the benches outside the pub. It was odd, when you thought on it, considering you didn't see that many white faces anywhere else in the area. But those George Cross flags blocking out the windows, ostensibly to shield the football on the big screen, also made their clientele crystal clear.

'And it never bothered you,' he said. 'All the … foreigners?'

Auntie looked around. 'What do you mean?'

'I mean,' he leaned forward. 'All the black people and wot not.'

'Ah,' said Auntie, her eyes misting with the memory, 'when we came down in the Eighties it was the West Indians and them Indian ladies with their lovely saris and the red dot on their forehead. Of course, I worked with them all,' – Auntie had been a dinner lady – 'very nice, very nice.' She took a handful of crisps, then a sip of Guinness. 'But they've gone now, I suppose. I mean, the folk from my generation. A lot moved out, to the suburbs. Brenda went back to Barbados when she retired. They'd built a big house.'

It was then that Stuart's phone buzzed. It was an email from Uber. *As you will be aware,* it read, *as part of its Phasing Program, the UK's Uber fleet is being renewed with the goal of becoming fully self-drive. From tomorrow, we are delighted to announce that London will become Britain's first fully self-drive city. Your services will therefore no longer be required. Uber would like to thank you for your valued contribution. As a small token of our appreciation, we are pleased to offer you three free* Uber Self-drive™ *journeys of up to ten miles (total). All of us here at Uber wish you good luck and hope you will choose* Uber Self-drive™ *in the future!*

'All right, pet?' asked Auntie. Stuart put his phone down, cleared his throat.

'Fine, Auntie.' He stood up. ''nother?'

'Ooh you're spoiling me.'

*

Across the city, the sun was also shining, although if the prevailing mood was anything to go by, dark clouds should have been louring.

'I don't see the Turners here,' said Juno with a gleam in her eye.

'Who are the Turners?' said Meena.

'We did invite them,' said Phillip, 'but they're on their hols. Antigua. They go every year, apparently.'

'And they are?' said Meena.

'Fascists,' said Rory. He shouted toward the garden fence: 'Fascists!'

'Our neighbours,' said Phillip. 'They've just moved in.'

'Why are they fascists?' asked Meena.

'*Tories*,' said Juno with gusto. 'And how about you, darling. Happy?'

Meena was startled. 'I'm sorry,' she frowned. 'What do you mean?'

'About *Shared Values. You know* – the religious ones.'

There was a moment of silence as Meena, along with everyone else around them, tried to digest the origin of Juno's question – after all, no one who had set foot at Bryan and Phillip's, at least until the recent visit by the Turners, would have been expected to vote for anyone other than Labour, or at a stretch the Greens or the new Socialist Party, but that, clearly, was not the distinction Juno was making.

'Why … do you ask?' said Meena finally, speaking for everyone.

'Well, I mean,' Juno's eyes bulged like someone who had caught an animal in their headlights and decided it was too late to swerve out of the way, 'because *you're* religious, aren't you.' She gestured, wine slopping over her fingers. '*Headscarf*,' she announced as if the prosecution rested its case.

The sharp intake of breath audible in the background may have been Emma's.

'What…' – Meena spoke slowly – 'has that got to do with the election?' She hadn't been singled out for her faith for as long as she could remember.

'Yes,' said Sanjay. 'What *has* that got to do with it, Juno?'

Juno looked between him and Meena as if she were now that animal.

'Oh, I know *you're* Labour, Sanjay,' Juno's voice rose when she may have meant it to drop. 'I just wondered about Meena, that's all.'

'That's all – what?'

Phillip glanced over at Bryan, who was with the kids by the pond, and tried to capture his attention.

'Well, because I know she – I mean, you, Meena, I'm sure you don't need your husband to speak on your behalf...'

'I *don't*,' said Meena.

'Well, you're religious. Isn't that's what it's all about, your headgear and everything? So...'

'So?'

'So that's the same as these Shared Values, right? "Traditional" families. Eye for an eye. RE, all that.' What she might have hoped was a mischievous smile came out more like a drunken smirk.

'How dare you ...' said Sanjay.

'Sanjay,' said Meena, 'please.'

'That's completely unacceptable, Juno,' said Emma. 'Diane!'

'I don't need my "husband" to talk for me either.' Juno sloshed more wine on to the ground.

'You've had a bit too much, love,' said Phillip, gently. He turned to Meena. 'I'm sorry,' he said.

Meena shook her head. 'Juno's got one thing right,' she said. 'I can fight my own corner. So you thought I would be happy about Shared Values just because I'm *religious*? Have you any idea what they stand for?'

'Bryan,' Phillip called. Bryan looked up, distracted. Phillip's expression said all he needed to know.

'Well, it's what you believe in, isn't it?' Juno seemed to expand into the space around her, almost as if she was giving one of her performances, albeit to a hostile audience. 'I mean, that's why it's called Shared Values, right? Because it's for all those people who share "traditional values", and you're "traditional", right?'

Meena shook her head sadly. 'You don't understand,' she said. 'I...'

'What the hell are you on, Juno?' said Sanjay. 'If you want to talk about Islam, I'd say you're making a good argument for sobriety.'

'Now you actually *are* sounding like the Patriots, Juno,' said Rory. 'No joke!'

'And you were saying about the Turners?' said Bill.

'Come on,' said Diane, wading through. 'I'm taking you home.'

'I'm so sorry,' said Bryan, as the afternoon drew to a close.

'Will you please stop apologising,' said Meena. 'It was just Juno. We all know what she's like when she gets drunk.'

'No, it was completely unacceptable. Drink doesn't excuse it. Really,' he took her hands, 'I hope this won't affect our friendship. We love you, you know.'

'Oh don't be silly.' She gave him a hug.

'I'm sorry,' Bryan said to Sanjay. He held up his hands.

'It's what we're up against, all of us,' he said. 'It's a reminder. To stay united.'

They got into the car and pulled out.

'Okay?' said Sanjay. Meena gave him a tired smile.

'Fine.'

'Juno's a bigot,' said Sanjay, 'even if she is gay. People forget that – sexuality doesn't necessarily make you Left. There are plenty of right-wing gays. Funny, really – there we were, talking about prejudice because of the election, and then it happens in the last place you'd expect.'

'She was just drunk,' said Meena. 'And maybe, in her own way... scared.'

'Scared? Of what?'

'I'd never thought of it like that.'

'Like what?' said Sanjay.

'The new government. Gays. *They've* got nothing to be afraid of, have they?'

'Gays?'

'Because we were talking about racism, Islamophobia, but what about gay people?'

Sanjay sighed. 'Some of the guff Shared Values put out ... at least the Patriots keep morality out of it. Shared

Values have made it their *raison d'etre* … Gays, Trans, sex education… That's what all their talk about "moral leadership", "traditional families" is really all about. They seem to think "the permissive society" is at the root of whatever their gripe is with the modern world.' He shrugged. 'Although that still doesn't excuse Juno …' He shook his head. 'But look – I've been thinking it through, after our talk earlier. We really don't have anything to worry about. The government will have enough on its hands to affect the likes of us. Their plans to bring back hanging, for example …'

'Shared Values only got four per cent,' said Meena 'That's just a few seats, isn't it?' Sanjay nodded. 'So they can't have *that* much influence, can they?'

Sanjay glanced in the mirror at Aisha, fast asleep in the back seat. He shook his head. 'No, love. Not that much.'

Bryan, Phillip and the kids were tidying up in silence until Hallie found her latest boyband on Spotify and it blasted over the speakers. 'Noooo!' Ben protested.

'We've been listening to yours all day,' shouted Hallie.

'I was the DJ! It was old people's music!'

Bryan and Phillip exchanged a smile.

'Now the old people have gone,' said Hallie, boogying across the room with a pile of plates.

'Careful you don't drop those, chick,' said Phillip. Hallie laid the plates down and wiggled back outside.

'Dads!' said Ben.

'I rather like it,' said Bryan, dancing outside after Hallie.

'God!' Ben covered his face in embarrassment.

'Come on!' Hallie said. 'There's work to do!'

'God!' he said, but went out after her.

They had almost finished and Hallie had already gone upstairs when Ben, fresh from switching the boyband to some indie music, sidled up to Bryan and Phillip at the kitchen table as they polished off a bottle of wine.

'I preferred Hallie's music,' said Phillip.

CANARIES

'You *would*,' said Ben. The men grinned good-naturedly. Their son was clearly straight and, what's more, just entering that awkward stage.

Untypically for Ben – who would invariably be ensconced in his room playing Warcraft or heaven knows what at this time on a Sunday evening – he came to sit beside them, dabbing at his phone.

'Anything interesting?' said Bryan. Ben looked up.

'Sorry?'

Bryan nodded at his phone.

Ben shook his head. Dabbed a bit more. Then, without looking up, said, as if the thought had just occurred to him: 'I was just wondering about what Auntie Juno was saying …'

'Oh don't worry about Auntie Juno,' said Phillip quickly. But Bryan shook his head.

'Go on, Ben.'

'I was looking at their site …'

'Whose site?'

'The Shared Values Allies.'

'Okay,' said Bryan.

'Is it something about gay people, Ben?' said Phillip. Ben nodded.

Then it happened. A dollop of water on the phone. Another.

'Oh, Ben, my big soldier.' Phillip put his arm around him while Bryan reached for some kitchen roll. 'What is it, kid? What's the matter?'

More tears fell as Ben stared at the phone.

'They say you're unnatural.'

Both men inwardly flinched. This was precisely the kind of thing they had always tried to shield their children from.

'You're grown up enough now,' said Bryan carefully, 'to know there are plenty of bad people out there, don't you, son?' Ben nodded, as Phillip gently took the phone. 'They try to take out their own failings and frustrations on those weaker than them. You've been studying what happened to the Jews in Germany, haven't you?'

At this, Phillip shot him a warning glance and Bryan realised too late. The tears started up again.

'They're not going to do that to us?' said Ben in the whiney voice that reminded them that he was still, at least partly, a child.

'No, son,' said Bryan. 'No of course not. I was just using that as an example ... of bad people picking on people for no reason. There's nothing to worry about, honestly.'

'But they're *the government*,' said Ben.

'Well,' said Bryan, 'it's complicated, but only a very little bit. Shared Values have got thirty seats in a parliament of six hundred and fifty MPs. Nothing's going to happen to us, I promise.'

'We have the law,' said Phillip. 'We're protected by the law.'

'That's right,' said Bryan. 'Honestly, son, there's really nothing to worry about. Auntie Juno, well, you know her, she's an artist, she's always exaggerating ...'

'The whole world is a stage for that one,' said Phillip.

'What we should be more worried about,' said Bryan, trying to steer the conversation onto safer ground, 'is the awful Patriots Party. They want to bring back executions, bully Muslims like Auntie Meena and Uncle Sanjay, and be even more horrible to Europeans living here. I mean, for all the Polish people, the French ...'

'Audrey and her family,' said Phillip, meaning a school crush of Ben's. 'For them, it really is a nightmare, to have those idiots, with hundreds of seats, in government. Compared to them, that handful of cretins can't do a thing.'

Ben looked at them through his tears. 'Do you really believe that?'

'Absolutely,' said Bryan. Ben seemed about to add something else, but he looked back down.

'What is it, Ben?' said Phillip.

Ben shook his head. 'Nothing,' he said quietly. He reached for some kitchen paper and wiped the phone screen. 'Sorry,' he said.

'Don't be silly,' said Phillip. 'We love you. You know that don't you.'

'I know.'

After Ben went upstairs, the two men continued drinking in silence. Finally Phillip said softly: 'Do you think it was it true, what I said?'

'What do you mean?'

'About us having nothing to worry about.'

Bryan considered this. 'Yes,' he said. 'Realistically, what can they do?'

'They can ... turn back the clock.'

Bryan sighed. 'I suppose they can *try*. But times have changed. You can try to turn back the clock, but you can't turn back time.'

Phillip frowned. 'Isn't that a song?'

Bryan smiled. 'It is, isn't it. Is it?'

'I think it is.'

'Anyway,' Bryan squeezed his hand. 'We'll be all right. The kids, well, they're not gay. I suppose they'll be all right. It's the young people. The young gay people that might really suffer, from the prejudice, ignorance.'

Phillip nodded. 'It never stops, does it.'

'What?'

'The struggle.'

7

After the second pint came a third, and after the third came a fourth. Stuart kept drinking long after Auntie had fallen asleep in her chair.

He kept drinking as the sun moved across the green with its ratty slide and swings, as it crossed the car park and began to cover the terrace in shade. As the lights came on inside the pub and the terrace emptied. As the barman called last orders and The Oak began to close up for the night.

'Oi! There's still some left,' he said, as the glass collector reached out. The collector drew back. He'd seen his sort often enough. So pissed they'd be swinging out before you knew it. Before *they* knew it.

'Closing time.' He walked away. Stuart pulled himself up, then sat back down. He tried again. This time he made it to his feet and managed to extract himself from the bench, even though it involved half crawling across the ground before standing up straight.

He headed into the darkness across the green in the general direction of home. Silhouetted by the streetlight, he looked like one of those zombies on TV. A slow moving one.

'Hey!' came the call. 'Hey!' It was only after the third 'hey' that he swung around. That bastard glass collector was standing there. 'You forgot something!'

Stuart stood there, swaying, his fists clenched, trying to focus. Then he realised the dark shape by the man was Auntie. He made his way back while the glass collector kept his distance. Stuart took the handles of Auntie's chair and swung her around, pushing her straight across the grass when he would usually have taken the path. Auntie didn't seem to mind, she was snoring and that.

Then they were back at the flat, Stuart lifting her out of the chair and laying her onto the bed. He took off her jacket and shoes and put her inside. He closed her bedroom door and went into the kitchen to see what else he could find to drink. Then he remembered: only the other day he'd bought a six-pack of Stella for the weekend. He swung open the fridge door. There it was. He hung his head inside the opening in thanks, or perhaps because he was feeling a bit woozy, and pulled out a can.

*

His phone was ringing. He was blinking in the morning light. A string, a tangle of thoughts: where was he? What was he doing here? Why wasn't he in bed? Why did he feel so shit? *So* ... shit. Then the memory rushed up at him out of the darkness. He'd been fired. Well, not fired exactly, but it was the same thing. And ... his phone was ringing. Maybe it was a work offer! He fumbled for it between the empty cans ... Maybe Uber had changed their minds, though he'd never spoken to anyone as such. Did they even have his number? The phone rang off and he cursed himself for messing up. That's you, Stu, one great fucking fuck up. Not his words, Jacky's. Her arms crossed at the front door, barring entry. The kids out back, didn't even know he was there. Her new man, Darren, the one with the leased Audi, out somewhere. Stuart knew – he'd been hanging around, waiting for him to leave. Gave it a few minutes, then strolled up the path. *His* path. *Their* path. She should have been afraid of him, talking like that. She was only a wee lass. But she knew her power over him. She knew her power over everybody. That's what he'd fallen for. She knew what she wanted. She wanted him when times were good. But when they weren't, and he couldn't find the words (and it was all to do with words these days) and 'step up', smooth talk, get the work, well, then she wanted someone else. She shook her head. 'Don't think I don't know what you're up to, Stu,' she'd said, 'waiting for Darren to leave, thinking you can come round without any appointment. I'm not having it.' She pointed a finger. 'I'll get a restraining order.'

He finally found the phone, and the fear that had been

buzzing about his head became real. It was her number. That's you, Stu, one great fuck up. He had a new message. Her voice, it almost had a ring of delight: 'You think it's clever, do you, you think it's grown up, calling at one in the morning so pissed out of your fucking head you can barely speak. Us thinking something terrible had happened, frightening the kids half out of their minds you fucking *creetin*. And there's you supposed to be setting an example!

'What a waster you are. What was I ever thinking? Fuck. What a mess. Well. Since *you rang*, just to let you know ... I mean, I was going to try and break it softly like, but fuck it, you just aren't worth the effort you fucking waste of space. Now the divorce is sorted, Darren and me are getting married, and the kids, who love him, *who look up to him*, will be taking his name. Just to let you know – we won't want any more calls, no more visits. *No more late night weepy calls, Stu.* But don't think this lets you off the hook, neither. Don't worry, the payments is one responsibility I'll hold you to. It's not fair Darren has to take on all the father's duties and pay for it too. See if there's *something* you can do right, you fucking *loser*.'

Stuart dropped the phone. Dashed to the bathroom and threw up. Threw it all up. Had his head half down the bowl as it poured out, like a fucking firehose it was, scorching the back of his throat. Two, three further convulsions until he finally slunk back, hanging on to the bowl like a life belt, gasping for breath, his eyes streaming, sobs escaping like coughs, coughs dissolving in sobs.

The silence of that pale olive-green bathroom, the silence of that city, the city that was never, ever truly silent. The clunks and the clanks of the flats, the muffled voices, a distant siren. Stuart stayed there a while before finally getting to his feet. Looked at himself in the bathroom mirror. When he was in his twenties they used to say he resembled England and Newcastle's former star player Gazza, what with his round, wide open face, his square jaw. Now, a couple of decades on, he was more like the old, alcoholic Gazza, pale and drawn, with fat in all the wrong places. He'd lost his smile, too, he noticed, that wedding day smile, that maternity unit smile. Like Gazza, he'd lost his smile.

Stuart heard her coughing, Auntie's. Remembered where he'd put her, what he'd done. 'Fuck,' he said to his reflection. 'Fucking fuck *fuck up*.'

He knocked on Auntie's door but there was no answer. He pushed it ajar. The curtains were open – but then, he'd forgotten to close them – and Auntie was still in bed, her face poking out from beneath the duvet.

'Auntie?' She looked startled, her half-closed eyes ranging slowly toward him.

'Frankie,' she said, meaning her late husband, 'is that you, Frankie?'

'It's Stuart, Auntie,' he said. 'Are you all right? Can I get you some breakfast?' He thought about the mess in the living room. 'In bed?' He said. 'How about that, breakfast in bed, for a treat.'

'Frankie?' said Auntie, coughing. 'You'll have to get it yourself, I'm poorly.'

'Auntie?' said Stuart. He went over and felt her forehead with the back of his hand. It was hot. He pulled back the duvet and realised she was still in her clothes. And they – her clothes, the sheets – were damp. Auntie was burning up, feverish. He pulled the duvet back up. 'You just take it easy, Auntie,' he said, backing out of the room and closing the door behind him. *Oh Jesus*, he thought. *Oh sweet Jesus. What have I done?*

What should I do?

*

'We have the law,' his dad had said. 'We're protected by the law.' But Ben knew it didn't really work like that. What were laws but rules? Rules for grown-ups, just like school, with punishments and everything. But when it came down to it, it was all rubbish, something Ben understood even if his dads didn't. Or at least he didn't want them to understand. *If they knew* ... but maybe there would be no stopping it. Maybe *he* couldn't protect *them*. His dads were beginning to learn what Ben had this past year – that bad didn't care about rules. Rules were only for the good people to follow, and what was true for school, was true for the rest of life. It made sense, didn't it, that the bad, mean, cruel children grew up to be bad, mean, cruel adults.

'Watch your backs! Bendover's arrived!' There were nervous sniggers around the form room as he came in. These days he almost always left it until the last minute to coincide with the teacher so as to avoid what had become a morning ritual since Todd had come into the class, appeared one day, out of the blue, and Ben's whole world had changed.

It's not like Ben didn't know he was different, he wasn't *stupid*, he knew it was funny to have two dads, two gay dads, but that was how he had grown up and when he had moved schools, enough of his old friends had followed him for it not to be a big deal, for it to be *almost* normal. He had his *posse*, Gray and Taylor and Chris, and in time other boys came and went, factions forming, un-forming, like in Warcraft.

But one day, there he was – a pale kid with blond hair, those bright blue eyes. Right from the start Ben had sensed there was something wrong about Todd that made him keep his distance, but Gray ended up sitting beside him, and then he was at their table at lunch and then he was hanging about with them in the playground. At first Todd seemed shy, before he'd settled in. Looked at you, then away, reminded Ben of a dog with its tail between its legs. But it didn't take long. It didn't take long for him to turn them all against him.

The question had been respectful. He had trotted beside him between classes. 'Is it true you've got gay dads?'

Ben's senses prickled, but what could he say? 'What about it?'

'Just wondered. What's it like?'

Ben looked at him. It seemed like a genuine question. He wondered if Todd himself was gay, or going to be – they were getting to that age. 'All right,' he said. 'Normal.'

'Normal?' Todd said. Then he smiled. It was the first time Ben had seen Todd smile *properly*, not the nervous, eager to please smile he gave to everyone else. 'But it's not,' Todd said. 'Is it.'

'What?' Ben stopped. The others were filing into class. Ben's inner-warning siren began to sound along with the bell.

'It's not normal,' Todd was shaking his head, a joyous grin now plastered across his face. 'Not *normal* at all. I'll tell you what it is: it's fucking *queer*.'

Ben opened his mouth, but nothing came out. Todd was still shaking his head as he went into the classroom. 'Fucking queer,' he said.

This was the opening shot, the beginning of hostilities in the war with no end. No end in sight: just the daily grind of the trench, the constant bombardment by a foe who took extreme pleasure in attack. 'Watch out lads!' The cry in the showers when Ben came in. 'Backs to the wall!'

But how had this even happened? Wasn't school LGBTQ+? Rainbow flags and rights? "Celebrating diversity"? And anyway – why did they even *like* Todd? Couldn't they see what a bastard he was? His old school friends … Gray had been the first to crack, laughing when Todd had whispered, *sotto voce*, 'bum brothers', meaning him and Chris, sitting together. Worse: Chris had heard it too. And next lesson, he was sitting at the back beside Taylor. And the next – Ben had to sit beside one of the girls. Cue more sniggering.

'Cut it out,' said the teacher. 'What's so funny?'

'Nothing Ms.'

Then it was lunchtime, and those four – Todd and Gray and Chris and Taylor – they had disappeared, were ahead of Ben in the queue, so he had to wait on his own, and then, when he had come over to the table, they'd all shut up, finished quickly, and were off, leaving him on his own. He picked at his lunch, and wondered ... what was he going to do?

That evening he'd logged onto Warcraft and tried to hook up with them in the latest Dungeon, but it was the same story: they kept running away, and there was this new character – a Death Knight by the name of Fenlun Todie who could only be *him* – who kept saying 'watch out! Princess Bendover will get you!'

The next day at school that was what it was: 'Princess Bendover'. Then just Bendover. Even when the teacher picked him, said 'Ben', there would be these sniggers behind him and he knew Todd, or one of the others now, was ending it 'dover'.

Bendover; that was his name, that was what he became. 'Oi, Bendover,' some kid in another class would shout. He was now always on his own in the playground. Infected. Everyone knew to steer clear of him in case they caught it too – the virus. Of course, Hallie spoke to him, but he didn't like that because she was a girl, even though she was his sister. He told her to steer clear. He didn't want to be seen with girls. Only gay boys hung out with girls. What's wrong with being gay, she said. He just gave her a look. She was only twelve, but she understood. She said they should tell their dads but he pleaded with her no, no, no, whatever you do don't tell them.

'Why? They can help!' Ben shook his head as if she was mad.

'They can't *help*,' he said. 'They'll only make things *worse*.' She looked at him. She understood. They both understood – school was like prison. The guards could say whatever they liked, whatever sugary words about peace, love and understanding, but everyone hated a snitch.

The worst thing was, it didn't end there. Even if Ben had told Phillip (he *certainly* wouldn't have told Bryan, who would have wanted to *do* something however much Ben explained why he shouldn't) he knew that his father would not be able to help. Because it wasn't like the old days, he supposed, when at least you could escape at the school gates, make it home in one piece, and turn on the telly. When you were cut off, safe, nothing could touch you.

Now it followed you. It followed you into the world; that other, invisible world you carried with you at all times, where there were no gates, boundaries, safe spaces. Not just Warcraft. It was everywhere, forums, social – TizWoz, ChitChat, Videoworlds. That was the worst: being bombarded by pictures of dicks and friend requests from paedos who had somehow gotten his name ('I hear you like it up the arse') or maybe they were all just him, the Death Knight, stalking him through this other world, this world without end.

The only thing that would make it stop, if it ever *did* stop, *ever ever ever*, was for Todd to go away, to disappear. For his dad to get a new job and them to move. But Ben knew not even this would necessarily do the trick. The only thing that would *really* do it, was for Todd to *die*. As soon as Ben thought it, he stopped himself, shocked that he could even think such a thing. He had never thought anything like that before. But it was true, it was a bare fact: this evil, even if it moved schools or whatever, he knew it would never go away, it would always be there, would dog him for the rest of his life, or at least as far ahead as a thirteen-year-old could see.

The only thing that would save him was if this evil was dead, and Ben found some relief in imagining the multitude of gory ways Todd could die, very rarely quickly. Sometimes it was from a slow, but not too slow, illness that made all his bits rot off, other times maybe he had been kidnapped by a serial killer who had decided to experiment on him. Yes, that gave Ben the most satisfaction, was one of the few things that would help him drop off to sleep, imagining his adversary nailed to a wall as a ravening psycho carved him up. Slowly.

CANARIES

Hallie did tell in the end though, but not the dads. She told Simon and Claire – Juno and Diane's kids – when they came over that election night. They were a couple of years older, fourteen and fifteen. They wanted to play Warcraft but Ben looked glum and Claire said, what's up Ben? And Hallie said: 'He's being bullied.'

'Hallie!' Ben exploded.

'*Sorry*,' said Hallie. 'It just came out.'

'What's this, Ben?' asked Claire.

'Nothing,' he shook his head, looked at his hands.

'Secret's out now,' said Claire, who Ben couldn't look at properly at the best of times because. ...well, *you know* ... and now it was even worse.

'Please don't tell,' said Ben, the tears beginning to fall. He wiped his face with the back of his hand, and then Claire was holding him, and he was crying all the more, but at the same time, sort of melting into her arms.

'It's all right Ben, of course not. 'course not.'

'You will,' he said. 'You'll tell your mums and they'll tell our dads.'

There was silence, then he heard her say: 'No. We won't tell if you don't want us to.'

Ben looked up at her, her long hair trailing across his damp face. 'Promise?'

Claire nodded solemnly. 'Promise.'

So he told her. He told them everything, even stuff Hallie didn't know, and then she started crying too, and they had to comfort her.

'Has it ... ever happened to you?' Ben asked Claire. She shook her head.

'Not really. Nothing that bad. I think everyone's a bit afraid of my mum.' They all nodded. They knew which one she meant, and it wasn't Diane.

'I have,' said Simon. Claire looked startled:

'You didn't tell me!'

He shook his head. 'Marcus found some of mum's porn stuff. Was sharing it around the class.'

'What did you do?' asked Claire.

Simon shrugged. 'I followed him into the loos, then

when he was at the urinal I punched him until he went down, then I took his phone and stamped on it, then I said "if you do that again, next time it will be your face".'

'Fucking hell,' said Claire.

'You should do the same,' Simon leaned forward. 'It's the only thing they understand.'

8

Stuart jolted awake. He hadn't realised he'd been asleep, but he must have dropped off. He looked around, panicked, afraid he might have missed his number, but no – there were still, what? A dozen people ahead of them? Auntie was slumped in the wheelchair in front of him, the waiting room still bursting to the brim, as it had been for the past, how long? Ten? Eleven hours?

When Stuart first arrived at Casualty, he'd gone to the desk and asked for Auntie to be seen immediately. The woman – little more than a teenager, not a nurse, just a teenager in ordinary clothes, had asked: 'Was she brought in?'

'I brought her in.'

'Not an ambulance, then.' She did something with her computer. 'Will you be wanting Priority?'

'What's that?'

The woman looked at him like he was stupid. 'To be treated as a priority.'

'Yes. Yes, she's a priority.' The woman clicked something else.

'Cash or visa?'

'I'm sorry?'

'Will you be paying cash or visa. It's two hundred pounds for Priority.'

'I have to pay?'

The woman looked irritated. 'For Priority, yes.'

'But I thought it's free, the NHS. Free.'

'It is,' said the woman. Stuart kept looking at her. 'But if you want to be placed in the Priority queue you have to pay.' Stuart felt for his wallet, but he knew he had neither the cards nor the cash. He put his hands back flat on the counter. 'So, I'll assume no, then,' she said.

She had directed him to this other room where he'd had to look twice at the number the machine gave him to even believe it. In fact, before a seat became free he was standing there, around the wall with Auntie breathing heavily in her chair, when this bloke approached him. He showed him his number – it would be coming up in about ten goes.

'Hundred quid,' he said.

'What?'

'Yours for a hundred quid. Your old lady ain't looking too clever. Yours for a ton.'

'But it's free,' Stuart said. The man nodded.

'Eventually. You want to wait that long?'

'I ... I haven't got the cash.' The man shrugged, wandered away. Five minutes later he saw him give the ticket to a man with an unconscious kid in his arms, palming the money he gave him as if he was selling drugs.

Then Stuart saw another man going through the rows. Stuart realised – the numbers were being inflated by touts. They got batches of tickets then sold them off. He went over to a security guard who was standing half outside the door, vaping. 'Have you seen that? What's happening?' he said. The man looked at him, resting his palm upon the end of his baton.

'There,' said Stuart. 'That bloke there, he's selling tickets to get seen.'

The man shook his head. 'I don't see nothing, mate.'

'He's not the first, this other bloke tried to sell me his for a hundred pounds!' The guard shook his head.

'Not my problem,' he said.

'But it's got to be wrong, doing that.'

'My advice is to mind your own business, mate.'

'But it's not right! There are sick people.'

'That your granny over there, is it?' said the guard.

'My Auntie, yeah.'

The man dropped his voice. 'Listen, *cunt*. If you want your granny, auntie or whatever to get seen, then you'll shut the fuck up. Otherwise I'll have you kicked out and she can just sit there pissing her panties, got it?'

Stuart backed off. He returned to Auntie. Watched as through the night the touts came and went, watched as they smoked and joked with the guards at the doors.

They had only five to go when the young woman came up to them. She looked really sick. Pale. She was clutching her stomach. 'Please,' she said. 'Please. I've been bleeding since three o'clock. I'm afraid I'm going to lose my baby.'

'I'm sorry, love,' said Stuart, his face creasing with anguish. 'I would, but we've been here all day now. We can't wait any more.'

The woman nodded like she understood, then she leaned over and looked at Auntie. She didn't even seem shocked. Perhaps she was in too much pain.

'But she's gone, mister,' she said.

'What?' Stuart got to his feet. It was true, he knew it as soon as he saw Auntie. Her eyes weren't even closed. They were open but unseeing, a pair of watery grey discs. Her mouth hung down, there was white where the spittle had been smudging the corners of her mouth but dried.

'Auntie,' he said, pulling her back upright. 'Auntie, come on. Come on now.' But her head lolled about. Her throat, her face was cold. 'No, this can't be. It can't be.' Holding onto her, he began pushing her towards the double doors that led to Treatment. They'd swung open electronically when he'd been watching them, but now they remained closed. He tried to open them but they wouldn't budge. He began banging on the door. 'Open up! Open up!' He tried to ram them with his shoulder, but next thing he knew there was a baton beneath his chin and he was being wrenched backwards, crashing onto the ground. Two of them were on top of him, flipping him over, wrestling his hands behind his back and snapping on plastic cuffs. They pulled him to his feet, then pushed him against the wall. 'Auntie!' he shouted as they ran him outside. He glanced behind and the doors were finally opening. A pair of weary looking nurses in hospital greens were bending over Auntie. He tried to break free but was thrown to the floor again, one of them kneeling on his back while the other got on his radio. While he was lying there, his cheek flat against the cold pavement, he felt someone going through his jacket pocket. It took all his strength to twist his head over to the other side. It was the woman, the pregnant one. 'I'm sorry, mister,' she said, and took the ticket.

9

What was needed was a government of national unity, the Prime Minister declared, and in due course the somewhat precarious parliamentary coalition firmed up into the 'Patriotic Alliance', adding to its number a handful of rogue MPs from both of what used to be called the mainstream parties (but what *was* 'mainstream' these days?) not a few of whom announced it was their 'patriotic duty' to 'answer the call' in the UK's 'hour of need', while casting a scornful eye across the aisle at the depleted opposition benches.

Thus in the mid-Twenty-First Century, Britain's old political settlement – almost a gentleman's agreement – between the Labour and Conservative parties, stood in ruins.

And yet, despite the 'saloon bar revolution' as Bill had coined it in one of his columns, the English sun kept shining or, more usually, the rain falling. The Premier League played on. Public transport ran late, or not at all. Celebrities were born, blazed, then faded away. Church bells – where they rung – kept ringing, and still, hardly anyone went to church. The call to prayer – where it was permitted – was still sung, and almost everyone went to mosque. Everyone Meena knew, at any rate. It would be unthinkable not to – it was their community, right? – and maybe there were even a few new faces after the general election, worried about the likely political changes, but they dropped off once the initial surprise had sunk in and the scare stories seemed to have been just that – stories.

Meena's mosque had been one of the first to sign the loyalty pledge, or Covenant of British Values, as it was officially known, and the sky hadn't fallen in. In fact, the 'CBV' turned out to be open to all houses of worship and was entirely voluntary, although it was true the only ones the media reported on were mosques, and the only ones that piqued their interest were those that hadn't signed, rather than the majority that had.

While Sanjay had plenty to say, Meena found it hard to

get too worked up about it. After all, the CBV applied to everybody, and no one could deny there was a problem with radicalisation that, in turn, led to terrorism, which did nobody any favours, least of all ordinary Muslims.

And it wasn't like she didn't have work to do. The sector was booming. A new Cabinet post had been created for Housing, which was something she had always dreamed about, to be honest – finally, they were getting the recognition they deserved. All right, it had gone to Our England's sole Cabinet minister, which had made Bryan groan out loud when the news broke – 'God help us. They've put a Nazi in charge of Housing!' – but, despite her misgivings she had to admit (if only to herself) she was quite impressed: after years of Tory (and Labour!) intransigence, the new minister was driving forward a massive house building programme. Admittedly he had said 'our people' would be first in line for the new homes, but legally that meant *British citizens*, whatever their origin. What Meena had not heard was the kind of racist or Islamophobic language Sanjay had worried about.

She was on a trip out of the office with Nathan. Meena would have preferred to go alone, but Bryan said he wanted Nathan to get the experience, although Meena suspected it was actually more about him being concerned for her safety. The past few years had certainly seen a rise of crime in what used to be called, before gentrification, 'the inner city', or at least the areas where Meena and her colleagues did most of their business – the council and social housing estates that had resisted the march of the middle classes.

This was despite the fact that London had weathered political and epidemiological storms rather well, its endlessly inventive finance sector coupling with infinitely flexible governments to ensure the softest of landings, at least for England's South East. In a way London was even, little by little, actually regaining some of its old, edgy reputation, albeit more for being flush with laundered cash than for a cutting edge music scene.

The exception was the estates, still dotted across the city much to the pattern of devastation created by the Luftwaffe almost a hundred years before. In what had become a more or less annual occasion like the Notting Hill Carnival or Lord Mayor's Parade, every June or July, usually when the days were at their longest and hottest, these would erupt in violence.

The trigger would be a heavy-handed arrest or fire that got out of hand. The police would move in and it would turn into a pitched battle between local youths and the forces of law and order, which would then spread across the city, fanned by social media. The anger and impotence of the poor would percolate into the richer areas – even Kensington High Street and Mayfair had been hit. Hundreds, if not thousands of people would 'go shopping' – looting, in other words – while the police tried to cope, with varying degrees of success.

Among many of Bryan and Meena's clients it was commonly believed that the police themselves had a hand in the trouble, their own *agent provocateurs* inciting the riots in order to justify the maintenance of their funding, and although Meena wasn't inclined to entirely buy into this, it was unarguable that the disturbances were mentioned whenever talk of further cuts came up.

Certainly, Meena never felt threatened when she set foot on the estates – she knew so many of the women and kids, had provided homes for them – even if they were unofficial no-go areas.

She only felt a little nervous now, entering with Nathan. If anybody looked like a target, it was him, although she suspected he would have been the last one to realise. In his hoodie, ripped jeans and trainers, he presumably thought he was blending right in, but Meena knew that to the folk around here, he might as well have been wearing fancy dress. He looked every bit the posh boy coming to visit a drug dealer with a wallet thick with cash. Meena only hoped *her* presence would protect *him* from any unwanted attention.

Their first call was on an Iranian family who had just been

provided with accommodation. Meena always enjoyed these 'Welcome Visits' as they were called. The Farahanis were expecting them, and had plainly made an effort for the occasion. Mrs Farahani greeted them with a warm smile and, after they had removed their shoes, she bade them enter the spotless living room which already, albeit intangibly, since it consisted of little more than a futon sofa, a cheap rug and a few potted plants, seemed somehow reminiscent of Tehran. Mrs Farahani went to make some tea while her husband stood grinning opposite them, their two small children peeking shyly behind his legs.

The tea arrived and the father and children sat on the floor, while Mrs Farahani perched upon a stool – they insisted their visitors took the sofa.

'Lovely,' said Meena, even though the tea was a little sweet for her taste.

'We discovered a street, not far from here, where there are many Turkish and Kurdish shops,' said Mrs Farahani, who had been an English teacher. Her husband, Dalir, had taught Persian literature and had enrolled on an English language course arranged by Meena.

'Very tasty,' he said, pointing at the baklava. 'Eat! Eat!'

They were such a lovely family, almost refugee pin-ups. Meena thought about the last election, all the anti-immigrant rhetoric, the hostility that existed out there to families like this. In fact, they were lucky to have got in – one of the first things the government had done after the general election was 'suspend' the United Nations Convention on Refugees.

'Have you heard anything yet?' said Meena. 'From your sister.'

Sadness swept Mrs Farahani's face. She shook her head. Tehran had been badly bombed by the Sunni Federation, in coalition with the Americans, Israelis and, of course, the British government. Meena, a Sunni Muslim herself, felt deep shame for the actions of her co-religionists and had done everything she could to help the Farahanis and families like them, despite some of the talk at the mosque that the Shiites were finally receiving the reckoning they deserved. In fact, these reactions more than anything had shaken Meena's faith in her community. Muslim idiots carrying out terror attacks was one thing – it was easier to disassociate herself from them because they were so self-evidently different – but when people she had grown up with said the Iranians, the Shiites, were getting their just desserts and God was punishing them, then she thought – hold on, how are you any different from supporters of the Patriots? Shared Values? Our England? All the bigots who blame everything on Muslims? And then she realised, actually – they weren't. They weren't any different at all. They were just people – prejudiced, ignorant people.

'There's a great Persian restaurant in Shoreditch,' said Nathan. 'Persepolis.'

'Shore-ditch?' Mrs Farahani said.

'It's in East London,' Nathan said enthusiastically. 'The digital hub.'

Mrs Farahani's eyes swam. She plainly had no idea what he was talking about. 'It's where they have a lot of companies that work with computers,' explained Meena. 'Social media. Apps, for phones.'

'Ah,' Mrs Farahani smiled. Nathan nodded encouragingly. Mrs Farahani, Laleh, was twenty-three. She was a year younger than Nathan, Meena thought, but she seemed as if she was from another generation, another time.

Her husband asked her something, and she explained in Persian. She switched to English. 'Thank you.'

Meena smiled. There was no way they could afford one of Nathan's trendy restaurants. Maybe she and Sanjay should take them. She waved at Roshni, their little girl, just a year older than Aisha, who hid her face behind her hands, then sneaked a peek between her fingers.

Meena and Nathan's next stop was two floors up, to check one of their disabled residents had got safety rails installed. Geoffrey, who was of West Indian descent, was only in his late fifties but looked about seventy. He had been a bricklayer, as far as Meena knew, but in the end his knees and hips had gone from the heavy lifting and he had become increasingly immobile and obese.

They rang the bell, heard a thud and then scraping from inside. This would be Geoffrey hauling himself to his feet. He made his way slowly to the front door.

'Who is it?' he called through the panel.

'It's Meena, Geoffrey,' she shouted. 'Meena, from Housing.' There was a rattle as he undid the chain.

'Hi Geoffrey,' Meena smiled. She always put on her cheery smile in situations like this. She hoped that behind her Nathan was following suit. Geoffrey was in a tracksuit and flipflops. She looked away from his unclipped toenails. 'Here to check they installed everything properly,' she said.

'You don't have to shout, woman, I'm not deaf.' He turned around, leaving the door open, and waddled up the corridor like an old woman.

'Have you lost a bit of weight, Geoffrey?' Meena inspected the rails that lined the corridor. 'Brrr,' she said. 'It's a bit chilly in here. Saving on the heating?' She turned to Nathan, who was surreptitiously pinching his nose. She scowled at him. 'Can you take some photos, please,' she said. 'For the record.'

She followed Geoffrey into the living room. At least it was an improvement on before, she thought. He had cleaned the place up: there were no pizza boxes, old newspapers or plastic bags stuffed with the detritus of takeaways surrounding his battered old recliner. That's when she realised there was something else missing too.

'Where's your telly, Geoffrey?'

He had slumped back down on his recliner. 'Listen to the radio,' he said, nodding to a tiny thing on the floor.

'But you loved your telly, didn't you?' She wandered into the kitchen. There were a couple of pots and pans in the sink. A bowl ... she glanced across the living room. Geoffrey was watching Nathan, who was standing with his back to him and looking out of the window. Meena knelt down and opened one of Geoffrey's cupboards. It was empty. She stood up and checked another. The same. She looked inside the fridge – a few old ketchup and soya sauce packets, the rank residue of a bottle of milk.

She came back into the living room. Nathan was still looking out of the window. 'Has something happened, Geoffrey?' He looked up at her.

'Who's he?' he said.

'Nathan,' said Meena. 'Would you like to introduce yourself?'

Nathan jumped. 'Oh, yes.' He turned around, gave a half-bow. 'Nathan. Drake. Housing officer.'

'So, where's the TV, Geoffrey?' said Meena. 'Come on, I know you love your TV. Fifty-five inch, isn't it? My hubby's always on at me to get one of those.' She walked over to the dusty wooden platform on which it had sat.

Geoffrey made a congested sound that emerged as a kind of sigh. 'Sold it,' he said.

'Sold it?' said Meena. She gave him another look. 'And you *have* lost some weight. What's going on Geoffrey?' Another rumble.

'Disability,' he said. 'Stopped it.'

'Stopped it?' she said. 'But we've just had all this stuff installed. We had to get a doctor's certificate and everything.'

'Said I fell outside their category. Was "mobile". Could work.'

'So you sold your TV,' she said. 'And this is why there isn't any food. How about the food bank?'

He looked up at her. In those large, blood-rimmed eyes she saw a look of sheer terror. 'It's too far,' he said. 'Tried, but couldn't make it.'

'Couldn't you ask someone?' He looked at her again, then away. There was no one Geoffrey could ask. 'So you were just going to sit here, then? And *starve*?' Meena felt a sudden surge of anger. That was precisely what Geoffrey was going to do, she thought. 'Nathan,' she said. 'Go to the food bank on Tyham Corner and get a week's groceries. Say Meena sent you.'

Nathan couldn't get out of there quickly enough. Why did he even bother, thought Meena. 'While we're waiting,' she said to Geoffrey, 'why don't we put the radio on?' She picked it up, but immediately realised it didn't have any batteries. She looked at him. He had been sitting here starving, with nothing to watch or even listen to. He gave her that look again. 'Don't worry,' she said. She took his rough hand. 'It'll be all right. I'll make sure it'll be all right.' That was when tears began to moisten his eyes.

'You're all right,' he said. 'You're all right, miss.'

She was there for a good couple of hours, much longer than planned. Nathan took his time getting back with the groceries, then Meena wanted to make sure Geoffrey had eaten something (beans on toast) before they left. 'I'll speak to one of the churches,' she said to Nathan, as they were heading down the walkway. 'Or a mosque.'

'You can't get them to reverse their decision?' he said.

'Of course I'll try,' she said, not holding out much hope. She checked her watch. It was almost the end of the working day, but it was Sanjay's turn to pick up Aisha, and this should only take a minute.

They crossed the common and went into Trellis House, just across from where Geoffrey and the Farahanis lived. Meena reached into her bag and pulled out a clear plastic bag containing a set of keys.

'The old lady who lived here died in hospital,' she said. 'Can you take some photos again? We'll need them for the clearance.'

'No relatives?'

Meena shook her head and opened the security gate, then the front door, which swung open easily, surprising her. There would usually be a pile of junk mail. Had someone been collecting it, she wondered.

The flat had that musty old lady smell, but was warm, warmer than Geoffrey's place, any rate. She stepped into the hallway. Behind one of the closed cream doors, she heard a clunk.

10

Meena froze, Nathan stumbled into her. 'Hello?' she called. 'Is anybody there?' She backed against the wall, and elbowed Nathan back, too – she didn't want any trouble. If it was burglars, she wanted to give them a clear route of escape.

There was another clunk and the far door opened. A man, a very white man, was standing there, naked except for a pair of pale blue Y Fronts and socks. He rubbed his eyes. Then, in alarm, clutched his hand first over his crotch, then retreated into the room, closing the door so only his head was visible.

'What the fuck? Who the hell are you?'

'I'm sorry,' said Meena. 'We were told the flat was empty.'

'Well it's not!' he said.

'I'm sorry,' said Meena. 'I'm from the council. Housing. This is the late Mrs Armstrong's flat, right?'

'Auntie? Yes.' He looked down. His voice cracked. 'Yes.'

'And you are? I'm sorry … she was your auntie, you say. So you're living here …?'

'Stuart.'

'I see, Stuart, so you've been living here. I see. Look. Shall we give you a moment, to put some clothes on? We'll wait outside.'

'All right,' he said, and closed the door. Meena pushed Nathan back.

'He's not supposed to be here,' Nathan said. 'I thought they said there weren't any relatives.' Meena shrugged.

'Mix-ups happen.' They heard the door open. Stuart came toward them in jeans and a t-shirt.

'Sorry to disturb you like that,' Meena held out her hand. Startled, he took it. 'We were told the flat was empty.'

'Well, it's not,' he said again.

'And Mrs Armstrong was your auntie?' Stuart nodded.

'My mam's sister, that's right.'

'We're very sorry for your loss,' said Meena.

'Well,' said Stuart. 'Yes …'

'Look,' said Meena, 'this is a bit awkward, but we had come to inspect the property, now your auntie has passed away. If you like, we can make an appointment and come back another time.'

Stuart sighed. 'Nah,' he said, 'you're all right.'

'Thank you,' said Meena. 'That's very kind. We won't be long.'

They weren't. Stuart watched the Pakistani lady duck into various rooms with the lanky bloke, telling him where to take photos. 'Do you mind?' she said when it came to his bedroom. He felt (or at least, he would have felt, had he not felt so down) a bit embarrassed but he said, go ahead. It was a right mess, he knew, what with the clothes and takeaways and empty cans, but what the heck. 'Thank you,' she said, back at the front door in no more than five minutes. 'Really sorry to disturb you, Stuart.'

'That's it, then?' he said.

'Well,' she said with an apologetic smile. 'For now. You see, we were told Mrs Armstrong hadn't any relatives. That was why we were here, to see what could be done with her … furniture and so on. But now you're here, perhaps you can help us with that.'

Stuart looked confused. 'Okay, except …' He scratched his head. 'I'm not sure what you mean.'

'Ah, yes.' Meena looked at Nathan, then back at Stuart. 'Well, you see, because Mrs Armstrong has passed away, her property is now officially considered to be vacant. That was why we were here – we were told that there were no relatives, so we had come to see about removing her belongings so we could let the property to another tenant.'

'But I'm here,' said Stuart. Meena understood what he was getting at but decided to pretend she didn't. Hopefully he would get the hint.

'Yes,' she said. 'So that means that you can decide what to do with her property, rather than us calling a clearing service. Although I would be happy to give you some numbers if that would help.'

'No, what I mean missus,' he rubbed his face, 'is that I'm living here now, so that won't … you know, be necessary. I can pay the rent, and that.' Behind her, Meena heard Nathan scoff.

'I'm afraid … it doesn't work that way, Stuart,' said Meena. 'You see, there's a waiting list, a rather long list, based on need, and how long people have been resident in the area, and so on. Unless you're on the list?'

He shook his head. 'A list you say?'

'Yes. I'm terribly sorry …'

'And how do you get on this list?'

Meena dug into her bag and pulled out a leaflet. 'This explains what you need to do,' she said. 'There's a website.'

'All right,' he said. He looked satisfied. He obviously hadn't understood, thought Meena, her heart sinking.

'But I have to tell you, Stuart,' she said. 'Even if you do get on the list, because of the rules, it is very unlikely that you will be able to stay here.'

He shook his head. 'But it was Auntie's.'

'You don't *inherit* council property,' said Nathan.

Stuart glanced at him, then back at Meena. 'So, what you're saying is: I can't live here?'

Meena nodded. 'I'm sorry, Stuart,' she said.

'But where will I go?' he said.

'I'm … sorry,' said Meena.

'How long have I got?'

'Well,' said Meena. 'You don't have to leave straight away. I would say you'll have about a month? I'm afraid that part isn't really in my hands. There's quite a lot of pressure on us to place people – families, and this is a family home – living in quite difficult circumstances.'

Stuart nodded, looking down at the leaflet. 'All right,' he said quietly.

'I'm sorry,' said Meena. Stuart shook his head.

'Nah,' he said. 'Are we done?' Meena nodded.

'Cheers.' He closed the door.

11

The March Against Capital Punishment was one of the largest the UK had ever witnessed. Over five million people were estimated to have mobilised across the country, while more than a million marched in London itself. It was the first demonstration Bryan and Phillip had been on for years, and the first ever for Ben and Hallie. There was the sense, thought Bryan as they gathered at the assembly point beneath Waterloo Bridge, that it was not only the reintroduction of capital punishment they were marching against, but the loss of so much of what their country had once stood for. One banner being held by a clearly affronted middle-aged man in brogues and a beige corduroy jacket seemed to say what so many of the mostly white, middle class demonstrators were thinking: WE WANT OUR COUNTRY BACK.

Not everyone was white, though. In fact, Sanjay had been instrumental in getting the group of friends together as he was organising the local Labour Party's contingent, so they just fell in behind their banner.

They began moving slowly forward, Big Ben looming up ahead of them, a sea of protesters filling the Embankment behind. 'It's so big, isn't it!' Hallie said, full of excitement. 'They've got to listen!'

'Let's hope so,' said Meena.

'But there's millions of us. They have to!' said Hallie.

Meena couldn't dampen Hallie's enthusiasm. 'I'm sure they will,' she said.

'I wrote,' Meena heard Bill say to Bryan, 'that this is what it must have felt like to be a German, I mean a decent German, in 1934 – watching while your entire country loses its mind.'

But although she would never have dreamed of saying so, Meena couldn't find it in herself to fully agree with her friend's sentiment about capital punishment. After all, many countries executed people, and although she didn't agree with it in all cases – and they weren't talking about all cases anyway, only the most serious ones like child and mass murderers, police killers – she wasn't one hundred per cent opposed. Could she forgive someone who hurt Aisha, for example? Never.

The demonstration snailed past Parliament. She looked at Ben and Hallie, alongside Juno and Diane's kids, who were hooting and chanting with their painted faces and homemade placards. Then she caught Juno's eye, which she had been avoiding since their first awkward reunion at the bridge.

Juno came over. 'I'm sorry,' she said immediately. 'I should never have said what I did.'

Meena noticed Bryan looking at them and she immediately wondered if there had been some kind of conspiracy to force Juno to apologise. But it was difficult to imagine forcing Juno to do anything, and she did seem sincere.

'Don't worry about it,' said Meena. 'Water under the bridge. We were all ... you, know. Stressed.'

'I had had a bit to drink, that's true,' said Juno. 'But I can't just blame it on that, even though everyone thinks Juno drinks too much.'

'That's not true ...'

Juno shrugged. 'I'm sorry, anyway – picking on you. That was really, really wrong. I was just angry, and stupid. And wrong. And, okay, maybe also a little drunk.' She gave her forehead a loud slap. 'Stupid Juno!'

'Don't worry, please ...'

'I respect your beliefs, honestly, I do.'

Meena gave her a sardonic look. 'Now don't go too far – I know you're an atheist.'

Juno smiled. 'Well, I didn't mean that, obviously. You won't see me in a burka! I mean,' she said seeing Meena's look of alarm, 'you know, covering my head. But I respect you for standing up for what you believe in – your identity, culture, despite the fact you spend half your time surrounded by queers and unbelievers.' Juno shrugged. 'You know, you and me have a lot in common.'

CANARIES

Meena couldn't conceal her surprise. 'What do you mean?'

'Oh, I know who you see when you look at me, but I'm not like these people.'

'Really?' To Meena, Juno appeared to be precisely like the rest of the crowd.

'It's what's on the inside. I'm not posh like most of them.'

'With a name like Juno?'

'That's not really my name,' she said, 'I thought everyone knew that! It's my stage name. Porn name. Because of my big tits. My real name is June. I was brought up on an estate in *sarf* London, but I ditched the June, along with the accent, after I came out. No one would have taken me seriously, otherwise.'

A chant rose up around them: *'No to the noose, No to injections, Yes to love, And new elections!'* After it had petered out, Juno continued: 'I never went to university or anything. In fact I didn't do much school, truth be told. Did my first porno at sixteen, although I said I was eighteen!

'That's why I ask questions you're not supposed to, I guess. Because I'm ignorant.' She saw Meena's sceptical look. 'Oh, I don't mean thick, at least I don't think I'm thick any more, not like I used to when I was first surrounded by people like Diane.' She grinned. 'But because I don't come from ... *all this*, I suppose it provokes me sometimes. Everyone's so bloody right-on, you know? I get bored. Say things I shouldn't, what's on my mind without really thinking it through. Sometimes I'm right, not that I get credit for it, other times wrong. Like this time, *that* time, I mean. That was cruel and unfair. You were the last person I should have picked on. I'm sorry.'

'Why "the last person"?'

'Well,' said Juno as if it was obvious, 'you're not one of them either, are you.'

Following the cacophony as the demonstration swept past an empty Palace of Westminster, came the trudge up broad, characterless Victoria Street on the way to Hyde Park. Meena had by now separated from Juno, using the excuse of Aisha's tears to get away from her unsettling confessions. She lifted Aisha off Sanjay's shoulders and put her in the buggy. Bryan joined them.

'How's it going?' he said.

'Fine,' said Meena.

'I saw you speaking to Juno,' he said.

'It was fine,' said Meena. She smiled. 'Friends again.'

Bryan nodded. He wasn't going to push it. 'Have you seen over there?'

At first Meena struggled to recognise him out of context, and he was further obscured by the homogeneity of the group around him, young and hip beneath their ECO INSURGENCY banner, sandwiched between columns of drummers, but it was Nathan, his face painted purple, red and green, including his handlebar moustache. He was jigging with the drums, arm-in-arm with a pair of similarly painted young women, one of whom Meena recognised as Sasha.

'He seems to be having fun,' said Bryan. Meena nodded.

'Well,' said Bryan, 'we were young once.'

Meena let out a laugh.

'What?' said Bryan.

'I was just thinking,' she said. 'About our rather different youths.'

Bryan grinned. 'Well,' he said, 'we're all together now.'

'Even Nathan,' said Meena.

'Even Nathan,' said Bryan.

But it wasn't the million-plus crowd the demonstration become known for, it was an incident toward the end of the day.

It had been a beautiful afternoon. The friends had

stretched out on the grass under clear blue skies as a succession of speakers took to the stage and renounced the government's 'barbaric fantasies', as the leader of the Labour Party put it. In fact, it turned into something of a picnic. Meena had brought some food for Aisha and Sanjay, which she shared out. Rory, Bill and Phillip went to the Marks & Spencer at Marble Arch and returned with shopping bags full of goodies, along with a couple of bottles of wine and some beer. As they were breaking the French bread Meena heard Bill say: 'Anyway, there are lots of police.'

'What's that?' she asked.

Bill popped a bottle of Peroni. 'Our England,' he said.

'Nothing to worry about,' said Rory. 'A handful.' He looked around the park. 'They're hardly a match for us.'

'But we don't want any trouble,' said Emma. 'Especially not with Hamish and Isla here.'

'Really, love,' Rory said to his wife, 'it's nothing.'

Phillip said to Bill: 'Have you ever seen him in a fight?' He meant Rory.

Bill grinned. 'There was that one time a drunk local wanted to knock my lights out back when we were students, and he tried to reason with him.'

'A civil servant even then,' said Phillip. 'What happened?'

'He hit you, didn't he, Rory?'

'I ducked,' said Rory, 'then we ran.'

'Discretion the greater part of valour,' said Phillip. 'Very wise.'

They enjoyed their bread and cheese and cold cuts. The kids had a run around. The speakers' voices blew loud and soft with the breeze. Bryan hung his head back and soaked up the sun's rays, only half-listening to his friends' chatter. Despite the somewhat sombre occasion, it was hard to think that anything very terrible was really happening to the country, or at least, anything worse than usual. Then why did he continue to feel anxious? Experience that vaguely disquieting state of unease he had registered years ago, and which had never entirely gone away?

He could date its arrival to the morning he had woken to discover the result of the Brexit referendum, the referendum in which, to his lasting, secret shame, he had not even voted, so certain was his twenty-year-old self that it was a done deal to Remain. Certainly, since then nothing had ever truly felt the same. The European identity that had run in ripples through almost every aspect of his sense of self – from the food and furniture he preferred, to the certain knowledge that he was free to roam, and perhaps one day even live, across a whole continent; that he was, in fact, a citizen with another flag – azure blue with golden stars – had felt ripped from him in 'an outbreak of democracy', as a youthful Bill had posted on what was then called Twitter, 'the cultural equivalent of open heart surgery with a rusty spoon.'

But, like everyone else, Bryan had had little choice but to get on with it, and since then, of course, 'the outbreak' had spread, albeit taking different forms, across the western world. Indeed (although he was loathe to admit it) Bryan had almost started to come round to the idea that England's spiritual – if not practical – dislocation from the 'European Dream' may have marked a lucky escape from the kind of Continental excesses Englishmen across the ages had traditionally viewed with lofty disdain from the White Cliffs of Dover – the mass round-ups, deportations, camps. Despite his sexual orientation, progressive politics and general aversion to the banal predilections of his own people, Bryan's faith in traditional British values – common sense, fairness, moderation – had turned out to run even deeper in his veins than azure blue and gold.

Then came the general election. The result had rocked him again. He simply hadn't seen it coming. For the second time in his (political) life, his complacency had been shaken to the core. It 'couldn't happen here'? Well it could and it bloody had, and that sense of disquiet that had followed the first winds of Brexit had re-asserted itself... chipped away behind his apparently unflappable façade.

CANARIES

Yet sitting here with his friends on this very English summer day in Hyde Park, drew its sting. Chill out, Bry. Nothing terrible was really going to take place. *He* was certainly not going to murder anyone and face the noose. In fact, despite its current semblance of strength, the government was unlikely to survive the full five years. Then sanity would restore itself, Labour or the Tories would get back in, and Great British Decency would return. Little would change for families like his – there would still be friends, kids, parties, picnics, and Marks and Spencer sandwiches.

The children were growing restless, a chilly edge was coming to the late afternoon air. They began to make a move. While the others headed off towards Knightsbridge – Emma said she wanted to take Hamish and Isla to Harrods for the first time, while Diane and Juno lived in that direction anyway – Meena and Bryan's families set off towards Marble Arch to catch the tube going north. Bill tagged along – he was planning to meet a friend for a drink in Soho.

It was as they neared the triumphal arch, looming above the hedges that bordered the entrance to the park, that they began to hear the noise. The klaxons, megaphones, the chanting like a football crowd. Bryan and Phillip exchanged a glance – both were thinking the same thing, but they were now in a bottleneck, thousands deep, flowing toward the exit and it would be almost impossible to break away, especially with the kids. So they found themselves shuffling forward as the noise grew louder.

Meena picked up Aisha, drifting between the four men. She gathered Ben and Hallie around her, too, as they neared the gate. Surrounded by this wall of bodies, most of the people taller than she was, she felt panic flutter from her chest to her throat, but she knew she had to stay calm for the kids.

'What's that noise?' asked Hallie.

'Don't worry about that,' said Meena, 'it's just the demo.'

'But I thought the demo was over,' said Hallie, who had made it clear she was tired and wanted to go home.

'Don't worry,' Meena gave her a brilliant smile, 'we'll be at the Tube soon.'

'I need the toilet,' said Hallie.

'Me too,' said Ben.

'Me too,' said Aisha.

'Once we get through the crowd,' said Meena, 'we'll find a McDonalds or pub or something and you can go there. Just stay together,' she said. 'Stay with me, okay?'

They would watch the Sky News helicopter footage on YouTube later, with its hundreds of thousands – ultimately millions – of views, with commentary and superimposed arrows and lines: *'This is Our England.' The journalist outlined the dark blob of bodies shifting in slow motion in red felt tip. 'And you see here.' He drew a ragged blue line. 'This is where the police are holding them back, and this,' he drew a series of yellow arrows above another blob, 'is the crowd exiting the park. Now let's watch what happens next.'*

You could see the yellow arrows flowing out of the park while the thin blue line waxed and waned against the red bulge. That was the helicopter-eye view – to Bryan and Meena there was nothing but tightly-packed bodies and noise which grew louder as the crowd contracted ever closer as they passed the counter demonstration.

'Careful,' said Meena, to the people around her, 'there are children here. Children!' It was so loud the kids were cupping their ears, their faces pictures of fear.

'Keep going, come on, keep going,' she said, praying: please let this be over, let this be over soon.

'Now,' said the journalist, 'you see, here, the breach.'

The red blob burst through the blue line.

12

Meena had never screamed, at least not since she had been a kid in the playground, but it escaped involuntarily, a piercing, primitive cry that shocked even her as she made it, as the crush hardened around her like concrete.

It may have been enough, just enough, to save them. To jolt Bryan, Phillip, Sanjay and Bill into equally instinctive defence-mode. To stiffen against the weight of bodies that ploughed into them. They bent against it, but did not break, as Hallie too, and Ben and Aisha, added their animal sounds to Meena's.

The men pushed back. The wall held. It held. Then the pressure began to give. Suddenly there was space, air. There was a moment, just a moment, when the men looked at each other with relief.

Then they realised, together – they could see between the heads, over the shoulders, four ranks distant, those ranks dissolving rapidly – the enemy. Its spiky gelled hair, its sneering white face; its gold-ringed fist, its lunging white trainer, its banner – JUSTICE – smacking down on a prone, balding head and splintering. Sanjay turned to Meena: 'Run,' he said.

He barely had time to turn back before a fist came at him, cuffing his ear. He pushed the man and the blond-fringed thug in a Chelsea shirt fell onto his arse. Sanjay glanced right to see his friends grappling with more Our Englanders. He looked back just in time to see another fist. Too late, this time. It connected full with his cheekbone and he went down.

Make no mistake, Bryan recognised them – over the weeks it had taken him to recover from his Manchester injuries, the wounds and cracked rib to heal, the months, even years for those deeper, psychic scars, he had had plenty of time to ponder his assailants – who had never been brought to justice, incidentally – to see them in every hoody-clad youth, even glimpses recently in Ben and his friends, which he had been obliged to suppress (he and Phillip had never mentioned the bloody coda to their romantic encounter to their children) and now he was ready, even in a sense welcomed the opportunity to confront these 'ghosts that only come out at night' during the day. In a sense, he had been preparing for years.

Certainly, he was bigger than most of their attackers and had less of a problem fending them off – in fact they seemed to mostly go for the others. His first instinct was to shield Phillip, who was being attacked by a shaven-headed taxi driver-type who brought a stick down on his shoulder. Before Bryan had even thought about it, he had the bastard by one of his pug ears and was twisting. 'No you don't,' he was saying, 'no you don't!' He was twisting it, this piggy ear, with his left hand, and punching him with his right, Bryan's big, soft fist connecting with the man's face. He punched again and again, until it became wet. He thought it was the man's tears, he thought the man was crying and let go. The man dropped while Bryan examined his hand. It was dripping with blood. He looked at Phillip with surprise. But Phillip was darting around him: Sanjay was being kicked and stamped on by three of them.

'No you don't!' roared Bryan. He picked up the stick and walloped one of them clean around the face. Blood lashed the pavement. The thug stumbled away, clutching his cheek. Bryan realised there was a nail protruding from the end of the stick. He threw it away and lunged at another, who simply skipped back, giving him the finger.

'Fuck off, granddad!' He backed off. Bryan looked around for someone else to fight, but the jackals were all keeping their distance.

Phillip was beside Sanjay. Bill was standing, swaying, nearby, holding a bloody nose.

Bryan searched for the kids, for Meena, for her mauve headscarf. He saw it – he thought he saw it – behind them, up there, on the grass.

Police reinforcements began to run between them, their black batons raised. They weighed into the baying Our England mob.

'Come on.' Bryan lifted Sanjay to his feet. 'Come on,' he shouted to Bill. Bill joined them.

'I think my nose is broken,' he said.

'It's all right, it'll be all right.' He took Bill's arm, he took Phillip's arm. The four of them, arm-in-arm, brothers-in-arms, made their way through the police lines toward the grass. Bryan felt wetness on *his* face now, but he knew what that was, and it wasn't blood.

Meena had seen it, she had seen them, even as she had been pressing Hallie and Aisha's faces to her chest, even as she reached out and grabbed Ben by the wrist, dragged him back onto the grass, yelled: '*Ben*, stay, here!'

'I've gotta help!' He strained against her. 'They're my dads!'

'You'll stay here!' She squeezed even tighter.

'That hurts!'

'Do as I say, Ben!'

'Dads!' Tears streaming down his face.

'Look away, Ben,' said Meena. She yanked him back, pressed him against her. 'Look away, my love.'

Then, suddenly, it was over. Did it last a minute, two? The children, Hallie and Ben, at least, would remember it for the rest of their lives. But here they now came – the four men, the brothers-in-arms.

'What are you doing here?'

Meena was watching her husband, the other boys. She was so delighted to see them in one piece, well, more or less.

'Don't you hear me, sister? What are you doing here? Where's your husband?'

Now she looked up. It was a Community Support Officer, what was colloquially known as a 'Plastic Policeman'. He was Asian like Meena and sporting a bushy black beard. To the 'proper' police on either side of him, Meena knew he would just be another Muslim, but Meena could tell, from his untrimmed beard, from 'sister', from his question, that they were worlds apart.

She ignored him. She let Ben go. He ran into the arms of his fathers.

'You shouldn't be here,' the man continued, 'see what happens? You should be home, kept safe. Where's your husband?' Now Meena looked: at the police officers flanking the CSO, the white policewoman, especially, she looked her in the eye. The policewoman looked away.

'I'm quite all right,' she said, 'thank you.'

'Yeah,' he said, 'looks like it.'

'Is there a problem?' it was Sanjay, his cheek already coming up bruised, blood smeared across his teeth. He was still fired up.

Meena said: 'Sanjay.'

'I was just saying, bruv',' said the CSO, 'to your wife? I was just saying, she'd be better off at home.' He shrugged. 'You can't say I'm wrong.'

'What business is it of yours?' said Sanjay.

'No need to get stressed, bruv'.'

'And I'm not your fucking "bruv".'

'Hey, bruv',' he grinned. 'Chill.'

'Everything all right?' It was the male cop. He looked at the CSO. 'Problem?'

'Nah, guv,' he shook his head. 'No problem here, is there, bruv'.'

The friends drifted away – dispersed, as the police would put it, along with the rest of the crowd.

They made their way out of the park. The initial rush of adrenaline draining along with their conversation. They just felt tired now, more than tired – exhausted, shocked, bruised as they made their way in silence toward Oxford Street and public transport.

Bill peeled off at Kings Cross and headed straight to hospital, turning down Bryan's offer to accompany him (it turned out he did, indeed, have a fractured nose – all those years dodging punches at discos, he would later joke, to catch one now I'm grown-up) while the two families went straight home, the adults feeling a mix of shame for having exposed their children to violence and a deep, almost bottomless, gratitude that they were all okay.

Meena and Sanjay gave Aisha a bath then both sat with her as she went to sleep, seemingly the least troubled of the lot by what had happened, while Ben and Hallie lingered downstairs with Bryan and Phillip that evening. They joined them in front of the telly and watched Channel 4 News, where the first item was the death of 'at least four' of the protestors – a middle-aged man had suffered a heart attack after being beaten by the Our England mob (Bryan remembered the chap he had seen falling beneath that banner) and three others who had died in the crush.

Meena, also watching the news a few miles away, remembered the moment the crowd had closed around her and felt, literally, sick.

'Idiots,' said Sanjay. 'What were the police thinking?' He shook his head. 'I can't believe it was a mistake.'

'What do you mean?' said Meena.

'I'm not saying it was deliberate but ... well, it's clear whose side they're on. The first thing the government did was give them a pay rise, just like Thatcher in the Eighties. Now this legislation, aimed at "cop killers". It's clear where their sympathies lie, so what if a few lefties get their skulls cracked? They've always hated us.'

'I don't think it's that simple, Sanj,' said Meena.

'They must have seen it coming, but they let it happen, just long enough for the fascists to teach us a lesson ...'

'People make mistakes,' said Meena, 'shit ... happens.'

'The funny thing is,' said Sanjay, 'that shit happens more to some people than others.' He shook his head. 'I don't like the way this country's going, Meena.'

There was something in his tone that made her ask: 'What do you mean, Sanjay?'

'I've been thinking. About my cousin, Aameen, in Toronto.' It took a moment for this to sink in, then Meena said:

'You're thinking about Canada, Sanjay?' She was stunned. She had never heard him mention it before.

'New country,' he said. 'New opportunities. We're still young, and the legal system isn't so different from our own, I could do a conversion course …'

'How long have you been thinking about this, Sanj?'

He shrugged.

'Sanj.'

'A while. I mean, with the election, this "loyalty test" …'

Meena gave him an exasperated look. 'When was the last time you even went to mosque, Sanjay? You get so worked up about a piece of paper you didn't have to have anything to do with. Now you want to leave the country? We're *British*. Our families … my brothers and sister, mum and dad, your family … *our friends.*'

'But what does "British" really mean?' he said. 'Our parents were born in India, and Pakistan, right? They left to improve their lives, do the right thing for their kids. The question I've been asking myself is: is this the right place for Aisha for *our* kids, our grandkids? And, you know, Meena, I'm not sure anymore. I ask myself,' and here his voice broke, 'am I half the man my dad was? Or am I just letting all this shit wash over me just because I've – because *we've* – got good jobs, for now. Am I being complacent? Should I be thinking that maybe there's something better out there? Better for all of us? I mean, you saw those savages …'

'But that's not *Britain*, Sanjay. Britain's our friends, our families, our lives here …'

He shook his head. 'Britain was the election – the millions of people who voted for parties that hate us. What happened today – that's just as real as our lives. More so, probably. It's the sharp end, but behind them are all those people sitting at home and quietly nodding their approval.

'We might not want to see it, we hope it'll just go away, but,' he stroked her cheek, 'there's no ignoring it when it's kicking you in the face.'

'You're upset, Sanj,' said Meena. 'After what happened, but it could have happened to anybody … what I mean is, if we'd been among those people watching at home, you wouldn't be saying this now … The government's only got five years. Next time round I'm sure Labour, a left-wing alliance, will get elected …'

But Sanjay was shaking his head.

'What?' she said.

'It's not that simple,' he said. 'It's not just about politics. It's the temperature of the times … *they're* setting the agenda now.'

'Who's "they"?'

'The bastards,' said Sanjay. 'The opportunists, the ideologues; all the power-hungry shitheads. They saw the opportunity – once authority, once trust, had just *disintegrated*, Meena – and they seized it. While we wasted all that time standing around scratching our heads wondering what the hell was going on, they picked up the ball and ran with it. Sure, today the issue's the death sentence or a loyalty test but they're not going to stop there,' he shook his head. 'They're just getting started.'

13

The celebrations went on through the night and Stuart was at the centre of them. Not that they were celebrating him, mind, but he was right there, in the pub, nursing his Coke at the bar while the party went on around him. The news was playing with the sound turned down on the screen above their heads, all about 'the ambush' as they'd talked about it for ... well, weeks before it had kicked off. 'Catch them on the way out – you see, there, the bottleneck,' Vince had said when they were at the planning stage. 'We'll hold a couple of counter protests – just a handful of troops here, here and here. Let the press talk us down, take the piss, say only a few of us turned out. Then we'll melt away, re-group, and the rest of us will go here.' He prodded on the map.

It had gone precisely as planned. Better than planned, judging by the delight displayed by Vince, Mike and the rest, who appeared utterly unperturbed by the reports of serious casualties. 'Turn this bit up,' shouted Mike. The bartender dutifully raised the sound. They were interviewing a woman, her eyes red with tears. 'They just came at us,' she said. 'They were animals!'

'Oooh, *animals*!' said Mike. 'Woke bitch!'

'Needs some cock!' shouted someone.

'Help me! Help me! I'm being oppressed!'

'Fuck me! Fuck me! I'm being oppressed!'

The pub roared with laughter. Stuart grinned. Times were good, he thought. Things were looking up.

He'd come a long way since the day that Asian lady turned up at the door. He'd really thought he'd had it. He'd already got the Child Support on to him – Jacky had wasted no time in telling them he'd missed *a single payment* – and he still felt terrible about Auntie ... so when that woman appeared along with that lanky, laughing, posh git, he thought – well, it's only what I deserve isn't it. He hadn't bothered with the housing list, telling the social or whatever. He knew where he was heading – he only had to look outside, to the street.

He began going through Auntie's stuff. Her albums and that. Her and mam, all of them together, laughing by the seafront at Roker. Her wedding, together with her friends from when she was working. Her kid, his cousin, who'd died in a car crash. She never mentioned him, had always put a brave face on it. You've just got to get on with it, was as much as he could remember her saying – and that was to Stuart, when he'd first come down, after being kicked out. 'You've just got to get on with it, pet,' she'd said. And he'd understood that this was her philosophy of life, and if it was good enough for Auntie, it would do for him, too.

He'd been running out of money, which is why he hadn't made the childcare payment. He'd gone through her jewel box – no fear, pet, you've just got to get on with it – and dug out some trinkets, a couple of rings, a necklace. Brought them to the pawn. The bloke had looked down his nose. 'But that's a diamond,' said Stuart.

'Paste,' he said.

'Gold. That's got to be worth something.'

'Melted. People don't buy this stuff anymore. I can give you forty quid for the lot.'

'The lot?' He took the money then went straight around the corner to a Wetherspoon's where he had a couple of pints and a burger. He'd raised his glass to Auntie. 'Cheers,' he'd said, and later, when he was still sitting there, alone, after a few pints more, 'I'm sorry, Auntie. I'm so sorry.'

Time was ticking. He'd had a couple of letters from the Housing people and a bloke had come round. Apparently he was the Asian lass's boss. He'd been all right, apologetic and that, but firm, too. Said they'd 'be forced' to evict him if he hadn't left in a couple of weeks.

'But what about this list?' said Stuart, even though he wasn't going to bother. Bryan crossed his arms.

'The truth is, Stuart …'

'Aye?'

'As a single, working-age male, your chance of being rehoused, let along keeping this place, are pretty much zero.'

'I suppose they'll give it to immigrants.'

'It's a question of need, it's not about where they come from.'

'So what am I supposed to do then? Go on the street?'

Bryan sighed. 'Look, there are these five tests. You can apply to our homeless unit, but to be honest, I don't think you'll pass any of them. You're not … ill or anything, are you?'

He shook his head.

'But you're not from London. You don't have any other links here? You could try getting in touch with the authorities where you come from. They may have something …'

Stuart thought of the months he'd spent in the benefits offices back home, the disappointments, the coming home to … well, to all of that. He shook his head.

'I'm sorry,' said Bryan. 'I really am, but there's nothing I can do to help you. It's the law – we have to take possession of the property.'

So one day Stuart had just up and left. He'd gone through the house, seeing if there was anything else of much value – only Auntie's digital radio that he'd bought her from his first month's money, really – along with the photo albums, some of her documents and that. He'd packed up and slammed the door, posting the key back through the lock. Altogether, even along with his own stuff, it had barely been enough to fill the boot of his Prius, the one thing Jacky had let him hang on to, presumably so he could keep paying her bills.

He wasn't really sure where to go. In the end, he simply drove up to Finsbury Park. He got out and went for a wander. Sat outside the café and had a cup of tea. Watched the families, the mums, mainly – it was the middle of the day – around the boating lake. Took out his phone, flipped through photos of his kids. Would they remember him? They were only five and six. He looked into their eyes, *his eyes*, everyone said. Did he remember much from that age? He shook his head. The revelation came with cast iron certainty: they would call this other bloke 'dad'. And if Stuart's name ever did come up, *she* would do her level best to blacken it.

He looked around: the unkempt middle-aged men, blacks and whites, scattered about the park benches, smoking, drinking cheap cans, abandoned here like dogs, he thought, like unwanted dogs. That's all we are.

He looked back down at his phone, looked back into those eyes – *his* eyes – and thought, I'll be fucked if this is it. I may be a fuck up, but one day, one of them – maybe both – they'll come looking for me, and they'll see I'm all right. They'll see. They'll see me for what I am, and her for what she is.

Stuart pulled the card out of his pocket. Turned it over in his fingers. *Vincent Cave, Welfare officer ...*

Vince had listened to what he had to say and told him to come right over. Half an hour later Stuart was pulling up to the old factory. It all seemed pretty quiet, then he saw Vince come out of a doorway.

'It used to be called the Shoe Factory,' said Vince. 'It *was* a shoe factory, when they had factories. Then when the area became trendy, the council turned it into studios, for *artistes*. But that didn't last neither, cos then they sold it to a developer who planned to turn it into trendy flats, at a million a piece or some shit. 'course the council said they needed the cash, but funny how it never trickles down to the likes of you and me, eh?

'Anyway, when the builder buggered off, the place was left empty. A bunch of nonces – the same artists who'd had it before – tried to get hold of it, but we showed them a bit of muscle and reclaimed it for the English. Follow me.'

They walked into a posh reception area, with a desk

and everything – 'To keep the riff raff out,' said Vince with a smile – then went through to the lifts, which were nothing like the ramshackle, piss-smelling ones at Auntie's. Waiting for them was like when he'd taken Jacky and the kids on holiday to Tenerife, splashed out the last of his redundancy money. Jacky had insisted they stay at this pricey hotel, had gasped it was like paradise when they got there but then spent the rest of the fortnight ignoring him and uploading stuff to Instagram. It wasn't soon after, he guessed, she started seeing that fella.

They arrived at the first floor, which was the same chichi design, all gold and bronze with low lighting, real yuppy, but as they got out of the lift, facing them was this huge OUR ENGLAND banner with a good-looking white family against a backdrop of rolling green hills, sheep and so on. All the apartment doors were open too, boxes of leaflets, t-shirts, badges and that, filling the corridor.

'This is the nerve centre. Not bad, eh?' The flats – or that's what they had been – were now offices, with desks and computers sitting beside the large picture windows that overlooked the canal. It was mainly women at the computers.

Stuart felt immediately ... strangely, moved ... It was like that banner when he came in, like something from the olden days, it was like one of those movies he'd seen about the war. There was this energy, Blitz spirit you might call it.

'Take a pew,' said Vince. 'Cup of tea?'

He returned with an Our England Cross of Saint George mug and an older woman – Linda – who had blonde hair. She was holding a clipboard. 'I'll leave you with the lovely Linda here,' said Vince. 'And when you're done, come and see me – I'm in the office at the end.'

Linda sat down on the corner of the sofa. 'Vince tells me you're looking for somewhere to stay, Stuart?'

'That's right,' said Stuart. It all felt slightly unreal. He hadn't been expecting this – he'd explained his troubles to Vince, but Vince hadn't specifically mentioned anything on the phone about helping him out. Just said 'come over'.

'Do you have a passport, love?' she said. 'We need it for our records.' Funnily enough, Stuart did. It was one of the few things he hadn't left in the car. 'Lovely,' she said, and went off to copy it. 'Collins,' she said when she came back. 'Viking name. But of course it would be, you being from the North East. I'm Saxon – Garside – but I come from Essex. We're all Saxons there. Now, what's your line of work, Stuart?' He explained, then Linda asked him some other questions like whether he had any qualifications (yes – a few GCSEs and a forklift licence), a criminal record (no) and then read from this weird list where he had to say how strongly he felt on a scale of one to ten about all sorts of things, ranging from immigration (initially 4 for slightly concerned, but when Linda pressed him on it, about how it affected his work opportunities, housing and that, he changed it to 2 for angry) to Europe (he didn't have a problem saying 2 to that) to gay rights (well, he said, he'd never really thought about it. 'It's all right, Stuart,' said Linda. 'It's not a trick question – you don't have to worry about the politically correct brigade here.' He noticed her pencil hovering over the 2, so he said that). Linda gave him a very white smile. She looked back down the list. 'All twos, lovely. Vince said you were sound.' She reached out and squeezed his bicep. Stuart had to make an effort not to jump. 'It's that Viking spirit! Vince said you've got your stuff in the car. Would you like to come up and see the flat?' Stuart still wasn't entirely sure what was going on, but said okay and followed her to the lifts. 'That's my granddaughter,' said Linda, pointing to the banner, 'though those aren't her real mum and dad, they've split up.'

They went into the lift up to the fourth floor. When they stepped out there was another Our England banner facing them, this one simply like an elongated Cross of Saint George with OUR ENGLAND stamped diagonally

CANARIES

across it. Up here the doors were closed, but there was a kid's tricycle in the hallway, and a buggy outside another door. 'People just leave stuff lying around here,' said Linda. 'They don't worry about it being stolen.' She unlocked a dark wood door that opened onto the living room of a posh flat, with polished parquet and all. There was a modern sofa facing a huge TV and a kitchen-diner with that same view over the canal. 'You'll be sharing the use of the kitchen,' said Linda. 'But you'll have your own room, obviously!' They walked down a narrow corridor to a modest sized bedroom with a mattress and some bedding rolled up. It was otherwise bare, although there was a glass door that opened onto a small terrace, itself looking onto another part of the former factory. 'It's not much, I'm afraid,' said Linda. 'But Jamie has taken the bigger bedroom. Will this do?'

Stuart's mouth was dry. 'It's ... lovely,' he said. 'But ... well, Linda, I don't think I could afford ...'

Linda looked puzzled, then let out a laugh like a bark. 'Didn't Vince tell you, darling? It's free. It's our service, it's what we offer. You're more than welcome,' she gave his arm another friendly pinch. 'For as long as you need it.'

He stood there trying to understand. This morning he'd been imagining finding a quiet place to park his car for the night, put the seats flat, and try and kip, now here he was being offered a room in a luxury flat for nothing. Linda could see he was confused. 'It's part of our social project,' she said. 'Our England's social project – to look after the forgotten English, the folk the elite don't give a toss about. Well, someone's got to, haven't they?'

Stuart nodded. Linda handed him the keys. 'It's all yours now,' she said, going out. 'You take your time.'

'Linda's sorted you out? Good.' Vince was sitting behind a large modern desk in the corner office, which was probably meant for one of the top of the range flats, the picture windows on either side of him taking in both the canal and the rest of the industrial estate. He was dressed smart casual, in the usual polo shirt and dark jeans. There was a single faded tattoo spread across his bicep, half covered by the shirtsleeve, but put him in a suit and tie, Stuart thought, and he could be any company boss. 'Flat all right?'

'It's ... great,' said Stuart. 'I had no idea ...'

'Don't worry about it, mate,' said Vince. 'That's the whole point, isn't it – to help the English. Although we have been known to lend a hand to the odd Scotsman, too.' He winked. 'What do you know about us? Not much is my bet, from what I recall you saying in the car.'

Stuart shrugged. He had never taken much interest in politics. Vince gave him a sympathetic smile.

'The lying media, the mainstream politicians, call us fascists,' he said. 'Do you even know what fascists are, Stuart?' He shook his head. 'Me neither. They say we're "far right". But right of what? Actually, financial-wise, they might have a point – because we don't believe in handouts, from the government, that is. We believe they make you weak – they've been made, or used, by the elite to make us – the English – weak. Have you ever read Brave New World, Stuart? No? Well, in Brave New World, which is this book from years ago, there's the rulers, the Alphas, who lord it over the rest of them who they keep addicted to this drug called Soma. And the lowest of the low are the Gammas, who aren't hardly human. And that's what they've done to us, Stuart, the elite: they've turned the English working class into Gammas, addicted to benefits as their way of keeping us like sheep, lambs to the slaughter. To stop us seeing what's going on, and being bloody angry. So we're against benefits. We help people, we'll help *you*, but to help yourself. And be bloody angry about it, too. To *not* be all right with your lot.

'They call us racists.' He grunted. 'But we don't think we're better than the other lot. On the contrary, mate – we know we're in *competition* for whatever scraps the bastards throw us. The Alphas want us at each other's throats – divide and rule, just like they did in the empire – but we're not stupid, we know what's going on.

'They think it's *their* England, see. The rest of us are just here to serve *them*... cannon fodder like World War One. But fuck that – it's *our England*, Stuart, and we're going to take it back.'

Vince grinned. 'Apologies,' he said. 'I've been known to get a bit carried away. Anyway, like I was saying, we're not here for handouts but to help you get back on your feet. The ladies will have put you on our database and will let you know as soon as something comes up – but, as it happens, I am in need of a driver ...'

Vince's licence had just been suspended for three years. 'It had to happen,' he said. 'What you'll find out soon enough is the elite regard the English as far more of a threat than any bloke called Mo with a stick of dynamite up his jacksy.' He shook his head. 'They don't really give a shit about that. Containment, that's their policy – keep a lid on the likes of us. *We're* what they're really afraid of.' He chuckled. 'They might think they've played a blinder with the new voting system, brought us inside the tent. But we're going to beat them at it – beat them at their own game.

'Anyway, cut a long story short, they've been on my case since forever. Every minor infringement, I get pulled up. In the end, they managed to do me for dangerous driving, jumping a red light they said, and sure enough there on the film it's red, but at the time? Not in a million fucking years – don't they think I know what they're up to? So I've lost my wheels. Mike usually gives me a lift, but he's got responsibilities, a job, family, all that, and the girls out there have been on to me to get a proper, trustworthy bloke for ages. So, what do you say, Stuart?'

Stuart said yes.

14

Vincent Cave was not the only person to have recognised the game-changing potential of the new electoral system. After the Liberal Democrats had pushed it through, Bill had penned an opinion piece for *The Herald* with the headline BE CAREFUL WHAT YOU WISH FOR.

'Just as Gorbachev was a true believer in communism,' he wrote, 'and in his naivety hastened its downfall, so the Liberal Democrats, and all the so-called progressives who call for a more democratic form of government, should be careful what they wish for. Their support exists, much as they do, within today's political space. If we enter another electoral universe, who knows what aliens might appear out of a nearby black hole and, instead of coming in peace, gobble them up?'

But the trouble with being a columnist, Bill thought, looking around the office and noting with a sinking heart that he was, as usual, by far the oldest one there, was that it was not enough to have opinions – didn't everyone? – but to have fresh, yet consistent, opinions every week.

He'd got a lot of mileage out of the Capital Punishment demo. There had been the subject itself – DEAD AND CIRCUSES had been the headline and his drift, examining the primal appeal of executions, albeit ones held behind the prison walls, and predicting the next step ('in our apparent acceleration toward the past') would be for them to be broadcast – then his first-hand experience at the demo itself, along with an account of the moment the cordon had broken and they had been set upon. He'd got some TV out of that, which had kept his head above water (as he always saw it – his career on a national news website felt so precarious he was only ever one column away from the next cull of senior editorial staff). Finally he had even done a light-hearted one about how his broken nose had affected his appearance and how, although it had made him, in his words, look like 'a second-rate boxer', the ladies appeared to find him more attractive, after which Phillip had messaged him: 'You wish!'

So Bill had managed to get a full month out of one march, and had plans on the backburner to use it again by later seeking out the loved ones of the victims, along the lines of 'the headlines may have changed but the heartache never goes away'. But it was still too early for that, even though since the demo three murderers had been executed to widespread public approval. Of course, the authorities would insist that they had simply been following the new rules, but Bill doubted it was a coincidence that all of them were specimens nobody, except perhaps their mothers, would mourn – a couple of child killers and one of the terrorists behind the massacre at the Bluewater shopping centre. The trouble with populism was, he thought, its sheer bloody popularity. And of course the judicial killings had distracted nicely from the permanently dismal economic news.

All those abstract figures – GDP, interest rates, inflation – were beginning to drill ever more deeply into the real world – people's wages, their access to credit, career prospects. The pound had plunged back off the cliff ('a currency that dives more often than a Chelsea footballer' Bill had written, and received the usual abuse from Blues fans) and it was presumably this, as much as the current spate of terrorist attacks, that was hammering the final nail into the coffin of the big malls. Bill wondered what online shopping figures were looking like these days, whether he could make something out of them – IS THIS THE END OF THE CATHEDRALS OF SHOPPING? If shopping replaced religion, what would replace shopping? Have we entered a Houellebecqian, *Atomised* society? He sighed. Of course we bloody had. That was old news.

Don't look at what they say, he thought. Look at what they *do*. It was a mistake to think the New Right were cynics like the old order. That was the easy excuse, and one still trotted out by much of the Left, puffed up with outrage at the latest evidence of right-wing 'hypocrisy', or whatever.

But the reality was more likely the opposite: in many respects the New Right was the mirror image of the old. While your Labours and Conservatives had become steeped in a sense of defeat when confronted by the helplessness of the nation state in a globalised world, the New Right really *did* seem to believe they could change things and didn't give a damn about global norms – as demonstrated by the messy mass deportations in France and Italy, the camps (*camps!*) set up in Germany.

While the old parties attempted to conceal their impotency, if anything, the new ones sought to hide their potency.

After capital punishment had come the BBC. The Alliance delivered on the long made threat by successive Conservative governments – in this age of streaming, that it was absurd to retain a Cold War, socialist anachronism.

The Commons vote won a healthy majority – backed, as it increasingly was, by the Tories, who could see what side their bread was buttered – to break up the Corporation. Cheered on by the privately-owned media, the only squeaks of protest had come from a few minority-read news outlets like Bill's (he'd done a couple of pieces about it, naturally) and, of course, their readers, who shared self-righteous social media posts among themselves.

Bill shook his head. You had to admire the government's hubris. Ministers had long refused to give interviews to the 'biased-BBC', limiting their appearances to GB News and similar outlets, but even an MP exploded with outrage when one presenter observed that it was the 'end of the era of public service broadcasting'.

'Are you saying that *you're* not fulfilling a public service? Surely it's time to move on from the myth that only the public sector can provide a public service!'

A throwaway line that would prove prophetic when it came to the fate of 'our NHS', as they habitually called it.

The 'trillion-pound sell-off' for which the public would be supposedly compensated by annual 'vouchers' covering their care, had disaster written all over it, *But the NHS*, thought Bill, rubbing his face ... *Again* – he'd said it all, repeatedly, and yet the Titanic continued to steam toward the iceberg. It was almost as bad as race. The danger for a columnist was to develop a reputation as a Cassandra. The 'loyalty test' for example, about which he had written a very doom-laden article, but which had ended up being watered down to the Covenant of British Something or Other. Dreary, dreary, dreary, but then, he looked out of the window at the slate grey London sky, isn't the devil in the dreary? He thought about the chat he'd had that Sunday with Bryan and Phillip when he'd been invited for lunch. They'd been on about the gay stuff, of course.

The signs had been there from the beginning – the 'direction of travel' of the new government, what with the Ulster Dems, Shared Values and Our England – but, for the most part, 'the gay thing' had been overlooked, given the *sturm und drang* of executions, broadcasting, 'Covenants' and privatisations, so the new Education Bill wound its way slowly through both Houses, tucked among the guff about promoting 'this Island's story' a couple of clauses limiting sex education to over-16s and banning teaching that homosexuality was 'normal'. So far, so Maggie Thatcher.

The LGBTQ+ community had acted with appropriate outrage, although it had not registered much elsewhere. Then came plans from the new Ministry of the Family for an increase in the Married People's Tax Allowance, only in the tiny, ten-point end-notes adding 'for the purposes of this bulletin, the first tranche of Married People to benefit from the changes refers to couples wedded before 13 March 2014', which was the date that gay marriage had become legal in the UK.

Bill had actually been the first mainstream journalist to pick this up after Phillip had forwarded him the article in *Gay Times*, and he had noted sourly that of all his pieces – some of which attracted hundreds of comments – this had received the least reaction: only about thirty. People were suffering from outrage fatigue, he thought. When we're euthanizing undesirables and closing down treasured public institutions, what does a footnote about an allowance matter?

Gay activists had mobilised for their generation's fight for equality, but deep down there still remained, perhaps even among them, a sense that this would be a passing aberration; that despite the reactionary gale, history was on their side and good would, eventually, prevail. Certainly few people, not even Bill, had expected what would come next.

The White Paper on Family Values – consciously echoing the political party that had brought the government to power and controlled the Ministry of the Family – was seen nationally, and internationally, as a moral line in the sand.

'The guiding rule,' said the Secretary of State for the Family, that *'horrible woman from the radio'* Juno's friends could now never picture without being menaced by an over-sized sex toy, 'is to recalibrate our moral compass, and it very definitely sits alongside … it *complements* our other reforms, which are all about taking responsibility for yourself, standing on your own two, good, feet, and grabbing life by the horns.'

'You're doubling maternity leave and providing generous tax breaks to married couples, as long as the woman stays at home,' said the TV presenter.

'We want to empower women, we want to strengthen families, we want to create a more inclusive society.'

'Yet at the same time you're repealing the law on gay marriage. Some might say – that's not very empowering, or inclusive.'

'I appreciate, Adam, it's difficult, I can see that,' the Secretary of State looked, momentarily, pained. 'But sometimes life *is* difficult. We've inherited a nation, a country, a society, which for too long had been under a kind of spell, an incredibly damaging illusion – a tax-draining health service, the biased BBC – that life can just be handed to us on a plate without having to do anything in return. The world can be any way we want it to be. Anything we want to have, well that's just fine, we'll take it. Life exists to serve us. A "me first" society. And look where it's got us! Just look!'

The presenter shrugged. 'It looks all right to me.'

'Well,' said the Secretary of State, an edge of steel entering her voice, 'here we are in London, in the centre of London, this metropolitan bubble... I can assure you, Adam, it might look okay to you, but out there, across the nation, it does not look "all right" at all.'

Just as I'm becoming accustomed to my flattened nose when I look in the mirror, Bill wrote, *tomorrow I'll be risking my good looks again to join my gay friends.*

His phone buzzed. It was a message from Vincent Cave.

'I'm outside,' it said.

15

As soon as Bill stepped through the glass swivel doors of The Herald's HQ he recognised that other bloke – Mike? – stood looking like an off-duty bouncer, a black bomber jacket covering his black polo shirt, a cigarette smouldering between his thick knuckles. He nodded, unsmilingly, and dropped the fag.

'Vince?' said Bill.

'In the car.' Mike nodded toward the white Prius on the corner. He fell in behind him as Bill headed over. There was a driver he didn't recognise, looking straight ahead. Vince was in the back, on his phone. Bill paused, for a couple of reasons: part uncertainty (should he knock on the window and wait for Vince to get out or lean over and let him in?), part a distant warning signal from the depths of his consciousness that reminded him that although he may not be in immediate danger, these were dangerous men, and did he really want to get in a car with them?

In any case, before he had had a chance to make up his mind, he was being frisked from behind by Mike. When he had finished, Mike opened the door. Vince looked up.

'Clean,' said Mike. Bill dutifully climbed in, Mike got in the front, and the car moved silently off.

Vince was grinning. 'Fucking hell,' he said, still holding on to Bill's hand after he had shaken it, 'that's quite a kink you've got in the nose department. Is it true the birds prefer it?' He shook his head. 'Sorry about that, mate. They really fucked you up. Obviously, if we'd *known* …'

'If you'd known,' said Bill, 'you'd probably have told them to look out for me and I'd be in traction.'

Vince looked mock-offended. 'Now that's harsh. You don't think I had anything to do with it?'

Bill shook his head. 'It's not funny, Vince. People died. Innocent people. It was a fucking disaster, a tragedy.'

Vince nodded, this time with, apparently, more sincerity. 'It was a tragedy,' he said, 'a fuck-up.' He shrugged. 'But don't you think that's what the authorities wanted? Do you really think it was an accident?'

'Hold on,' said Bill. 'Are we about to go on record?' He took out his phone and went to the recording app, but Vince plucked it from his hand and laid it on the armrest between them.

'No,' he said. 'I don't want to get into their narrative …' For all his proletarian credentials, Bill remembered, Vincent Cave was highly intelligent and, it was said, actually the brains behind Our England. 'They know it, we know it – they lightly policed that section precisely so it would get out of hand and we'd be discredited as thugs.'

'Well,' said Bill, touching his nose, 'what do you call this? Come on, Vince…'

'I'm not saying there aren't some … elements among our supporters, and look, no one's more sorry about what happened than me. But the police knew what to expect. *You* knew what to expect…'

'Frankly,' said Bill, 'no. Otherwise we wouldn't have taken that route – when I first saw your people, there were no more than a dozen.'

'You saw us?' said Mike from the front. 'You should have come over and said hello.'

'It was my day off.'

'Still,' Vince gave him a sly smile, 'it might have reminded them whose side you're on, saved your good looks.'

Bill shook his head. 'What makes you think I'm on your side?'

'That's what I say,' said Mike.

Vince's smile grew into a grin. 'More than most, any rate.'

Bill shrugged. He had, after all, carved out a place for himself as one of Fleet Street's token 'working class' journalists (as his opposite number on the *Guardian* had remarked after they bumped into each other on the same miserable Midlands housing estate – 'every up-market paper has to have one') and had become the go-to man for stories north of Watford or outside the fashionable postcodes.

Although Bill himself was far from being a son of the soil – he'd had an ordinary upbringing, gone to the local comprehensive then a decent university. But once he had stumbled into the national press through a mixture of raw talent and good luck, this ordinariness had marked him out in an environment dominated by a clique which, be it liberal or conservative, struggled to make sense of a nation with whom it shared little in common other than the colour of its passport.

Bill had first come across Our England at an editorial meeting. The partner of the arts editor had put in a bid to convert an office block into a series of design and performance spaces under the LondON initiative, designed to breathe life back into the city after the commercial market collapsed, but had backed down following 'a campaign of intimidation by skinheads'.

'What would skinheads want with the building?' said a colleague.

'They claim they want to use it to house poor families.'

The editor shook her head. 'Whatever next,' she said. 'Skinheads running housing programmes! Bill?' everyone looked at him.

'I'll check it out,' he said. 'Could make some kind of feature.'

'It's got to be bullshit,' said the arts editor.

Ever heard of the housing crisis? Bill thought. Still, he couldn't pretend he wasn't a little uneasy as he approached the factory – he had done a bit of asking around and established they were indeed from some kind of far-right group that wouldn't necessarily welcome a reporter from *The Herald* – but there was no turning back.

A group of tough looking men were gathered outside, smoking. As he approached them, they stopped talking. Bill grinned.

'I come in peace,' he said.

They glared at him. Then the oldest – who he came to know as Mike – said coolly: 'And you want?'

'A word with your leader. I'm a reporter. A journalist.'
A shiver of hostility ran through the group.

'Fuck off,' said one of the younger ones.

Bill clamped his hands behind his back, pressing his nails into his palms. He managed to look Mike steadily in the eye.

'Who for?' said Mike.

'*The Herald.*'

Mike shrugged. 'Not a proper paper, then.'

'That's what I tell them,' said Bill.

'I'll see what I can do. Wait here.'

Bill waited, the men regarding him with continued hostility. Finally Mike returned. 'All right,' he said.

That was when he had first met Vince, in that corner office with his desk upside down, screwing on the legs. He'd stood up and shook Bill's hand with an iron grip. He was wiry with short black hair that ran in a straight fringe along the top of his forehead and had a ferretish, Cockney face, while Mike was bulky with the look of a angry Irishman, albeit he spoke with a throat full of London gravel. Vince might have been an electrician, Mike a builder, but he knew to take this with as much salt as his own 'hail fellow, well met' *shtick*. His colleagues might file them under 'tradesmen', but Bill knew the instant he encountered them – these people were *serious*.

'I'd offer you a pew,' said Vince, 'but we're still putting the place together. What can I do for you Bill …'

'Richardson, *The Herald.*'

'Yeah, Mike said you were some bigshot journo.' He smiled. 'Why would *The Herald* be interested in us, I wonder.'

'Heard you had moved in here, were planning some kind of … social housing project?'

'You're interested in our social housing project, Bill? Really? Hold the front page, Mike! They'll be splashing big on Our England's social housing project!'

'Our England? That's your name?'

'Well, it is our England, isn't it? Same as everybody else's?'

CANARIES

Bill took out his pen. 'So, Vince …'

'Cave. With a "c".' He grinned. 'Good English name, that, although I've had a few nicknames in my time, not all complimentary.'

'So, Vince, would you characterise your group as nationalist?'

'Well, William, I'd say we were patriotic, but another outfit's already grabbed that name.'

'So you're in the same … vein as the Patriots?'

Vince shrugged. 'You could say that, except that they're mostly a bunch of blokes from the Home Counties moaning about foreigners from the comfort of their armchairs. They're dreams of bygone Empire, all that tosh, whereas we're your more practical sorts. We're here to make an actual difference, on the ground, for the English people. Them that got left behind.'

'You keep saying "English". By that do you mean *white* English? And what about Scots, Welsh …' He glanced at Mike. 'Irish.'

Vince nodded, making it clear he knew exactly where Bill was coming from. 'Oh we're not prejudiced against our Celtic cousins,' he said, 'but we're saying English, because someone's got to, haven't they? Someone's got to speak for the English.'

'The white English.'

Vince's grin widened. 'The working class English.'

'So you'd accept black and Asian families here, then?'

'Anyone is welcome to apply for help,' he said. 'Although I won't pretend that our priority is not to help the ethnic working class English. The ones left behind. There are already groups representing the other minorities – Caribbeans, Muslims, Chinese – so why not them?'

'You're claiming that the white English are a minority.'

'Well,' said Vince. 'Aren't they?'

Bill shook his head. 'No,' he said. 'Quite obviously they're not.'

Vince shrugged. 'I'm not sure where you're getting your figures, but the last time I checked the census, just

35 per cent of London's population was classified "white British". Now, if we estimate that a good ten or fifteen per cent of them will be posh folk like you and your mates, London being the social magnet what it is, that leaves twenty per cent that have been left behind.'

'But ...' Bill scratched his head. 'You talk about London, but you're not calling yourself *Our London*, are you.'

'It's the same across the country. In all the big cities. It's a *trend* is what it is. We're being displaced – what's called "internally-displaced". Refugees, in a word, in our own land.'

'First time I've heard moving to the suburbs called that,' said Bill.

Vince grinned, teeth straight and hard. 'Keep laughing, mate,' he said. 'You just keep laughing.'

It had been some time before the election that would cement the power of the right, but even back then there had been signs.

For a start, once it would have been unthinkable for an avowedly white-ethnic group to take over a formerly council-owned building in what remained a left-leaning London borough, and Bill had expected soon after the publication of his article, alongside an opinion piece penned by the partner of the evicted artist, that Our England would simply be booted out. He had left the polemics to his colleague, but felt his piece – quoting Vince's unapologetic words – spoke for itself.

Yet despite a couple of demonstrations by the Reds, who had evolved from the anti-fascist/globalisation movements in much the same way as Our England had from the far-right, plus a few complaints to the London Mayor's office (which had fallen back into Tory hands) nothing much happened.

It was as if there had already been a change in the political climate even Bill – who was, after all, paid to have his finger on the pulse – hadn't quite registered. He thought back to a follow-up interview he had done with an imam at a local mosque, who didn't seem particularly perturbed by the development down the road. 'They're looking after their own,' he had said. 'Providing they do us no harm, how can I condemn them for that?' Bill had left this quote out of the article – it would never have got past the editor in any case – but it had troubled him for some time afterwards. The thought of Vince's cheerful, Cockney face, the creeping sense that Our England, not Bill Richardson and his peers, was ahead of the curve.

So he had kept an eye on them and had actually appeared alongside Vince a few times on Channel 4 News and BBC's Newsnight as they began to rise in prominence. Again, Bill was always careful to steer clear of the polemics – he had noted how Vince had a tendency to tie the presenters into knots whenever they tried to nail him as a racist or Nazi.

Now, of course, both the BBC and Channel 4 were counting down to their impending demise while Vincent Cave and Our England were riding high.

'So,' said Bill. 'Where are you taking me?'

'Somewhere you'll be all too familiar with,' Vince said sadly. 'The hospital.'

Bill followed Vince past reception, through the crowded casualty department and along the corridors lined with stalls set up by enterprising locals selling snacks, soap, toilet paper and the other sundries no longer supplied by the hospital free of charge. They entered a ward where they bumped into a guy and two little girls. Vince embraced them. 'Well,' he said. 'I hear that at least nothing's broken that can't be fixed.'

The man shook his head. 'Bastards,' he said. 'Cowards.'

'How long do they say she'll be in?'

'At least a fortnight.'

'And Mike's sorted you out? You've got everything you need.'

The man nodded. 'Thanks Vince. You're a diamond.'

'Don't mention it, it's the least we can do. We're here for you, through thick and thin.'

Bill followed Vince down the aisle to a bed where a blonde woman lay, her head wrapped in bandages, her face bruised and puffy, lip cut, arm in a sling.

'One of our welfare officers,' explained Vince. 'The Reds must have followed her on her rounds. Mandy,' he said, sitting beside her, taking her hand.

'Vince. Mike said you'd be coming. Thanks for …'

'Don't be silly, Mand. I've already told your old man, we're here for you. Most important thing is for you to get on the mend, asap. Have the police come?'

Mandy nodded. 'Can't say they seemed to give a shit.'

'You don't know that, Mand.'

'*Come on*, Vince.'

'You gave them a description?' asked Bill. Mandy squinted at him with her uncovered eye.

'Who's he?'

Vince smiled. 'A friend, Mand. Journalist. He's on our side.' Mandy's voice hardened nevertheless:

'They were covered up,' she said. ''course. Daren't show their faces. All CCTV round there …'

'She means the Cohen Estate.'

'But I knew who they were, all right. They *wanted* me to know. While they were kicking … said it was Red territory. Said they were taking it back. Said if they saw me again, they'd throw me off the roof.'

Vince looked up at Bill. 'A woman,' he said.

'I'm sorry,' she said.

'What are you sorry for babe?' He leaned over and kissed her on the forehead. 'You rest now.'

They walked back along the corridor.

'I thought you should see it,' said Vince. 'I know what you lot – even you, William, I'm not thick – really think. That we're all a bunch of hooligans. I wanted you to see what's really going on, what we're up against. You think it's all one way, and, all right, like I said, it was a fuck up at the demo, but this is what we have to deal with day in, day out.'

'I'll speak to the Met press office,' said Bill. 'They'll give me a few paragraphs... it's terrible, I realise that. But ...'

'And if it had been anyone else? If this had happened to the Reds? A *woman*? You lot'd be over it like a rash.'

Bill shrugged. Vince nodded. 'I get it,' he said. 'I just wanted you to see. It's getting worse, William. It's going to get a lot worse, and it'll not be of our making. What you'll be looking at, sooner or later, my friend, is a war. A fucking civil war.'

Stuart was waiting around the corner, watching the world go by. Every day, waking up in that nice apartment, with the view and everything. Taking the car for a wash, keeping it nice inside. Hanging around the office, having a laugh with the girls. Running the odd errand, making the odd delivery. It wasn't like work really, but he was getting paid, *and* square with the Child Support ... he'd never forget how close he had come ... but Vince, Mike, Linda, *Our England*, had saved him. There were still people that gave a damn. There was still a future, even for people like him, the people that built this fucking country, even though they'd been tossed aside by the powers that be, as Vince put it.

Divide and conquer, Vince had said, that was their game. It went all the way back to when William the Conqueror had nabbed the nation from our rightful king, Harold. Did Stu know the people on the top, the people in the fancy houses, all had Norman names? They'd been doing it for a thousand years! They did it the same when they had the empire, too, with the Hindus and Muslims in India, then brought Indians in to run businesses in Africa. And they were doing the same at home, getting the little people to squabble over the crumbs while they sit at the table. Of course, in the long-term, the foreigners would have to be got rid of, just like Idi Amin had done in Uganda when he put them all on a plane, when they were invited over *here*, but in the meantime, the first thing we had to do was get our country back.

And I'm part of it, thought Stuart, the insurgency. It was as if he had woken from a dream – or a nightmare, at least that was how it was coming to seem – and he now saw everything as it really was. He wasn't a failure, a *loser* – these were just labels society put on him, wanted him to think to keep him down, keep him passive, a ... what was it Vince called it? *Gamma*. No – he was the backbone of this nation, one of them that fought the Jerries, Frogs, all them others. He was not a nobody, he was a somebody, he just hadn't realised it.

He thought back to his life before. Just existing, really. Doing what was expected of him, not thinking about it any more than a cow in a field. And look how that ended up – when he was no longer any use, even to fucking Uber. He might have been dead by now ... he might as well have been dead as far as society was concerned.

But he didn't just exist. He was part of the resistance, a hero in his own way, just like those generations that had come before. But instead of fighting for *them*, the Normans, to line *their* pockets, he had woken up.

Stuart had woken up, and become a warrior for his people.

He watched Vince coming down the ramp with the reporter. Vince leaned in the front of the car. 'I've got some business in the centre, Stu, so we're done for today. But would you mind giving Bill here a lift north, if you're going that way?'

'No worries,' said Stuart. He watched them shake hands, and then the reporter was getting in the back.

'Thanks very much for this,' said Bill. 'I said I could get the tube but Vincent insisted.'

'No worries,' said Stuart. 'Where is it you'd like to go?'

'Harringay, if you know it? Green Lanes.'

'No worries,' said Stuart. 'It's on my way.' He smiled. Of course this posho journo would live there, where it was all chichi coffee and burger bars; multiculti central,

Mike called it, and they'd actually shot one of their election ads there as a backdrop. 'Say no more,' Mike had said. Of course this journo lived there.

'Vince has come up in the world,' said Bill, 'having a driver and all.'

Stuart shrugged.

'You're from the North East,' said Bill. 'Sunderland, is it?'

Stuart was surprised. 'Aye,' he said. 'Thereabouts.'

'I spent a lot of time up there,' said Bill.

'Oh aye? What were you doing?'

'University, then work,' said Bill. 'Reporting, on the industry and so on. Do you miss it? The North East? I loved the coast, and of course, the people. You're friendlier than us lot down here!'

Stuart glanced in the rear mirror. 'People say that,' he said. 'But Londoners are all right. They've been all right to me.'

'So are you a member then? Of Our England?'

Stuart shrugged. 'I suppose. I'm a driver. I don't only help out Vince ... Vincent. Mr Cave. I also do the deliveries. For the families.'

'It must feel good,' said Bill. 'Helping people out like that.'

Stuart nodded.

'Are there a lot of families these days?'

'Well,' said Stuart. 'I'm kept busy.'

'Two or three deliveries a day? How many families, would you say? Sorry about the questions. I'm just curious.'

'That's all right. I'd say ...' he thought about it. He was aware of three or four different addresses they delivered to, but there was always talk about others, and this was a reporter. What would Vince want him to say? 'I don't know, dozens ... More, maybe ... it's hard to say. Like I said, I'm just the driver.'

'It was shocking what happened to Mandy. To be honest, I had no idea that sort of thing was going on. Has it been happening a lot? The threats and violence?'

Truth was, it had come as a shock to Stuart, too, to all of them at the Shoe Factory. Yes, they had had the odd demo outside, even the odd bit of aggro on the way to a meeting, but the Reds, they were all mouth, like Mike always said, and they usually legged it after throwing a few punches. But then the attack on Mandy would fit that, wouldn't it: they were tough when it came to women who couldn't fight back.

'I'm sorry?' said Stuart.

'Has it been happening a lot? The violence.'

'It's been happening ...' What would Vince want him to say? 'Now and again. The threats and that. Graffiti.' He had seen the graffiti. 'I heard they put dog shit through letterboxes, that sort of thing ...'

'But this is the first time there has been violence like this.'

'Against a woman, yeah, I'd say so.'

They drove on in silence, Bill looking out the window. Stuart said: 'You've known Vi ... Mr Cave long?'

'A while,' said Bill.

'He's a ... sound bloke,' he said. 'He helped me.'

'He did?'

'I was out on my ear. Had nowhere to live, no job. He ... they. Our England. They ... they saved my life.'

Bill smiled. 'You owe him a lot.'

'I do. No one else is looking out for folk like me.'

'Yes,' said Bill, gazing back out of the window. 'I'm afraid you may be right.'

Stuart dropped the journalist mid-way up the Harringay Ladder, stopping outside a three-storey house in a tree-lined street.

'Thanks very much,' Bill leaned forward and held out his hand. Stuart hesitated, took it.

'I'm Bill, by the way, and you?'

'Stuart.'

'Stuart. Pleasure to meet you, and good luck with everything.'

Stuart had a moment of panic. 'You're not going to use what I said in your paper?'

Bill shook his head. 'Don't worry. In any case, you didn't say anything that Mr Cave wouldn't approve of, I'm sure.'

Stuart nodded. 'All right, then.' He put the car in first and headed up the hill (it was a notorious one-way system) onto Wightman Road, which would lead him directly to the Shoe Factory, but when he got to the turning, he carried on. He didn't know why. He liked returning to the flat – *his posh flat* – and didn't mind Jamie, a friend of Mike's who he shared with, though he didn't have too much to say to him. And he wasn't used to sharing with another bloke. Had gone straight from his mam's to his wife's. What was there to say to another bloke? Jamie always had the sport on, even boring stuff like motorbikes, all day, and there was only so much even he could find to say about the footie. Odds? Races? No idea. Stuart had never been a gambler.

That was how he found himself back at Trellis House. He parked the car outside the Oak and thought of Auntie. It was a bit too chilly for folk to sit outside, other than a few hardy smokers, but there was the bench where he had almost left her, where his selfishness, his drunken self-pity, had seen the end of her.

He looked up at the old flat. The light wasn't on. He thought about moving off, but he had nowhere to go, nothing to do now he was off the beer, so he got out and went for a wander. He walked across the green, stepping daintily around the dog shit, and, instead of taking the lift, went up the stairs. He was trying to get himself in shape – Mike said he should join a gym, not least because it helped avoid the booze, but Stuart hadn't got that far yet.

He was certainly puffing by the time he reached the fourth floor. He waited a mo before getting his breath back then made his way along the walkway. What was he intending to do? He wasn't sure himself. Curiosity, he supposed, he wanted to see who they had replaced him with. He half-hoped to find a family like some of them he had delivered to. That would mean in a way … in a kind of way, it would have been, well, not worthwhile exactly, but at least it would all have made some sense. He would ring on the bell, and see them, a nice family who would deserve it more than him, and that would make it all right, somehow. He could walk away with a spring in his step.

But he wasn't really expecting that. He wasn't that stupid. He was actually expecting a dozen foreigners who couldn't speak English and would tell him, in so many words, to bugger off. That was what he was expecting – because that was what they were up against, and it would prove it.

What he wasn't expecting, what really sent him reeling back against the wall staring in disbelief, was the steel door. The steel shutters. It being all shut up like that.

That bloke had told him he had to get out – there was urgent need. The woman had said the same. It was for them in urgent need, families. He wouldn't stand a chance, but there were foreigners, immigrants, families, who needed the place, urgently, right now, tomorrow, he had to go.

But would you look at that. The grubby steel door, already riddled with graffiti. The windows covered up. But … fuck. It had been *months*. Months they'd had it, months it had been empty. Months he could have been living here, instead of sharing, instead of relying on charity, but instead they preferred to make him homeless for the immigrants, only they hadn't even put any immigrants in! Make him homeless, that was all it was all about. Throw him onto the streets – *You're not from here*, that bloke had said, *why don't you try back home* – that's right, send him back to his reservation, like Vince was always putting it. They won't be pleased until they've put us all on a fucking reservation. Get him out, that's the most important thing. The fucking *cunts*.

Just then a neighbour came out. It was one of the Polish lads that lived in the flat next door. All those lads were in the building trade and Stuart had joined them for a pint a few times down at the Oak where they didn't seem to have any problem with all the flags and that, and the locals certainly left them alone, not least because they were built like brick shit houses. But they were friendly, too, and always keen for a chat to practise their English, even though one of them – Jacob was it? – had taken the piss, said if we talk too much to you Stuart, we'll end up speaking like you and no one will understand us! But they were good lads. This one, Havel, always had a smile.

'Alreet mite!' he said in a mix of Cockney and Mackem. 'We haven't seen you for a long time. What happen?'

Stuart shook his head. 'You've seen this?' He was still angry.

'They shut you out?'

'It was supposed to go to a family, when Auntie died. That's what they told me. But look, they just left it.'

'No one there,' Havel nodded. 'You forget something?'

Stuart thought about it. 'You wouldn't mind,' he gestured toward their door, 'if I took a look?'

'No, mite. Go ahead.'

The flats shared a balcony separated by a waist-high wall. That was how they had first met, when Stuart was helping Auntie pot some of her plants and the lads were checking the place out for the first time.

Stuart followed Havel down the narrow corridor, a replica of his old flat, although all the doors were closed and padlocked, serving as bedrooms for the Poles. They passed through a spotlessly clean kitchen and Havel opened the balcony door. Stuart stepped out. He felt a wave of sadness as he saw Auntie's flowers still there, lying dead in dried out pots.

With Havel watching, Stuart climbed over the wall, treading carefully between the pots, and tried the glass door. It was a bit stiff, but it wasn't locked (it couldn't lock – the frame had long-since distorted) and with a bit of a shove it opened up. There it all was – his, *their*, old life. Nothing had been touched. Didn't the woman say something about clearing it out? That was why he had taken all of Auntie's special stuff. The rest they could chuck. But they hadn't touched a thing. They'd just sealed it up, and left it – sofa, old TV, knick-knacks, magazines, a handful of Mills and Boon, some empty Stella cans (he looked away in shame).

Stuart walked through the flat, picking things up then putting them down, his rage and ... *contempt* growing. It was all fucking bullshit, he thought. All fucking bullshit. They don't even give a shit about the fucking immigrants. It's just like Vince says – a secret war against the Anglo Saxons.

'Mite?' It was Havel. 'You OK? Sorry, mite, I must go.'

'Just ...' Stuart cleared his throat. 'Just a minute,' he called back. He picked up a couple of other things – a stopped carriage clock that had been his uncle's retirement gift, a couple of the porcelain knick-knacks, a shepherdess and a pot-bellied boy – and came back out on the balcony.

'Mite, you alreet?'

Stuart nodded, passing him the clock and knick-knacks before clambering back over.

'Aye,' he said. 'Alreet.'

16

It seemed like ages since the friends had been on the demo against capital punishment, so much had happened since: Aisha going to infants, Hallie transforming, seemingly overnight, from a boyish girl to a girlish young woman. Sanjay had been offered a partnership in his firm, which he was still pondering – he hadn't given up on Canada yet, Meena knew, although he kept his thoughts largely to himself. It had been busy at her work, too: things had been moving rapidly forward on Our England's 'homes for heroes'.

Meena was in the centre of the largest overhaul in social housing for seventy years and found the planning process fascinating, especially now her borough had been granted special powers to re-purpose Green Belt areas. She had to admit she also got a bit of a buzz needling the mostly middle class objectors. They had fled the city for the building-restricted Green Belt, which had effectively become a social exclusion zone due to high house prices, and were now fighting a bitter battle against 'hordes of the great unwashed' (as she had overheard one gammon complain) moving in down the road.

Even the Patriots had pushed back Our England's proposal that 'white-British' families should receive priority, but she felt she could work with the amendment to 'families who had been born in England'. Although it meant revising their previous classification based solely on need, hadn't she and Sanjay also been born in the UK? And the plans didn't come cheaply – as the Secretary of State for Housing had said: 'You've got to have put something in to get something out.' Admittedly it was a move that would have been unthinkable a generation ago, but that was the past and, as the Prime Minister regularly reminded the nation: 'this is no time for looking over our shoulders.'

But sometimes it couldn't be helped – Meena still had nasty flashbacks from the capital punishment demo.

Nevertheless, she wanted to attend the gay rights one. It was important to show support.

'I'm sorry,' said Sanjay. 'I don't want you to.'

She looked at him. 'You're not forbidding me, Sanj?'

He shook his head. 'Of course not, but after what happened the last time, frankly, I'm worried. We can't have Aisha there.'

She had to admit he had a point. She *had* thought of that – she had actually thought Sanjay could stay at home with Aisha. But now she was faced with it, she realised that this wasn't going to work – it wasn't that Sanjay would have a problem looking after Aisha, he would be worried about her.

'Bryan and Phillip, Diane and Juno for that matter,' she said. 'They need our support.'

'I know,' he said. 'But they're not bringing their kids, either.'

'You've spoken to them?' She was surprised. Bryan hadn't mentioned anything about it at work. In fact, now she came to think about it, Bryan hadn't talked about the march for ages.

'I spoke to Phillip,' said Sanjay.

'What about?'

'The march. I said I would go.'

'You said that without discussing it with me?'

'There could be trouble, love. After what happened last time.'

'But that's precisely why we have to go,' said Meena. 'To show we won't be intimidated.'

'I'm afraid it could get ugly.'

'Then why do you want to go?'

He smiled. 'To show we won't be intimidated?'

In the end they arrived at a compromise: they would go as a family but when the march set off, Meena would take Aisha for a walk along the Thames and then head for home. Meena wasn't happy about it, but it did seem like the most sensible option. Certainly if it came to fisticuffs again, she wouldn't be much use.

She was going to mention it to Bryan on the Friday but she didn't have a chance to see him because she was out visiting clients all day, so it was only at the march itself that she had the opportunity.

There were none of the queues at the tube station to access the Embankment that Meena had experienced for the last march. In fact, it felt pretty much like any other Saturday morning in central London, with most people clearly arriving at the station for a day out rather than a demonstration.

But it wasn't hard to find them by the bridge. The first person she saw was Juno, who gave her a hug.

'It's good of you to come,' she said. 'But you shouldn't have brought the babe.'

'I'm not,' said Meena, apologetically. 'I mean, not really. We were worried after what happened last time, so we made a deal,' she pointed at Sanjay. 'He's the family representative.'

'Have you got your steel toe caps?' Juno asked him.

'I've got my running shoes.'

Bryan came over. 'I'm sorry,' said Meena.

'Don't be,' he said. 'Honestly, I should have said something, I was just tied up with work, life, you know …' In truth he hadn't wanted to pressure her after what had happened last time.

Meena looked around the demo. She frowned. 'The others?'

'Oh,' said Bryan, 'Bill – he's over there. Rory and Emma are away this weekend. France.'

'They still can't sell it?'

'Apparently not. Shame for them, really, as the pound's so low.'

'First World Problems,' said Meena.

Bryan grinned. There was an announcement over the speakers. The demo began to move off.

'Take care,' Meena gave each of them a hug. 'You take care!'

Meena pushed Aisha over to the pavement and watched them go. There were a lot of people, she could tell, but nothing like the numbers for the last demo. More like a Gay Pride parade.

As she watched them pass, Meena saw one smartly dressed male couple hand-in-hand, actually handcuffed together. No, not a Pride, she thought, there was no sense of celebration here. It felt much more solemn – a procession, definitely a protest, which she supposed was its purpose, but she had never witnessed the like among the gay community in her lifetime.

It didn't take long for the crowd to pass and Meena walked, as planned, across the bridge to take Aisha on a ride on the London Eye. From there, she had hoped to be able to point out the march as it passed Westminster, but by the time they had reached the top, the streets were full of traffic again. It was, thought Meena, as if they had never been there.

The demonstration didn't get much more upbeat. Indeed, once they had got going, apart from the upsurge of a chant which soon died out, the predominant sound as they made their way down Victoria Street, past indifferent shoppers and a small demonstration holding banners like HOMOS GO TO HELL, was their footsteps.

It was seeing that sign that pushed Sanjay to broach the subject.

He had been mulling upon it ever since meeting a colleague – a partner, actually, the one who was pressing him to come on board – for lunch.

The partner represented part of the business that provided consultancy to the public sector and, Sanjay knew, had recently been working with the Ministry of the Family on some very hush-hush stuff. Leaning forward mid-way through their main course, the partner had said: 'This repeal of, you know, gay marriage. They want to make it *ex post facto*.' He had sat back, surveying Sanjay while this sank in.

Sanjay had assumed his poker face, looked down at his plate and scooped up a forkful of sea bass. Before he lifted it to his mouth, he had raised his eyebrow and said, simply: 'Why?'

The partner snorted. 'Precisely,' he had said, 'well, story is, the minister just presumed by making them illegal, it would work backwards.'

'Ah,' said Sanjay. They had both shared a moment of amusement at the naivety of the non-legal fraternity. 'And you explained that it wasn't done that way... But *ex post facto*? Really? For something like this?'

'She's determined,' he had said. 'They all are. It's not until you see the whites of their eyes you realise what incredible *fanatics* you're dealing with. Do you know what one of them said? One of her special advisers – a young chap, thin as a rake, high as a kite on his juvenile power trip – said without any apparent sense of ... well, impropriety: "Otherwise what point would there be? Think of it as moral cleansing." I wanted to punch the little fucker in the face.'

'But you didn't.'

'No,' the partner had said wistfully. 'But I wish we were fleecing them for more.'

Sanjay took a deep breath and turned to Bryan. Then he changed his mind, but not quick enough for Bryan to notice and ask: 'What?'

'Oh,' said Sanjay. 'Something I've been wanting to talk to you about, but this isn't the place.'

'About Meena?' He shook his head. 'Not Aisha, I hope? You as a family?'

'No,' said Sanjay. 'Don't worry. We can leave it, until ... later.'

'Come on,' Bryan grinned. 'Now you've got me interested ...'

'We need privacy.'

Bryan took his arm to slow them down so they drew behind their friends. 'What could be more private,' he said, 'than a crowd?'

Sanjay shrugged. 'Whatever happens, you didn't get this from me. My career's on the line.'

'Of course.'

'It's about these new laws. Repealing gay marriage. How it ... may affect you.'

'Affect us?' said Bryan. 'It's awful, obviously. But it can't affect us: repealing a law is different from making something that was legal, illegal.' He shook his head. 'Well, obviously it does make it. Illegal, I mean. It's a tragedy for young people, for us as a community, and we're going to fight it, but it won't affect me and Phillip. I mean, we were legally married. You can't change a law in retrospect for the same reason that people can't be tried for doing something that was legal in the past like, I don't know, taking opium or something. Isn't that right?'

Sanjay nodded. 'Usually.' He felt his throat tighten. His voice dropped to the level it assumed when explaining obscure but potentially devastating legal points to clients. 'That's how it's usually applied, the law, Bryan. Here, and in most countries.'

'So, there we are,' said Bryan. He looked at Sanjay, his face suddenly shadowed by something like fear. 'Aren't we?'

Sanjay cleared his throat. He linked Bryan's arm in his and spoke softly into his ear.

'In this case, no. It's, um, going to be *ex post facto*. I've been told by one of the firm's lawyers who is working with the government. *Ex Post Facto* is a legal mechanism, one that only exists in the UK and maybe a handful of other countries, like Australia ...' Bryan gave him a blank look. 'It means that, basically, yes, laws can be retroactive. They've used it a couple of times in the recent past, for example over new evidence in murder cases, or tax evasion.

'It would have been difficult to push it through over ... something like this, which is dealing with, well, obviously, *non-criminals*, under the Human Rights Act... but now they've repealed the Act ...'

'Will they get it through?' said Bryan. Sanjay nodded.

'Otherwise the bastards wouldn't have had the guts to put it in in the first place. Nasty, vindictive, *evil* bastards.' He looked at Bryan, whose face had drained of colour but whose expression remained calm. Sanjay, who, of course, had thought all this through, wondered whether he should say the next part. Should he give this time to sink in and for Bryan and Phillip to work it out for themselves, then come running to him for advice? Or should he say what he had already concluded and save them the pain – at least – of finding out separately, and maybe buy some more time? What should he do? What should a friend do? He took a deep breath.

'Bryan,' he said.

'Hm.' Bryan looked a million miles away.

'Bryan,' he said, 'there's something else.'

'Hm?' Bryan looked at him.

Sanjay shook his head. 'Look, I may be wrong about this, I might have misread or misunderstood the proposals, the law or something ...'

Bryan smiled sadly. 'That'll be the day,' he said.

'It's just ... working through the implications ...'

'Implications?' said Bryan. 'We'll lose our Married Couple's Allowance, I suppose.'

Sanjay shook his head. 'It's not that,' he said. 'Look,' he pulled him closer, 'try to be calm about this, I'm sure we'll find a way around it ...'

'Around what?' said Bryan.

'Well, look: the Families Act says that only married couples can adopt or care for children who are not "naturally" their own.'

'But ...' said Bryan. Then he realised: 'They'll take Ben and Hallie away from us. You're saying that, Sanjay?'

Sanjay sighed. 'That's ... how I've read the law,' he said. 'And, frankly, their intent. Like I said, it's simply *evil*.'

Now Bryan pulled Sanjay toward him. 'Whatever you do,' he said. '*Don't tell Phillip*.'

*

Phillip would, of course, find out eventually. He would pull Bryan aside the evening after the details of the law were announced. They had cleared up dinner and were just settling down in front of the TV (the kids had done their usual vanishing trick) when he said: 'Did you see that article Bill forwarded?' The article that pointed out what Sanjay had been saying, flagging the removal of children as technically permissible under the law, but not going so far as saying it was likely, only that 'after this vindictive *ex post facto* amendment, it feels like anything could happen.'

'I'll speak to Sanjay about it,' Bryan said disingenuously.

'Because we could never let that happen,' said Phillip, levelly. 'I won't let them take my babies.'

'It won't,' said Bryan. 'I won't let that happen either.'

'But what can we do if it does?'

'Don't worry,' he laid his hand on Phillip's chest, felt his fast-beating heart. 'I won't let it. I promise you.'

But paradoxically, that article had given Bryan hope: Sanjay's warning had made the situation feel pretty desperate. Realistically – what *could* they do if the kids were taken away? They would have the whole weight of the State bearing down on them. But perhaps Sanjay *had* misread the situation – maybe not even *this* government would go that far. It wasn't the olden days: despite the bigotry of the ruling powers, the vast majority of ordinary people were pro-gay these days, weren't they? Surely the government wouldn't risk upsetting scenes of kids being dragged away from loving families? Bryan shook his head. Times change, he thought, this wasn't the Nineteen Thirties. They would survive. Get through it: quietly, sensibly, unremarkably. They would keep their heads down, pay the mortgage, carry on with their lives. This *was* still England, after all.

It wasn't as if he didn't have enough on his plate. The massive building programme was causing a huge headache, as well as this wicked business about British citizens being placed first in the queue. That was all very well to say, but what about need? Bryan spent days trudging up and down decrepit tower blocks with an assortment of translators, explaining why families of nine or twelve confined to three damp rooms were no longer considered a priority. No, being refugees did not count, according to the new points system. Yes, I can see that your children are sick, but I'm sorry, there's nothing I can do.

It was relentless, unforgiving, and unappreciated work.

Bryan spent the day his marriage was officially dissolved at a case meeting trying to work out how to prevent the children from a Ukrainian family being placed into care because their property had been condemned and they were about to be thrown onto the street.

But perhaps it was just him. Meena seemed her usual positive self, grappling tirelessly with every new challenge, and he was glad to be able to throw much of the Green Belt stuff her way – frankly, he felt soiled by it – while even Nathan seemed more engaged. His promotion had probably helped, although neither Meena or Bryan had been particularly keen, but what with the increased workload they didn't have a great deal of choice. They needed him to step up, and he actually appeared to have done so – from the first day in his new position, seemingly without any hipster irony, he had come to work in a shirt and jacket and sporting new look: his quiff and moustache replaced by a clean shave and smart crop, although this *was* in keeping with the fashion, Meena had explained to Bryan. Hadn't he noticed, she said, a lot of young men had it these days?

'And there was me thinking they were just fascists,' he said. He clicked on a round robin email from the Chief Executive – *Seminar on Compliance Certificate for Public Sector Employees*. Then his phone rang. It was Phillip.

'We've got a bit of a crisis,' he said.

You think it's going to get better. That's one thing they tell you, when you're a kid, that it's going to get better –

you've fallen and scraped your knee. Your dad wipes it clean, puts on the plaster, don't worry, my brave soldier, it's just a scratch. Then the scratch turns into a scab, which you can pick at, which is all right, and then it's gone. Clean, as if it never happened. Happy endings. That's what they tell you, in every story you're read to, or read, there are the happy endings, no matter how grim it gets. But in real life, as Ben had learned, it doesn't work like that. True, he hadn't yet cornered Todd like Simon had said, but the truth was ... *the truth was*, he was afraid. Put simply, Todd was bigger than him. More developed, more muscular, and he had *that look* in his eye, that dead-eyed look that Ben could see and he didn't understand why the others couldn't (although perhaps they could, perhaps they were afraid of it, too) which made him think that Todd just didn't care – that behind that quick smile he was capable of *anything* – and it scared Ben. What happened if Ben *did* creep up on him – he had run through it so many times – and Todd got the better of him? What then? He could easily imagine that delighted grin, those dead eyes looking down on him as he sat across his chest and smashed his face. And smashed, and smashed.

Then, while the dads were watching TV and Hallie was upstairs, he had gone into the kitchen and opened the knife drawer. He took out one knife after another and gripped it, making stabbing actions. Then he saw the stand of really expensive Italian knives Bryan had bought Phillip one Christmas and neither he nor Hallie were allowed to touch because they were so sharp, and he drew one out. It was so beautiful – sheer metal that melted into the sharpest edge – and it had this feel in his hand, this balance. He jabbed it upwards, once, twice. He imagined it sliding into Todd's belly, as if through warm butter. He imagined plunging it down, in a crescent moon, until Todd's insides fell outside like in that movie he had seen. This one would be perfect. Trouble is, he thought, his dads would notice it was missing right away.

Ben heard movement from the living room and slid it

back, bent down and opened a cupboard door, pretended to be looking for some chocolate biscuits.

'Oh, go on, then,' whispered Bryan, taking a couple from the packet. 'But don't tell Phillip.' Ben smiled nervously, and Bryan gave him an affectionate pinch on the cheek.

Ben opened the knife drawer again and picked up some of the other knives, which now felt light and ineffectual compared to the last one. Would they even work, he wondered. And what if they did? Only now did the potential consequences begin to enter into his mind, like dim lights in the distance. He would get into trouble, he knew, but wasn't he already in trouble with this evil stalking him day after day after day? What was the alternative? To kill himself? To end it all? For a moment the sheer bliss of nothingness, not having to hurt any more, cradled him in its arms. But then the thought of him dying and Todd living, going on tormenting some other poor kid, some other poor adult, filled him with fury. He pulled out a small, rubber-handled knife, one of those they had used for chopping before they got the posh set but now only peeled the potatoes with and, wrapping it in some kitchen roll, brought it upstairs.

Just knowing the knife was in his bedside drawer, hidden beneath a Harry Potter, gave Ben some comfort, enabled him to sleep well that night for the first time in ages. He slept so well, in fact, he actually forgot all about it and was half-way to school before he realised, and it was only then that the familiar sense of queasiness came and with it the dark cloud that seemed to hang over him even though it was a nice day.

Back in the war zone, nothing had changed. Still no one was talking to him – everyone in his year knew now, that if you spoke to Ben you were gay. Of course the girls didn't care, or mind that much, but they didn't count. He didn't want to talk to them anyway, even though his hormones were playing havoc with his feelings and every girl he looked at was somehow loaded with sexuality, and every boy now, too in a way – now that everyone thought he was gay. He had even begun to think himself, that maybe he *was* gay, even though he never felt funny or terrible or … whatever around boys, he never thought of boys like *that*, but maybe Todd had seen something in him that he couldn't see himself. And maybe *if he was gay*, if other people started thinking he was gay, then they'd start thinking his dads had made him that way, even maybe that his dads had been fiddling with him, and then they would come and take him and Hallie away and … the bell rang, he closed the library book – the library was the only place in school he found sanctuary, could sit and pretend to read or pretend to study or actually do both – and dragged himself to his next lesson, Religious Education.

Ben didn't mind it. The teacher, a proper Sikh with a turban and beard, Mr Singh, was all right and, at least until Ben's world had turned to shit, he had almost looked forward to his class because the teacher was so easy to steer off on tangents and talk about the stories in the Adi Granth, Bhagavad Gita, Bible, Tanakh and the Qur'an and their similarities and history and what life was like and how it was different and everything. Anything to avoid having to do any actual work. Ben hadn't noticed the difference about the classes being obligatory now or any changes in the curriculum, although in truth he hadn't noticed much more than his daily misery, even though Mr Singh had quietly noted the changes in *him*: how that inquisitive, bright boy asked far fewer questions and appeared to have been shunned by his classmates. Still, his marks, if anything, had improved – although that may have had more to do with him spending all his time in the library, alone, Mr Singh thought. It was subtle, but he put it down to that blond kid, Todd. A right little psychopath, you could tell, and Mr Singh had had a word with Ben's form teacher, but Glenn, a young guy just starting out, claimed not to have noticed anything. Still, Mr Singh would keep an eye on it and maybe probe Ben's parents (a gay couple, he seemed to recall, perhaps that was why he was being picked on?) when they came in.

'Today, I'd like to introduce you to Martin,' he said. 'From the Church of the Seventh Day Adventists.' It was part of the new curriculum – inviting one religious representative every month to talk about their religion – and although he had been initially sceptical, Mr Singh had to accept that it had helped the kids focus on some of the stuff they would need for their GCSE.

Martin from the Seventh Day Adventists had already been briefed, as all the representatives had, not to give too much of a sermon, but to focus more on the history, the demographics of the religion in the UK, why they worshipped the way they did, and so on, and, like most of the other Christians other than the ageing Catholic priest – who had been a bit tetchy and had had a vague whiff of alcohol about him – Martin went on to explain the peculiarities of his sect with patience and good humour.

He explained that they worshipped, and rested – which was when God took his rest – on Saturday, because in America, where the sect was founded, Saturday is considered to be the seventh day.

They tended to be vegetarians, he said, because they believed the body was a temple, so many of them also did not smoke or drink alcohol, and obviously, he smiled at Mr Singh, take illegal drugs.

When Ben had arrived – at the last minute as usual – he had been dismayed to discover that the only seat available for him was not only beside Kelsey, a girl, but directly in front of Gray and Todd, and his neck hairs had been tingling ever since he had sat down.

Now he heard a snigger, a hand raised behind him. He knew it must be Todd's. Mr Singh had spotted Ben's anguished expression even if Martin hadn't and would have ignored the boy's raised arm. Martin, however, had less sensitive antennae. He smiled.

'Is it true,' Todd asked sweetly, his blue eyes beaming Aryan innocence, 'in your religion, you believe that if you're gay you go to Hell?'

There was a moment of calm as Martin, looking uncomfortable, tried to formulate an answer; as Mr

Singh's features darkened, the air singing with tension, then ... an explosion. A human explosion.

Mr Singh had experienced it only a couple of times before in his career – once when he had been a trainee at a rough school in Hackney, and once, a couple of years ago, at this more middle-class comprehensive – an eruption of noise, movement, violence, that was more animal than human, an indication perhaps, he had thought after the second time, of how close we – or at least children, still half-formed – remain to animals.

And yes, that was what it was like – a brawl in a monkey house. Before he could intervene – and these kids, they moved quickly – the classroom had blown up, the children scattering in a high-pitched tumult.

Martin was stumbling backwards, desks were being swept aside, and Ben, good-natured Ben, who had one of the best disciplinary records in his year, had launched himself at Todd, first landing a haymaking punch on the side of his head and, as the boy fell into the aisle, grabbing hold of him and hurling punches with his right hand while his left held back Todd's flaying arms.

Mr Singh found his way blocked by a pack of kids and desks. As he pushed them aside to get to the teenagers, he noticed something in Ben's hand – a sharpened pencil.

He got there too late. He wrenched Ben back, his arms around his chest, as the boy's fist, clenched around the pencil, jabbed downwards. A bead of blood thrashed back and across the white shirt of one of the girls. She screamed. Mr Singh heard another teacher bursting through the door, pushing the kids aside.

It was Mike from History. He looked down at Todd, keening, scrunched up in a foetal position, hands covering his face, and shouted: 'Call a fucking ambulance.'

*

How long had this being going on for? It was difficult to know. At least, it was difficult to get it out of Ben. A few months, that was what Bryan and Phillip decided, although whether it had anything to do with when the compulsory religious education lessons had kicked in was moot. In any case, Mr Singh, the teacher, seemed conciliatory enough in the meeting in the Head's office while Ben sat, trembling, crying, still covered in blood, Todd's blood, in the corridor with Phillip.

'Be that as it may,' said the Headteacher, a middle-aged Welshman Bryan had never met but who had the smooth, capable air of his own chief executive. 'This kind of behaviour is unacceptable, and results in immediate expulsion. It can mean criminal charges.'

Bryan clenched his teeth and let out a long sigh through his nose. He didn't often look nostalgically back to the old days, but at least then a scrap between a couple of boys would be treated as a matter of internal discipline and dealt with by detentions. Throwing out Ben, who had a perfect record, as Mr Singh had pointed out ('Glenn', Ben's form teacher, who was supposed to be his 'advocate' as the jargon put it, had remained mute throughout) could have a catastrophic effect on his future. Everyone in the room knew there were no other decent state schools for miles, and who would take a pupil expelled for violence?

'You mentioned Ben's … reaction came after the boy …'

'Todd,' said the Headteacher.

'Asked a question about homosexuality,' said Bryan.

Mr Singh nodded. He looked at the Head. 'I could tell something was wrong,' he said. 'By the look on Ben's face as soon as Todd put his hand up. In fact …' and he took a deep breath. 'I had mentioned it to you, hadn't I, Glenn, that I was a bit concerned about Ben.'

Glenn glanced at the Head, then Mr Singh.

'I … yes.' He nodded.

'How long ago did you notice this, Mr Singh,' Bryan asked.

Mr Singh looked at the Head, who was his usual inscrutable self. He thought – *when you're in a hole, Seb, stop digging.* But that would be wrong.

'I'd say since the beginning of the year. He's been keeping himself to himself. Hasn't sat with the other kids. Hasn't been ... the same old Ben.'

Bryan nodded, wanting to die inside. To think his little boy had been suffering like this, while at home ... he remembered the tears over that website. He should have understood it was something more than that, he should have quizzed him further.

'Be that as it may,' he heard the Head say again, 'I'm afraid we have no option but to ...'

'Hold on,' said Bryan. 'Do you mean to say this has been going on for months and the school has done nothing about it? Homophobic bullying? What kind of school is it that allows homophobic bullying, then punishes the victim?'

The corners of the Head's mouth twitched into something that was almost a smile, as if the player opposite him had inadvertently revealed their hand. He glanced at Mr Singh, who felt himself disappear down a very dark hole, then shook his head.

'There's no evidence of that.'

'We just have to ask Ben,' said Bryan. 'Mr Singh here has said as much, and it has been endorsed by Glenn.'

'No evidence,' said the Head. 'Only his word against ours.'

'And your teachers,' said Bryan.

The Head shook his head. 'I can't stop you taking any action you see fit, Bryan, but the fact remains that Ben injured this boy. Todd. They had to take him to hospital.' He looked at Glenn. 'Condition?'

'Er ... stitches, I think.'

'He stabbed him,' said the Head. 'In the face with a sharpened pencil. Never mind the stitches, he could have blinded, even killed Todd. Not only that, but we had to send three of the girls home. For trauma.'

Bryan drew in another breath. Trauma. They were sending them home for 'trauma' now, after a kids' scrap.

'And Ben?' he said, exhaling slowly in an effort to control his rage. 'His trauma?'

CANARIES

The Head sat back. 'He didn't mention anything to you or your ...' he paused, 'partner, at home?' Bryan shook his head. 'We've got over a thousand pupils,' he heard the Head say. 'I'm afraid these things can happen among children.'

Bryan nodded. 'They do, which is why we will be prepared to put aside Ben's *homophobic bullying* if he is permitted to stay at school.'

The Head shook his head. 'I'm sorry.'

'We'll see about that.'

The Head's expression hardened. Now he leaned forward, clasping his hands directly under his chin. 'Honestly, Bryan, I wouldn't, if I were you.'

'What?'

'Make too much out of this. Look, Todd's father is ... a successful businessman, who has already made an impact on the Board of Governors. Obviously, I have already had him on to me today, furious, as you can imagine. If we were to ... bend the rules for Ben, I can't imagine he would find that acceptable and, well, apart from making our lives very difficult indeed, I don't doubt he would do his upmost to make yours difficult, as well.'

'Ours?' Bryan said dumbly.

Irritation swept across the man's face. 'You must know what I'm referring to.'

But Bryan didn't, not straight away. It took more than a moment for the message to sink in – the confirmation of a fear he had been pushing aside for so long. Yet part of him still couldn't believe what he had heard, that this was happening to him, to them, now, in the 21st Century.

The Head let his gaze linger on him for a little longer, then stood up. 'Well,' he said. 'I'll leave that decision to you.'

The other teachers followed suit, but Bryan remained sitting there as the full horror sunk in. It was everything Sanjay had been saying and worse – the new legislation didn't just amount to a legal loophole recognised as a remote danger, a technicality that would never come to pass. The vulnerability of gay couples and their adopted children under the new law had already penetrated the consciousness of functionaries within the system.

Bryan finally got to his feet, stood there momentarily, like a tall building swaying in the wind. The Head was examining his phone, Glenn had shrivelled away to the corner of the room while Mr Singh looked grim behind his closely clipped beard. Nevertheless he, alone, held out his hand. Bryan shook it, then turned and walked out.

Phillip and Ben looked up at him. Ben's face was chapped with crying, Phillip looked just ... stricken. With a Herculean effort, Bryan forced a smile, holding out his arms. They stood to greet him and he hugged them both. They came together like a team. 'Everything's going to be fine,' said Bryan. 'Ben, I want you to know I'm so, so proud of you. You couldn't have made me prouder. Now, let's go home.'

'Am I suspended?'

'For now, son, but it's nothing to worry about.'

'For how long?'

'Let's talk about this later.'

Arm-in-arm-in-arm, brothers-in-arms, they walked out of the school.

17

'Just be careful.'

'Don't worry,' said Bill. 'It will probably be like that time when the local paper sent me to a haunted house. I'll be sitting up all night in the dark and nothing will happen.'

'You never know with that lot,' said Phillip. 'Violent extremists, on both sides. They won't be able to see you're a journalist in the dark.'

'Honestly,' said Bill. 'I'll be fine. More to the point, how's Ben holding up?'

'Okay …' said Phillip. 'In a sense, I get the impression he feels relieved more than anything. For it all to be out in the open, to not have to cover things up any more, although I think he was shocked by the violence.'

'He's such a gentle chap.'

'And of course, especially what with what happened between his biological parents. We've never hidden it from them, but I do worry that he thinks he could be like that, too …'

Bill looked around the office. Phillip had messaged to ask him if he wanted to go camping with them, but he had had this Our England thing so had given him a call. He dropped his voice. 'You're great parents,' he said. 'Just look how wonderful your kids have turned out. And look … I'm no psychologist. All right, maybe Ben has a more … violent side to explore. There's nothing wrong with that. Boys will be boys. But that in no way makes him … like his biological father. You probably need to speak to an expert, but I'd say if he is worried about it, then there's no point trying to avoid it. Maybe he could take up boxing, judo, or something. You never know – you guys could be rearing a future military hero.'

Phillip laughed. 'Wouldn't that be ironic.'

'Lawrence of Arabia was gay. Alexander the Great …'

'Although Ben's not gay,' Phillip said quickly. 'That's one thing we know for sure.'

'"course.'

'But it would be good ...' Phillip paused. 'If maybe we saw a little more of you? Now he's going through this ... awkward, heterosexual, stage, it might be useful to have a straight man about more. And you are his sort of godfather.'

'I am indeed,' said Bill, although he had never participated in any formal ceremony. 'Of course,' he said. 'I'll pop round when you get back.' He looked up. 'I've got to go, speak soon.'

'You take care.'

'Don't get too wet!' Bill switched off the phone. 'Ibo?' The IT guy grinned. 'So how does this work?'

'Simple,' said Ibo. He peeled on a pair of blue latex gloves and removed a small, round, white plastic box, the kind that would usually carry earbuds, but this had a pair of paper wallets. Ibo produced some tweezers and opened the first one, pulling out a semi-transparent piece of plastic shaped like a tiny boomerang. 'If you will just look toward the window,' he said. Bill did as he was told. 'Now,' said Ibo, 'stay still, as I place the receiver-transmitter behind your earlobe.' Bill felt a tingly sensation. 'Now, the second part – the recorder. This is slightly more conspicuous. You will have probably seen them?'

Bill shook his head. Ibo shrugged. 'Well, actually, this is top-of-the-line, police-grade, so if you're not looking out for it, you may not notice.' He reached into another wallet and pulled out another tiny plastic boomerang, although this actually seemed less substantial than the first, so light, in fact, that Bill had to concentrate to spot it crinkling slightly between the tweezers. 'Are you right or left-handed?' Ibo asked.

'Left,' said Bill.

'Okay. Now look at me.' Ibo leant forward and carefully placed the boomerang just above Bill's right eyebrow then flattened it downwards against his temple so it curved around his eye socket. 'Smile,' he said. 'Grin.' He rubbed it in further. It felt like some kind of cool gel, thought Bill, reminding him of the weekend he had spent at a wellness centre with Ulrika from Features. That was nice, he thought. Fun girl Ulrika. He should ask her what she's up to next weekend.

'All done,' said Ibo.

'That's it?' Bill moved his head, smiled, grinned. 'Are you sure it's inconspicuous? I don't look like one of those cyborgs from a 1990s Star Trek?'

'Take a look,' said Ibo, swiping the mirror function on his phone. Bill looked at himself. Leaned closer. Fair enough – he couldn't see a thing.

'And it works?'

Ibo took his mouse and clicked the private account page.

'Wow,' said Bill, sitting back. There he was on the same screen, repeated infinitely in high definition. 'So, basically, everything I see, hear, say – my experience, basically – will go straight to here. Pretty impressive,' he said, although like everyone else he had grown used to being impressed by technology and adapting to it almost instantaneously.

'How long does it last?'

'This will do you for forty-eight hours without a charge. The old ones only last for twenty-four. And remember, legally, you have to inform anyone you are talking to that you are broadcasting. I mean, most people don't bother, but this is business.'

'Too right,' said Bill. 'This is bloody journalism.'

Vincent had apparently 'received intelligence' (they really do think they're in a war, thought Bill) that the Reds were going to attack the Shoe Factory that night.

Bill had been right in predicting the paper would be lukewarm about the Mandy story and they had spiked it – it was just their word said the Home Editor. What do the police say? Not much, admitted Bill. The editor shrugged. 'She probably got beaten up by her boyfriend or whatever. It was "The Reds"! Sure.' Bill raised his eyebrows.

'What?'

'Well,' said Bill, Vincent's predictions ringing in his ears, 'don't you think that's a bit ... dismissive?'

'Come on Bill,' said the editor, 'do you really think the Reds did this? Don't you think you're being a bit naive?'

'How so?'

'They're buttering you up. They see you're a sympathetic voice, so they're spoon-feeding you.'

Bill was used to being patronised by colleagues but hadn't come up the hard way to let it get to him. He smiled. 'Maybe you're right.' She nodded. Of course she was.

The call from Vince had come through a few weeks later. The threats, he said, and the acts of violence, had been increasing. There had been scuffles in the street, some very ominous graffiti and, of course, 'the police do bugger all. If it was the other way around, you can be sure they'd be all over us.'

'What do you want me to do about it?' said Bill. 'I can't help you if you can't give me a solid story.'

'Do you think I would be calling you otherwise, William?'

That bloke, the driver ... Stuart, was waiting for him outside. Bill went around the front passenger side.

'Do you mind? I'm really not that used to being chauffeured, even if Vincent is.'

'Be my guest.'

'I suppose I should tell you,' said Bill. 'I'm wearing this contraption. You can't see it, but basically it's broadcasting everything I can see. Live, although I don't think anyone is actually watching at the moment.'

Stuart glanced sideways. 'I can't see anything,' he said.

'You see,' Bill pointed to his temple, 'there's a slight ... shimmer when it catches the light? It's some kind of light sensitive membrane, the tech guy was telling me. It's like the one you see on the police, security guards, but theirs are black strips.'

'So what are you doing that for? I'm on TV am I?'

'Online. Though like I said, no one's watching it. It's for this story Vincent's got me on, these threats you've been having …'

'Oh aye?'

'Well, I'll have one of the night editors monitoring it this evening, and if anything comes through, it will be beamed live through *The Herald* site.'

'So, people can see me now, can they?' said Stuart. He was thinking about his kids, Mary and Jaxon. These days, now he had got back on an even keel, he always seemed to be thinking about them. When he wasn't driving for Vince or doing the rounds. When he wasn't sleeping, he would think about them. What they were up to, at whatever time it was. Whether they were cleaning their teeth, going to school, watching TV, whatever. And when he wasn't thinking about them specifically, everything else he was doing would refer back to them. Oh, instead of spending that twenty quid, he would put it aside for the kids. Maybe she could buy Mary a nice dress, Jaxon could get that hoverboard. Or, even like now – so he was beaming live, eh? Maybe one of them had stumbled onto this website, and there he was, driving his car in London. Their dad, not the bastard waster loser they were told he was, but respectable, working in London, working to build a better life for them both. Working undercover, in the insurgency, for their future. A hero. He had always been their hero.

The Shoe Factory seemed pretty quiet when they arrived, except the gates were closed and there were signs of paint having been scrubbed off the front.

'Graffiti?' said Bill, but Stuart didn't respond. The gates opened and they went through.

Inside the walls things were different – there must have been a dozen useful looking blokes banging together sheets of corrugated iron backed by wooden beams and sitting on pram wheels. Bill got out of the car. He saw Mike was among them.

'What are these?' he asked.

'Barriers,' said Mike. 'Mobile barricades.'

'Bloody hell,' said Bill. 'The only thing missing is the M16s.'

'I wish,' said Mike. 'These are to stop Molotovs. You know, petrol bombs.'

'It's that serious? Really – if it's that bad, I can't imagine the police would ignore you.'

Then Vince got to his feet, his sleeves rolled up, hammer in hand. 'Isn't that your problem though, William? The whole lot of you? A lack of bloody imagination. Our mole tells us …'

Bill raised his hand. 'I should tell you.' The work stopped. 'I should tell you all, that by law … I am obliged to inform you, I am filming this conversation.'

Vincent didn't look surprised. 'Live stream is it?'

'Well,' said Bill, 'technically, I suppose. But truth is, no one will be watching or monitoring it until this evening, when the attack is supposed to take place. I mean, the attack on you guys. Until then, I'll be broadcasting but unmonitored and un-promoted. But it will be recorded so when I'm putting the piece together I can draw on any of the material I use before or after.'

'So you won't mention our mole, then?'

Bill shook his head. 'Not if you don't want me to.'

Vince laughed. 'He's … or she's, or they's I suppose I should say, our fucking mole William. So, no, we won't want you to fucking mention him, or her, or they!' He shook his head. 'Still, I trust you. I don't know why I do, but I do.'

'It must be my pretty face,' said Bill.

'Yeah,' said Vince. 'That must be it. Anyway, *our mole* tells us that they're fucking serious this time. It's been getting nasty, William. We've had a couple of our, male, organisers ambushed. No broken bones this time, but a few bruises. Came at one with a lead fucking pipe. If he hadn't moved his head when he did, we would be meeting again at the hospital, or worse. Really, mate, it's getting out of hand, escalating.'

'And you haven't been ... retaliating?'

'Here's a question, William. Do you think if we had you wouldn't have heard of it? Do you think if we had, and that lot were nursing a few bruises and hurt feelings themselves, they, and their buddies in blue, wouldn't be right on to you?'

'So, you haven't retaliated.'

'No, we haven't retaliated, precisely because we didn't want to fan the flames, so to speak. Which is ironic, really ... because now we've heard about their plan to burn the place down, with us in it, ideally. Come inside.'

Bill followed him. At every doorway was a bucket of sand and another of water. Garden hoses had been hooked up to bathrooms and kitchens. There was a group of women packing up papers into boxes and carrying them downstairs, where they were being loaded into cars. The computer equipment was being unplugged and placed in a corner under some kind of silver, flame-retardant sheeting.

'You're certainly taking precautions,' said Bill.

'We'd be mad not to, mate. You know, this time it's not just the Reds.'

'What do you mean?'

'Our mole tells us they've been working with Islamists. Using their "expertise", so to speak.'

'Come on, Vince,' said Bill. 'You lot always say they're working together, but you've never come up with any evidence.'

'Evidence,' said Vince. 'That's what *you lot* always say – "where's your evidence?" As if the evidence wasn't there in front of your eyes.' He shook his head. 'But you want "evidence"? That's why I've asked you here today, so you can see what we're up against. So you can't complain we're making it up. So you can *fucking live stream* it. Granted, I can't guarantee we'll catch ourselves an Islamist, but what I do want the viewers at home to see is that the Reds are no better than any other terrorists. No better than them that attack the shopping centres, and they should be treated just the same.'

'So have you set a trap for them? Is that what you're planning?'

Vince shook his head. 'Given the apathy of the authorities in defending the English people, our priority is to save our building here, to save everything precious we've built. This is going to be Rourke's Drift, mate. And just like the Welsh Guards, we may be outnumbered, but we're going to be prepared. And we might win a few fucking Victoria Crosses while we're at it, too.'

18

It had taken a while for 'the incident' at school, as it became known within the family, to be discussed in any depth but, gradually, the full story had emerged, and many tears had been spilt. 'I was afraid,' Ben said. 'Afraid of what you'd do. Afraid they would take us away.' Finally, and without any fanfare, Ben had produced the knife wrapped in paper and placed it back in the drawer. Both men looked pleased, but when he had left to go into the living room and play on his Xbox (a treat that had previously been rationed but Phillip had since suggested they would have to review all of his other online activities) their faces fell.

Phillip took Bryan's hands. He was about to say something but they heard Hallie coming in.

Then of course they had the tears all over again, and the revelation (which Ben had forgotten to mention) that he had actually confided in Simon and Claire, which at least gave the men some thoughts about how they might address this *as a community* and feel less alone.

The men shared a bottle of wine over dinner and they all watched TV together and finally the kids went to bed, though Phillip forbade Ben to go online – they would sort it out in the morning – and to wake them if he had any worries during the night.

Once Bryan and Phillip were on their own they allowed their facades to slip. 'It makes you feel so … impotent,' said Bryan.

'But let's face it – boys have always been accusing boys of being queers.'

'When we were kids, maybe,' said Bryan. 'But I thought that had changed. Come on – has this ever happened before?'

'Maybe they're getting to that age …'

'But it's the sense,' said Bryan, 'not just that they can bully Ben for being "gay", but that they think they can get away with it – and they *can*.'

He didn't need to explain: was it any wonder a brat at school was abusing Ben when the tabloids now revelled in using terms like 'Perverts Parade' to describe the gay rights demo? When they demonised any homosexual in public life who spoke out against the changes in the law?

The government's 'great bonfire of red tape' had sent most hate crime legislation up in smoke along with it. Ostensibly to 'free freedom of speech', as the minister had trumpeted it, in practice it had made permissible the expression of the kind of sentiments that hadn't been heard in public for over fifty years. Populist politicians appeared to be competing in making off colour remarks about 'poofs' and 'benders' within hearing of the press and/or someone with a video and, when questioned, laugh it off. It was almost a mark of being a 'man of the people' although, sadly, this behaviour wasn't confined only to men. There was a chill settling into public discourse, a kind of cruel relish in 'saying the unsayable'. 'The worm has definitely turned,' as one of them said, raising his pint, although for those subject to his 'bit of old-fashioned honesty', as he put it, there wasn't much to cheer.

But all was not lost. Calls were made. Emails and messages were sent. It turned out that Diane had a friend who was a teacher at a Steiner and she was outraged by what had happened. She promised to make enquiries to see if they could take Ben, even provide some sort of semi-scholarship given the circumstances.

Phillip and Bryan reviewed all of his online activity (at least the things he wanted to tell them about – they decided not to dig too deeply. In fact, Phillip said it explicitly: 'we're not interested in the porn, Champ, it's the social stuff we need to look at') and closed down all his accounts, including Warcraft. The poor kid was in such a state of shock that he demurred with hardly a word. In fact, he seemed almost relieved – and surprised – that you could just 'switch them off'. The men promised they would help him set up a fresh identity with new circles of 'trusted friends', and were delighted that Claire and Simon had already called him, and promised he could join their networks when he was ready.

Before they would do that, though, Bryan decided they would all take a break. They hadn't been camping in the New Forest for yonks, but the kids had always loved it and the men thought it would do them good to have a change of scene although, admittedly, when Bryan and Phillip proposed it, they did take some convincing.

'But it's freezing,' said Hallie.

'It's bracing,' said Bryan. 'Refreshing. Real nature!'

'We'll get *real* colds,' said Ben.

'Not if we wrap up nice and warm,' said Phillip.

'Will there be wi-fi?' said Hallie, who wasn't subject to the social media blackout.

'It's a campsite,' said Bryan. 'Practically a field.'

She looked at them. 'So there won't be wi-fi, then?'

'There's the wi-fi of nature,' said Phillip. Hallie turned to Ben.

'Is that a real thing?'

They loaded up and left London early in the morning, brilliant sunlight greeting their departure. Bryan didn't turn the radio on – they didn't want to hear any more bad news – instead he let Ben choose the music and was pleasantly surprised that, instead of inflicting his indie drone upon them, he chose their barbecue playlist, 'the old people's music' – because that was the sort of kid he was, thought Bryan, and was so proud.

The sky began to darken once they were off the M25 and heading toward the national park, and the car quietened. In solidarity with Ben, the men had switched their own phones off for the duration and felt a sense of peace themselves, barely exchanging a word as the playlist worked through the hits of the Eighties, Nineties and Noughties – 'the naughty Noughties' as Phillip had coined them, when they had first begun dating; before they had settled down, had the kids, when 'Progress' was spelt with a capital 'P' and they had been her high priests

– the first among their circle to get a mortgage, married … but their Goddess, was she dead?

Had she ever really existed at all?

They turned down a country lane in the driving rain, the windscreen wipers on full speed, and arrived at the campsite's flaking white iron gate, which was closed. Beyond them was a soggy, empty field.

'You called?' said Phillip.

'I dropped them an email,' said Bryan. 'To say we were coming, but they're always open this time of year: May to September.'

'And they didn't reply?'

'It was short notice,' said Bryan. 'You know what they're like. This time of year, there are always places.'

'There are certainly places,' said Phillip.

'Hold on,' said Bryan. Pulling on his anorak, he got out of the car and ran to the gate. Tried it, but there was a chain and padlock. He began to climb over.

'What's he doing?' said Ben.

'I'm wondering that myself,' said Phillip. Bryan reached the top and swung his leg over but he lost his footing and slipped, almost falling straight into the pool of mud on the other side. He lowered himself down and looked around. There was nothing – literally, nothing – not even the temporary bathrooms. What had happened? He had no idea. He looked back at the car, his family watching him behind the glass and windscreen wipers. He felt terrible. He had let them down. He had let them all down. The lights flashed on and off. It was Phillip, signalling him to return. He climbed back over the fence and trudged toward the car, had them lower the window.

'It's closed,' he said, standing there.

'Well,' said Phillip. 'Get in then.' Bryan nodded, ran around the rear, taking off his wet anorak and putting it in the boot, before running back and getting into the driver's seat. He sat there, looking at the gate through the rain.

'What now?' said Phillip.

'Does this mean we can go home?' said Hallie.

Bryan turned the car around and they began heading back up the lane.

'Let's go and get some lunch,' he said. 'Maybe it'll clear up.' He ignored the collective sigh from the back seats and Phillip's silence.

They found a pub and sat alone in the chilly dining room while the rain pounded down outside. The disinterested youths running the place managed to serve them some suspiciously microwaved-looking meals which tasted of nothing and, apart from Hallie, they left half eaten. When Bryan went to the bar to pay he asked about the campsite, but of course they had no idea.

'Do you know any that might be open?'

'This time of year?' said the girl. She shrugged. 'You could try Comely's down in Easterwhistle. That's a big one. They have events there.'

Bryan headed back to the table with this in mind, but when he saw them sitting there, staring out at the rain, he just didn't have the heart.

'Ready?' he said.

'For what?' said Phillip.

'I thought … well, the weather might cheer up, but it's not worth the risk. Maybe we should just… head home.'

The kids let out a cheer.

They got back in the car and began heading toward the motorway, which also happened to be in the direction of Easterwhistle. The rain actually did begin to ebb off and Bryan was almost on the point of suggesting the other campsite when he saw a glowing sign outside a pretty Georgian house set back from the road advertising VACANCIES. He pulled in.

'What are you doing?' said Ben suspiciously.

'I'll just be a moment,' said Bryan. He got out of the car and, tidying his damp hair, walked up the gravel path to the blue front door. He rang the bell, looking back across the front garden at his family. The door opened. It was a middle-aged woman with a wide, countryside face, and long, frizzy auburn hair. Behind her Bryan could see a welcoming, spotless hallway with a table laid out with tourist leaflets.

'Hello,' she smiled.

'Hello,' he said. 'I'm sorry, we haven't booked or anything, we were planning on going camping, but the site was closed ...'

'Oh?' she said. 'What site was that?'

'Mary's Camping, back in Marwick.'

'Ah yes, Mary's, but that's been gone for some time. That's back to farm land now.'

'Oh,' he said. 'I see. We always used to go there, so we just assumed it would be open. And then this weather ...'

'It's terrible, isn't it,' she said.

'And then I saw your sign, for vacancies.'

Her smile widened. 'Better here than in a cold damp tent, I bet,' she said. 'What is it that you would be requiring?'

'Well,' said Bryan, who hadn't really thought about it. 'I suppose that would be a double and two singles, for the kids.' He glanced over his shoulder at the car. When he looked back, the woman was still smiling, but her expression seemed to have frozen.

'A double,' she said. 'And two singles. Yes. I see. Yes. Well, I'd better check with my husband. If you wouldn't mind holding on for a mo'?'

'Not at all,' said Bryan. He turned around to admire the garden, its graceful mix of perennials and beds of late-blooming tulips. Sunlight began to break through the cloud and he breathed in the cool clean air. All right, they hadn't got off to a great start but it wasn't turning out so bad after all.

He heard a throat clear behind him. It was a man – the woman's husband, presumably, although she was nowhere to be seen. He was standing there, in his jeans and blue denim shirt as if he was blocking the doorway, although perhaps that was just his size. He crossed his arms.

'Hello,' he said. 'My wife tells me you're looking for some rooms. Two singles for the children, you say, and a double?'

'That's right,' said Bryan. The man nodded, looking at him, then over at the car. He shook his head.

'I'm sorry,' he said.

'Sorry?' said Bryan.

'We don't have them.'

'You don't have the rooms?'

'No.'

'But ... it says vacancies,' said Bryan.

'Yes,' said the man. 'But we don't have the rooms you require.'

'Really?' said Bryan. He looked over at the parking bay to the side of the house, which was empty.

'I'm afraid so.'

'Well, what rooms do you have?'

The man shook his head. 'I'm sorry. We don't have them,' he said.

'You *must* have some,' said Bryan. 'Otherwise ...' Then he understood. 'You're joking.'

The man shook his head. 'You can't make us,' he said. 'It's our house.'

'But you're a Bed & Breakfast. That's what the sign says.'

'Be that as it may.'

'There must be some rules.'

'That's where you're wrong: you lot can't order us about any more.'

'*I'm* not ordering anyone ...'

'Look,' the man said. 'Let's leave it at this, shall we? Neither of us want any trouble. You wouldn't want us bothering the police, would you.'

'I ...' Bryan looked back again at his family, then at the man. 'No,' he said softly.

'Good,' said the man. He stepped back. In the background Bryan could see his wife standing there with her hand to her mouth. 'Have a nice day,' he closed the door. Bryan stood looking at it. Then he went back to the car.

'What was that about?' said Phillip.

Bryan shook his head. 'I had a thought, for us to stay there. But there were no vacancies,' he said.

'But it says vacancies,' said Ben.

'Not what we are looking for,' said Bryan, starting up the car.

'Didn't they have anything?' said Phillip.

'Apparently not,' said Bryan. They pulled out and Bryan speeded up down the empty road. 'Sod the sodding countryside,' he said. 'How about tonight we have premium burgers in the big city?' Another cheer went up from the youth contingent.

As Bryan changed gear, Phillip reached out and rested his hand on top of Bryan's. Bryan felt warmth rise up his arm to his chest. Everything would be all right, he thought, so long as we have each other. So long as we have each other, everything will be all right. But when they returned to London they discovered Bill was dead.

19

The film would become famous, although largely for the wrong reasons. Over the years Bill's death, along with his identity, would become incidental in historical terms. What it would be remembered for instead was the first time the Boomerang Immersive Experience (or BiX, as it was branded) had gone truly global.

Up until now, BiX had been used mainly to play video games, watch extreme sports, porn or videos.

Simply by repeating the steps Bill had gone through, along with applying a pair of disposable contact lenses and ear buds, you could see and hear everything the 'broadcaster' was up to as they surfed the Big Sur, took part in an orgy, or raced shopping trolleys down a San Francisco hill. The fact that Bill had unknowingly, in so much as he had little idea BiX existed, and less interest, been fitted with the ground-breaking technology was purely a coincidence – because BiX could also be viewed as a simple video on a laptop or phone it had become the industry standard – but as a result, his death became known as the 'first BiX snuff movie'.

Part of the reason was because the intern tasked with monitoring the live stream hadn't been paying attention.

He had switched the stream on, as per Bill's instructions, after he began work that evening. There was a thirty second delay designed to act as a failsafe in case anything legally questionable happened (although the intern, who had been passed the job by another intern, was neither aware of the failsafe nor what legally questionable actually meant – he had grown up in an environment where open, immediate access was simply presumed) and in any case, when he wasn't playing on his phone he was expected to trawl through various feeds produced by news agencies and flag them up to the other, possibly more senior, young people on the news desks who were also working the graveyard shift, so he had plenty to be getting on with. In fact, he didn't actually realise anything had happened until the wee hours of the morning while he was scanning the feeds and came across a story that pricked his interest: UK REPORTER 'MURDERED BY REDS'.

It was only after he had clicked on it and watched some of the footage he made the connection and maximised the box with Bill's stream that had been nestled along with a dozen others at the bottom of his own screen and realised what had happened, but by that time the BiX had already been viewed several million times.

By scrutinising the full footage that had beamed overwhelmingly unwatched by the world until the AI at the heart of BiX detected visual and audio anomalies that indicated something interesting was happening and bumped Bill onto the Recommended chart, it was clear he had spent most of that evening doing next to nothing.

And in much the same way that the subjects of a documentary soon acclimatise to the film crew and forget the camera is there, the same could be said for the Our England members, who in any case appeared tied up preparing for the expected onslaught by the Reds and either ignored the reporter or, when they did notice him, like Barbara, a blue-rinsed pensioner, offered him some tea.

'Thanks,' he said, cupping the union jack mug. 'And how are you holding up?'

'Me love? I'm fine.'

'Aren't you a bit old for all this?'

'Who are you calling old!'

'I'm sorry. But you know what I mean.'

'We've got to stand together,' Barbara wagged a Bourbon biscuit toward him. 'It's what they want, to divide us.'

'Divide and rule. Yes, I've heard Vincent say that. It's Our England's pitch, isn't it, but come on, it's not really that simple, is it.'

'How so?'

'There's no conspiracy, is there. There's not anyone behind a curtain pulling the strings, like the Wizard of Oz. Otherwise ... well, you won the election didn't you. You're in power now.'

'Are you having me on, son?'

'What do you mean?'

'We "won", sure enough, but they're all still here.'

'Foreigners, you mean? Europeans? Or was it black people and Asians you voted against?'

'I voted to get rid of them all. For it all to be over, for things to go back to like they used to, but tell me, is it?'

'You can't go back, Barbara.'

Barbara shook her head. 'You think you've got all the answers, don't you, clever clogs.'

'Alas, no. That's why I'm in the business of asking the questions, it's much easier.'

'Ah, but that's the problem with our times, isn't it.' Barbara leaned forward. 'You see, "everything's too complicated", they tell us, "you can't go back", but you know what, son?'

'What?'

'That's complete balls. Look at Hitler.'

'Are you sure you want to make that comparison, Barbara?'

'There you go, *miss*-understanding, you naughty boy. I know your game. Of course I don't mean what he did, I mean the fact he bloody did it in the first place. All right, Erdogo-whatsit, that bloke in Turkey. Madame Le Pen. That one in Czech. Putin. People can do what they damn well please if they put their mind to it. If they don't listen to the "impossibles", "it's inevitables". If these foreigners can do it, well we certainly bloody can. Didn't we *stop* Adolf, after all when we decided to pull our fingers out, ignored the *appeasers*, the clever clogs? And that's what we're going to do again – wake the sleeping lion that is England. And when it wakes, young man, you had better believe it will fucking *roar*.'

'Well,' said Bill, sitting back. 'That's me told.' Barbara smiled sweetly.

'Biscuit?'

But it was not only the Our Englanders who appeared to overlook the filming. Bill himself quickly seemed to forget he was sporting BiX technology, availing himself of the Shoe Factory's amenities without pressing behind his ear to pause the device, so for years to come every last moment of Bill's life would be available online in excruciating detail. As Phillip later, much later, remarked: 'it could have been worse. His epitaph could have been: And He Didn't Wash His Hands.'

It was actually as he was coming out of the bathroom around midnight that Bill noticed a definite change in the atmosphere. The buzz of conversation had stilled. The lights had dimmed, phones darkened. Someone came up beside him. It was Mike.

'It's begun,' he whispered.

They went to the window. From three storeys up they could see some kind of movement by the closed gates, shadows. A dark figure dashed across the road.

'We chain the gates up at night,' said Mike quietly. 'My guess is they've got bolt cutters.' Sure enough, the gates began to slowly open. A murmur went up across the floor.

'What have you got planned?' said Bill. Then: 'You realise this is being filmed, don't you – I mean, if you attack them, even though you're defending your property, my film could be used as evidence and you could be had up for assault.'

'We're all above board here,' said Mike, producing his phone. He dialled 999, pressed the phone to his ear, scoffed. 'They've put me on hold.' Meanwhile half a dozen hooded figures darted across the courtyard. They stopped in a line cleaved by shadows. Finally, Mike said. 'Hello? Yes, I would like to report a break in. When? It's happening right now, at the Shoe Factory in Wood Green.

Where am I? I'm at the bloody Shoe Factory ... What? I'm sorry, I didn't mean to swear, but there are a group of masked men breaking in now and ... wait a minute.'

One by one, each figure was lit up by a flare of bright light. They held up bottles topped by burning material.

'Bloody hell,' Bill said. 'You were right – they're petrol bombs.'

As one, they were launched toward the building. The people fell back from the windows, yelling. The men dashed down the stairs to the exits, the women went to the bathrooms and began running water. Meanwhile flames shot up the outside of the building. Through the smoke, the figures outside fell back, but even as they did so, reached into their backpacks, and began to light up, and lob, more petrol bombs.

'Yes, we're on fire,' Mike was saying. 'We need the fire brigade urgently. What one?' He looked at Bill. 'She's asking me what one.'

'She means,' said Bill shielding his eyes, 'what service you pay for.'

''course,' said Mike. 'Group 5. Tell Group 5 to get their arses around here now.'

Mike switched off the phone. 'Fucking brainmelt,' he said. 'Come on, let's go down.'

As they entered the stairwell there was banging, a metallic thud. 'Thought so,' said Mike.

'What?'

'They're fucking shooting at us.'

It was true – when they arrived on the ground floor there was the definite sound of shrapnel hitting the corrugated shields placed at the entrances. Men were squatting behind them, trying to douse the flames with the water from garden hoses. Then there was a cry:

'Watch it!'

An explosion of white and orange above them. A Molotov had been flung over the barrier and smashed against the wall, raining petrol flames. Bill stumbled back, masking his face from the light and heat as screams filled the hallway.

'Get it off me! Get it off me!' one man charged at him, his head a ball of orange. He fell forward.

Buckets were thrown, the sound of sizzling. 'Ah, God,' Bill muttered, remembering to voice his impressions: 'Cooking smell. Pork. That's flesh. Human flesh.' He cowered from the shock of it, watched, broadcast, to an increasingly curious world. A woman dashed toward the glowing orange barrier and, despite the hose itself being on fire, picked it up and turned it on the men thrashing and kicking about on the floor. Water flooded the space. Someone screamed: 'Call an ambulance!'

Bill himself fumbled for his phone, dialled 999. On hold again. There was a private option, press number two. He went through to an operator: 'Crystal Healthcare. Can I have your eight letter combination code?'

'I need an ambulance, urgently, at the …'

'Can I have your eight-letter combination code?'

'It's an emergency … I couldn't get through …' The phone went dead.

There was no let up from the missiles hitting the barriers. One man was lying on his back, another on his side, a third propped against a wall, women dabbing ineffectually at their hands, their faces.

Finally, in the distance, the sound of sirens. Group 5? Bill was being hauled up by the arm.

'Come on.' It was Mike. 'You all right?'

'Have you seen this?' said Bill. Mike nodded.

'*Cunts.*'

'This is terrible. This is … it's like a war.'

'Come on,' said Mike. 'We have to get moving. It's not safe here.'

'Not … safe?'

Mike's stony expression cracked. 'Do *you* think it's safe? Think it's over? They haven't finished with us yet. They're coming through the back.'

Bill kept close to him as they went up the stairwell, passed men and women rushing downwards with slopping buckets of water.

They were back on the third floor, awash with orange

light from the fire in the courtyard, darkened by the shadows cast by billowing smoke from outside. 'Acrid stench of burning... plastic, plasterboard,' panted Bill. 'We can't stay here,' he said to Mike. 'We could die. Where are the fire exits?'

'Didn't you hear me? They've come in the back way. Fuck ...' Mike's voice dropped. 'Have you noticed?'

'What? And where's Vince?'

'He said he would meet us up here. But ...' He stepped back. 'We need to get out of here,' he said solemnly.

Hooded figures emerged from the shadows. Bill turned around. More of them. Their exit was barred.

'*Fuck*,' said Mike.

All of a sudden, Bill was plunged into darkness.

20

In the boot of something. The sound of an engine, the hum of the road. Muffled, excited chatter: 'You see how it went up, man! That's private sector cladding. Always fucking loopholes, they don't give a shit. Well, fuck them, I hope they fucking *fried*.'

'Send them up the chimney, fascist cunts. It's all they deserve.'

'Our England. *Fuck* England. Fuck them all. Racist fascist motherfuckers.'

'Please,' Bill shouted. 'I'm not who you think I am. I'm a journalist. From The Herald. You can check. I've got them here. My credentials.'

'Hear that?'

'It speaks!'

'Lickspittle media hack.'

'Please. I'm neutral. I was there to cover what was happening. The Herald. It's not a right-wing paper. I'm on your side.' A round of derisive laughter.

'Please,' Bill said weakly.

'Weasel words,' said one, almost to himself. 'Weasel words.'

The rumble of the wheels. Bill's broken breath. Finally, his low jittery voice: 'As you can see, I have been taken, I have been kidnapped, by whom I presume are Reds. I am in the back of a car, possibly a people carrier, somewhere in London. There must be some way to track me. If you are receiving this, you must be able to track me. Please, I implore you. Inform the authorities. Tell them where I am. Help me, please, get me help …' He repeated: 'Help me. Please get me help.' Kept repeating it, like a mantra, until the car slowed to a halt.

The banter stopped. Doors were slammed. Silence, only Bill's increasingly urgent breath.

The boot opened. Three of them looking down at him wearing those Anonymous masks popularised by the movie *V for Vendetta* and now almost a uniform for the Reds.

'Please,' he said, holding up his hands. 'I'm a journalist. I'm neutral. I'm on your side.'

They reached in and lifted him out. Placed him on his feet and pushed his back to the car. Bill looked around. He must have recognised this place: the old gasworks that had been converted into posh flats. The canal. Over there was a music venue. It was the centre of London, St Pancras. There – the station, glowing in the night.

Something was being stuffed into his mouth. Next Bill was spun around to face the three Anonymouses. Behind them the *Guardian* building was visible just a few hundred metres away, many of the lights still on.

'Bill Richardson. Oh yes,' the middle Anonymous said. 'We know exactly who you are. Lickspittle media come to spout right-wing propaganda in the guise of liberalism. And we know what you really are – an agent of the fascists, the oppressors, the status quo. The worst kind, because you pretend to be something else, to be "neutral". But there's no such thing as neutral, Bill Richardson. You think we're fools? You think we'll tolerate this? No longer. Bill Richardson, you have been found guilty of treason. There is no appeal. The sentence,' he paused, looking around. 'Is death.'

Bill's tried to speak despite the gag, shook his head, waggled his eyes. He tried to duck as the rope fell over his shoulders, but it was no good, they had him tight. They arranged it around his neck, Bill still bucking.

Then he was moving. Not under his own volition – they were almost carrying him – across one of those Victorian cast iron bridges that spanned the canal. Over his shoulder one of them expertly wrapped the rope around the handrail.

He was being lifted, rising, almost floating upwards. He was turned over, flipped, so he was looking down into the dark. The dark still water. He wriggled, struggled like a big fish, a fish about to be returned to the deep.

'Three.' The last thing Bill heard before the rope stiffened and his neck snapped with an audible crack on the broadcast being viewed by upwards of two million people.

There was a sort of shivering, a sort of hissing sound as the BiX picked up the final signs of life escaping from the journalist; as the rope creaked, as the *Guardian* building swung in and out of vision.

'*Fuck* Our England,' said a voice. '*Fuck* the English. Fuck you all.'

The sound of footsteps. Spent cans drumming the pavement, the rush of fire. A loud pop as the car went up. The dappled light on the canal from the flames. The awkward angle, part towpath, part *Guardian* building. Hundreds of thousands of viewers losing interest and clicking on to something else, the last moments of Bill Richardson doing the rounds forever.

21

The friends felt dwarfed by the occasion. The memorial service held at Saint Bride's, 'the journalists' church' in Fleet Street, was televised on the news channels and live-streamed by half the congregation on their mobile phones. At least one enterprising intern was BiXing 'in the spirit of Bill Richardson' and managed to garner a good few hundred thousand views.

They had met in a pub nearby, the first time they had all come together since it had happened. By now, three weeks after the event, they had begun to get used to the idea that Bill was gone, but the shock of it was still sinking in, particularly for Phillip and Rory, who had known him longest.

'As you know,' said Rory as they stood awkwardly by the bar with their drinks, 'I recently lost Dad, but this seems so much …'

'You expect it. To lose a parent, I mean,' said Phillip. 'But when it's a friend, someone you've more or less grown up with, it's like losing a piece of yourself. Because they are, I guess, a part of who you are … were.'

'Lost a piece of yourself,' said Rory. 'Yes. I can see that.'

Bryan checked the kids. He had said that they hadn't needed to come, but they had wanted to 'for Uncle Bill' and in any case, they probably would have taken Ben anyway, as he was still out of school. He tried not to fuss over his son too hard. He was so worried about him – what with 'the incident' and now this. He was such a sensitive boy … Bryan felt himself welling up, and looked away.

'It's time,' said Emma, and they set off toward the church.

'This fucking stinks,' said Juno, falling in beside Bryan. She was, predictably, angry, as she had been ever since the news broke. Bryan wanted to say *not now, Juno, leave it*, but everyone had their own way of coping. 'I mean, why would they? The Reds, I mean. Why would they kill a journalist?'

Bryan shook his head. 'Haven't you noticed?' he said. 'Times have changed. Nothing seems to make much sense these days.'

'It feels like a parallel universe,' agreed Juno. 'A parallel fucking universe.'

Yes, thought Bryan, perhaps *that* was it – they had somehow stumbled into a 'parallel fucking universe' in which everything they had once taken for granted had changed, whether it was acceptance of homosexuality, support for public institutions, or abhorrence of the death penalty. He thought back to what that woman on Bill's film had said – about the lion roaring, or some such rubbish. But it had already roared, and taken great bites out of the life he had known. Bill, in his ear: 'This is what it must have felt like to be a German, I mean a decent German, in 1934 – watching while your entire country loses its mind.'

You're right, Bill, he thought as they walked toward the church, the crowd, the barriers, TV vans. The Our England banners, megaphones. The huge arrangements of red and white flowers in the shape of the Cross of Saint George. Bryan winced: Bill's parents, stunned by grief, had allowed representatives of Our England access to the funeral, and to even, Bryan understood, pay for the hearse and cortège. They had been carried along with everyone else by the hysteria surrounding the attack on the Shoe Factory and the victims – an Our England activist had also died from his burns, while a further three had experienced 'life changing injuries'.

Bill would have hated all of this, Bryan thought. All of it – his parents, although proud of 'their boy', didn't have a clue. They didn't understand him. They were simple people, mystified by the child they had raised with his singular talent. They probably had more in common with Our England supporters, or at least Patriots, and had apparently, unthinkingly, accepted their support.

'Funerals are for the living, not the dead,' Phillip had

said, but it still left a bad taste in Bryan's mouth, particularly as they had excluded all of Bill's friends except Rory from speaking, and were permitting someone from Our England to say some words.

They had their invitations in hand as they passed through the cordon, packed on either side by strangers, England flags, Union Jacks, and dozens, if not hundreds of faces blotted out by the phones they were holding in front of them to record the spectacle. And then Bryan heard it: a sort of hissing. Beyond the general hubbub. Hissing as, up ahead, Meena and Sanjay showed their invitations. A prolonged hissing. Then a woman's voice from the crowd.

'What's *that* doing here?' Another:

'Shame.' Another:

'Scum.' Another:

'Murderer.' It only stopped when they had passed into the church. Phillip looked at Bryan and shook his head.

'God help us,' said Bryan.

'God's not here, love,' said Phillip.

They found themselves split up once they got into the church, but Bryan made a point of moving along the aisle and making it to Meena and Sanjay. She looked up at him when he arrived, her eyes wide, her small face pinched and drawn. He took her hand. Hers was trembling.

Bryan leaned down and whispered in her ear. 'You're very brave. Bill would be so happy to know you're here.'

She turned to him: 'Wouldn't have it any other way.'

The service was conducted competently by the vicar of St Bride's. He was nice about Bill (who had neither made a will nor indicated a preference for funeral arrangements) who he acknowledged was 'not a regular church goer, but who we hope would appreciate that, whatever he believed, our thoughts and our prayers are with him.' There was a reading by a lady from the Campaign to Protect Journalists, then it was Rory's turn. He just about held it together, his head bent down, only looking up when he appeared to remember it was required of him, and as a result his eulogy sounded more like he was reading out someone's annual performance review than remembering his much-loved friend. But it felt somehow apt, insomuch as it was how they all felt in a way in that unfamiliar setting, surrounded by strangers; the cameras, the indifferent multitude. It didn't feel the right place to share private emotion, sincerity, loss.

Then it was Our England's turn. The man was wiry, not very tall, slight, in fact, in his dark suit and black tie, bandages still wound around his hands – the vicar actually had to hold the paper for him – and didn't look very much like a stormtrooper. But this was Vincent Cave, apparently – Bill's contact at Our England, and one of its movers and shakers. He cleared his throat, looked down at his notes, then up.

'I want to thank Mr and Mrs Richardson for giving me this opportunity to speak, and I won't keep you long.

'I can't say I knew William well, but I do want to say that over the brief time I did know him, I couldn't help but be impressed by his professionalism and dedication. William was,' he looked down at his notes and swallowed. He looked up. 'The best of men. What I would call "a proper reporter", one that is not swayed by the crowd, or cowed by what his editors tell him. He was an old fashioned journalist who only cared about one thing – the truth. Something these days that is increasingly hard to find, and when you do find it, it can cost you your life.

'You only had to hear the words of his murderers to know why they did what they did – because the truth is something they fear, fear more than everything else. The courage to speak truth to power, the values woven into the DNA of this Island people, and embodied in Bill Richardson, along with the other victims of the attack, whose suffering, I can promise you, will not have been in vain.'

He stood looking at them. There was a smatter of applause. He nodded at the vicar (apart from that once, he hadn't needed to look at his notes) and left the pulpit.

'Blessedly short,' Phillip said in Bryan's ear.
'He's no fool,' said Bryan.
The congregation rose to sing Jerusalem.

They re-grouped by the river. Bryan had seen an exit at the rear and they had steered Meena and Sanjay in that direction. Bryan hadn't said it was to avoid the crowd – he hadn't said anything – but the others acquiesced without comment. It was all so ugly, they just wanted to get away.

Eventually Rory, Juno and Diane joined them. 'Emma had to go,' Rory said. 'Something at work.'

Diane looked around. 'It feels hard to believe – he's gone.'

'I don't believe it,' repeated Juno. 'I don't believe any of it.'

They looked at her but still didn't say anything. It wasn't just the conspiracy stuff – it was the thought that the Reds, whom they had always, informally, presumed to be 'their' hooligans, could have done something like this. That, by extension, they, in fact, could also be viewed as 'the enemy'.

They began to walk in the direction of the London Eye. Conversation petered out. Everything to do with Bill's death was just so ghastly, from what had happened, to how it continued to be shown on the screens of the world, down to the most excruciating detail. How their friend had ceased to be their own, had become public property, and somehow infinitely diminished because of it.

Meena gave Ben's arm a squeeze. There was a time, not so long ago, when it would have been his shoulder, but now he was much the same height as her. 'How are you doing?' she said quietly. 'Bryan told me what happened.'

Ben shrugged. 'All right,' he said.

'I'm so sorry, Ben. If we had known …' He shot her a wounded glance. 'But you did the right thing, standing up for yourself.'

Now he gave her a bitter laugh. 'Yeah, that's why they kicked me out.'

'Accidents happen. I mean, I know you didn't mean to ...'

He looked at her. 'But what if I did, Auntie Meena? What if I did mean to stab him?'

'The important thing is,' she said. 'No harm was done. Lasting, anyway. All of us ... none of us is perfect, Ben ...' She wanted to say, that's why we have rules – that's why the Qu'ran is a book of rules, even your Bible, although you've never read it – you don't even know you're Christian – says we are all sinners. She felt a flash of anger now, the first she had ever experienced towards Bryan and Phillip, who she had always considered such good parents, for not providing Ben and Hallie with any kind of religious upbringing. But they wouldn't understand – just as they didn't really understand her; had she and Sanjay down as 'nice', 'culturally' Muslim, just don't mention God. And yes, Meena was at fault, too, for letting them play that card, because it was the easy way, the *British* way – to rub along. After all, once you set off along the religious road, you could arrive at all kinds of uncomfortable destinations, end up where she had once found herself with Juno ... and then she thought to herself, with a spark of surprise, maybe Juno *had* understood something that she, that everyone else, had been intent on denying, wanted to avoid. Something that had been hiding in plain sight.

Being *nice* was not enough, Meena thought, not nearly enough. 'It was his bad luck you lost your temper, Ben,' Meena said. 'He shouldn't have pushed you like that. Bullied you. The world isn't a place of sugar and spice and all things nice, and pretending it is won't help anyone. It's a world of good and evil. And there's a constant battle between the two.

'*You're* good, Ben, I know it. I know you. But there's evil out there, all around us. It feeds on our weaknesses, the weaknesses of others. It's constantly looking for a way in, to take us over, to destroy us or to use us to destroy those we love. So sometimes we have no choice but to fight back. You fought back. As far as I'm concerned, you did no wrong. You only did right. I'm proud of you.'

Ben looked surprised but grateful. 'Thanks, Auntie Meena,' he said. Then he looked ahead at the others. 'They, my dads, I mean. Hallie. Everyone was really shocked by what happened ... to Uncle Bill, I mean. I mean, I was, too, obviously. But not for long. Hallie was saying why why why. My dads were crying too. I think they thought – I think they think – maybe I'm a bit odd. A bit of a psycho because I didn't cry. I tried, but I didn't. It made sense, you see. I wasn't thinking precisely what you were saying, but it all sort of made sense. Good and evil. That's how I think of it too – like a battle. The vicar said turn the other cheek ...' Meena thought about this, she didn't remember the vicar saying anything of the sort. 'But I don't feel like that. I don't want to forgive. Not Uncle Bill's killers or, not really, Todd, even though I said I was sorry. Actually I hope they both, I hope they all, burn in Hell.'

Up ahead, the others had stopped outside a pub. They were obviously deciding whether to carry on or go for a drink.

'Is that what it says in the Qu'ran, Auntie Meena?' said Ben. 'Do you think maybe I should become a Muslim?'

'I think,' said Meena, suddenly appreciating why she had steered clear of this topic in the past, 'it's a bit more complicated than that.'

22

Life gradually began to return to normal, or at least what amounted to normal in this 'parallel fucking universe' with its Bill-size hole. The news didn't linger – even Bill's funeral had been more of a footnote, an 'And Finally' moment if there still was such a thing – and the friends had to get on with their lives, too.

Finding Ben a new school had been a priority and after meeting the head of the Steiner, who appeared cautiously supportive (she spoke of a trial period to see how he gets along, which they took as code for 'as long as he doesn't stab anybody'), and having a look around the premises, which seemed a world away from Ben's old school, they decided to go ahead, even though there had been no offer of financial support. It would mean making savings, but Bryan and Phillip didn't need to discuss it – they were both desperate for Ben to be okay, and would do whatever it took.

Bryan looked at the photo of the four of them on his desk. It was a few years old now and, he supposed, how he still saw the kids – seven and six – taken on one of their camping holidays, although this time the sun had been shining.

The kids were dressed as Native Americans and Phillip had entered into the spirit of things with a painted bare chest and face and a headdress (where had he got that from? Perhaps a Village People fancy dress party?). And there Bryan was, with Hallie on his knee, squinting in the sun, rather less convincing in his t-shirt, although he had agreed to let Hallie apply some face paint (why was he so averse, he wondered. Then he remembered – it reminded him too much of make-up, all those nasty remarks when he was young) but in any case, there he was in the photo wearing such a happy, proud, joyful smile. The sunshine of their lives, or so he had thought. But even then, should he have seen the signs? Even then, were clouds gathering?

The rain rushed against the office windows. Meena got up and switched the lights on.

'Man,' Nathan sniggered down the phone, 'you crack me up.' It was an internal call so presumably someone else in the building and, judging by his prior conversation, something to do with his role as co-ordinator of 'small family units', the part of the housing scheme concerned with allocating two-bedroom apartments to families with no more than two children. He took particular pleasure in maintaining the Excel spreadsheet with the tenants' points and discussing them with other case officers as he might rival soccer teams, horse trading families and accommodation across the borough. Bryan and Meena continued to find his style disrespectful, but he had turned out to be very effective in matching people to homes.

'Tea?' said Meena.

'Lovely,' said Bryan. He clicked on an email from Phillip.

It was a link to a story in *Gay Times*. Above it, Phillip had typed URGENT READ THIS. Bryan clicked. It was a live news feed. The headline read:

SOUTHEND CHILDREN SEIZED

Summary at 1330:
- Early morning raids across Essex as social workers swoop on gay couples and their children
- Dozens of children taken into local authority care
- Appalling scenes as police arrest parents
- Southend's Mayor: 'We are obliged to fulfil our legal requirements.'
- Southend Council: 'Action taken after parents refused to attend meeting.'

1246: A police spokesperson has released this statement: 'At 0700 today Essex Police Service (EPS) supported social services in an operation across the county. EPS was acting following a request for assistance by the local authority, which was carrying out its duties under Section 3(C1) of the Families Act. In the course of the operation, a number of arrests were made for public order offences. No children were harmed during the course of the operation.

1130: *This is what we know so far*: In a county-wide operation across Essex this morning, but centring on Southend, at least nine children, all previously adopted by gay couples, were taken into care by social services. There has as yet to be confirmation, but an unofficial source has told *Gay Times* that they were placed into care under the Families Act, which has criminalised adoption by non-married couples, and which now includes formerly married gay couples. There were heartbreaking scenes as social workers, flanked by police in riot gear, took the children, many of whom were in their school uniforms. Some parents who resisted were taken into custody. Essex Council has stated that the raid took place after families failed to attend a meeting called by the council, although parents have denied this.

1030: Southend Mayor Rita Bairstow, of the Conservative Party, has released the following statement: 'I can confirm that social services took a number of children into care this morning. As a council we are obliged to fulfil our legal requirements and, of course, the welfare of our children is paramount.'

Bryan stopped reading. Out of the ether he heard Meena saying:
'Bry? Bry, are you okay?'
Bryan jumped to his feet, left the room, headed straight to the lavatory. He swung open a cubicle door, locked it behind him. Pressed his palms against it as if to further reinforce it from the outside world.

He was overwhelmed by a sudden urge to empty his bowels. He barely had time to pull his trousers and pants down before it rushed out. Sheer fear, he thought, even as it was happening.

This is sheer fear.

By the time Bryan had returned to his desk, Meena had taken a look at his screen.

'I saw,' she said.

He shook his head. His face was bloodless, his eyes darting around the room as if he was afraid the police were going to spring out of the shadows. Nathan was watching the pair of them, his ear still pressed to the telephone, although his colleague had long since hung up.

'Don't worry,' Meena said. 'It's going to be all right. Everything's going to be all right.'

'How?' said Bryan.

'I'll speak to Sanjay,' Meena said. 'You should go home.' She glanced over at Nathan, who looked at his screen. 'You're not well,' she said to Bryan. 'Come on.' She helped him up. 'I'm sure everything will be okay.'

After he had left, Meena followed the *Gay Times* feed for a while, then noticed the story had been picked up by the *Guardian*, although none of the other news outlets. She forwarded the story to Sanjay, writing – 'Poor Bryan's gone home, sick with worry. What can we do?'

Sanjay replied almost immediately: 'Awful. Not much. What's YOUR council doing?'

I don't know, thought Meena, but it was a good point. She did work for them, after all – and Child Services were just across the courtyard. Perhaps she could go over and speak to someone, find out something that might reassure Bryan and Phillip.

She looked at Nathan, thought about saying something about Bryan, but stopped herself. 'I'm just popping out,' she said. 'Mind the shop.'

Nathan nodded supportively. Meena put on her coat and left the office.

CANARIES

*

Meena had been there often enough for case conferences, so she knew the offices, and the staff, almost as well as she knew her own. She also knew the code for the security door that closed the department off from the outside world – a necessary measure given the sensitivity of their casework. She tapped in the combination and pushed the door open. She walked unremarked upon into the large open plan office.

Meena wasn't exactly sure what she was doing, only that she was looking for a friendly face – one of the social workers she got along with. But when she entered the section that dealt with fostering and adoption she immediately sensed something was wrong – there was none of the usual activity, the chatty, workaday atmosphere, even though every desk was occupied. The office felt subdued, tense. The social workers – all female – were sitting behind their computers. No one was on the phone, no one was saying a word. Meena paused by the filing cabinets. Over the other side of the room she could see their boss – Margery, a Glaswegian nearing retirement age – in her glass-walled cubicle looking very grave. With his back to Meena was a man in a police uniform.

Ordinarily there would have been nothing abnormal about seeing Margery in with a police officer – the police made regular appearances at the office – but usually they wouldn't have all that braid on their shoulders.

Meena was still standing by the filing cabinets when she realised Abidoyah, one of the social workers, was staring at her. Meena smiled, was about to come over when Abidoyah made a barely discernable shake of the head. She looked warily in the direction of Margery's office, then nodded meaningfully towards the Ladies.

Meena was waiting, with her back to the warm radiator, when Abidoyah came in. She looked along the stalls.

'There's no one here,' said Meena.

'Go to the basin,' said Abidoyah, opening her bag. She took out her make-up. She was a beautiful woman of Nigerian heritage who had modelled when she younger, but quit to 'give something back', as she once told Meena. She liked to keep up appearances though, and was the unofficial beauty consultant to every woman in the council.

'If someone comes in we're talking lippy,' she said. She looked at her in the mirror. 'You've come asking about your friend, Bryan.'

Meena nodded.

'Don't – Meena, darling, it's a shocker. Word has come down – from the Home Office – if anything leaks, if we warn anyone, we'll not only lose our jobs, our licence, we could be convicted. So we haven't spoken, right?'

'Right.'

'Promise me. Nothing on email, messenger, whatever. This is all you'll hear from me.'

'Promise.' Abidoyah gave her a searching look, then took a deep breath.

'Look,' she said. 'Those bastards are afraid the gays will be escaping the country with their kids after what happened at Southend. They've ordered a round-up this evening.'

'*No.*'

'Yes. There are eighteen families in the borough and they'll all be getting a visit.'

'I can't believe it.'

'Believe it.' The door opened. They both turned to face the mirror while one of the trainee social workers came in.

'Hm. It's a satin,' said Abidoyah, rolling the lipstick around her lips. 'What do you think?' The trainee went into one of the stalls.

'It's a bit dark,' said Meena.

'You think?' She dug into her bag and took out another one. 'I got this one.'

'What is it?' asked Meena.

'This is a satin, too, but it's a slightly lighter shade …'
'I mean what brand?'
'Max Factor …'

There was a flush and the woman came out. Abidoyah stood aside so she could get to the sink. They both waited for her to wash and dry her hands.

'Let's have a look,' said Meena. Abidoyah handed it to her. The woman went out.

'There's nothing we can do,' said Abidoyah. 'We've already complained to Margery but she's said it comes down from high. She's devastated, we all are. Even the police, they don't like it. But it's the law.' She shook her head. 'That's all I know. Look, my darling, I'd better shift, it's not safe. You go into a cubicle and wait. Give it a few minutes and get out of here. Don't say I said. I'll deny everything. Here.' She handed her the lipstick. 'Just in case, consider it a gift. God bless. God speed.' She picked up her handbag and left.

Meena went to sit in the toilet cubicle. People came in and out. No one said another word, but she heard one woman sighing heavily as she closed the cubicle door beside her. Then the sound of sobbing and whispered, incomprehensible, invocations. Finally, there was the sound of a toilet flushing, clothes being straightened. The door opened. Meena could tell from her shoes, it was Margery.

23

Bryan and Phillip were facing each other across the kitchen table, their arms stretched out, their hands clasped together, cooling mugs of tea sitting beside them.

It had been Phillip who had held Bryan as he crumpled into his arms, Phillip who had led him to sit down, listened as it all poured out – all the pain and fear Bryan had kept concealed behind the solid, steady front Phillip had always seen through, and was one of the reasons why he loved him.

It had been Phillip who made them a nice cup of tea and told him, for the 'enth time, to stop apologising, what are you apologising for, we're in this together, as a family, a *family*, and it had been Phillip who had said that rather than dwelling upon it they needed to think about practical solutions. It was also Phillip who took Meena's call on Bryan's phone as he was in the toilet. She was outside the council offices, on the high street.

'How's Bry?'

'He'll survive.'

'And you?'

'Oh, don't worry about me, chuck.'

Meena reported what she had heard. Phillip listened in silence. He mouthed 'Meena' as Bryan came to sit back down.

'Thank you, love,' said Phillip, 'we will, don't worry about us.' He turned the phone off. Let out a long sigh as if one of the kids had spilled something across the work surface again. He stood up.

'What are you doing?' said Bryan.

'Haven't you seen the time?' said Phillip. 'We've got to pick up the kids.'

They waited for Hallie with the other parents, mostly mums. Phillip chatted convivially with a few – presumably Todd's parents were not among them, thought Bryan. Perhaps they were hidden among the others, ignoring them or stealing curious glances. So far, so expected. Only one of the mums mentioned Southend – a Norwegian woman.

'Isn't it terrible?' she said, as the others looked at Bryan afresh and put two and two together. 'What are you going to do?'

'Well,' said Phillip, spotting Hallie among the crowd and waving, 'we'll cross that bridge when we come to it.'

'You must become refugees,' said the Norwegian. 'My country will take you.' One of the other mums let out a nervous laugh.

'I'm not joking,' said the Norwegian. 'What else can they do?'

'Well,' said Phillip, 'not a word to the kids, okay?' The mums nodded solemnly, although Bryan realised that would be asking too much: no doubt it would be all around school tomorrow. Oh Jesus, he thought, smiling at his daughter, oh God.

They got into the car, Bryan quietly proud that despite 'the incident', Hallie hadn't seemed at all bothered about him being there – she showed no sense of shame or awkwardness about having two dads. Tears sprung to his eyes again, but he surreptitiously wiped them away.

Phillip was driving – another novelty for Bryan, who usually took the wheel – and explained that Bryan had come home early from work with a tummy upset. They then went and picked up Ben, who Bryan was delighted to see already seemed to have made a couple of pals. He was tough, Bryan thought, resilient. Thank God.

The kids had their heads down over their smartphones, so it was Bryan who asked Phillip why were they taking this route home; Phillip appeared not to hear. He drove on, finally pulling up in a street about ten minutes walk from their own.

'This is where Rory and Emma live,' Bryan said dumbly. Phillip looked at him. He turned around to face Ben and Hallie. 'Okay troops, phones down. *Down*, I said.' They placed their telephones on their laps and looked at him as if they were waking up.

'This isn't the right street, Dad,' said Ben. 'Wasn't there parking?'

'Kids,' said Phillip. 'You're staying at Uncle Rory and Auntie Emma's tonight as Bryan and I have something to sort out. We'll come and pick you up tomorrow.'

The kids looked at each other. 'But,' said Ben, '… what about … clothes?'

'I'll pop them around later, and any other stuff. Message me what you need by … six.'

'But why can't we come home with you?' said Hallie.

'We're going straight out,' said Phillip. 'Last minute thing, a friend of ours is in hospital, sorry kids. Think of it as an adventure!'

Ben and Hallie didn't seem very keen. 'I'll need my charger,' said Ben.

'Just put it on the list,' said Phillip, opening the door.

'What's going on?' said Bryan as they walked up the street behind the kids, whose heads were once again bowed over their phones. Phillip told him what Meena had said. Bryan was beyond shock. He drew to a halt, absorbing this. Finally, he said: 'Will anybody even be at home?'

'One of them always is – kindergarten finishes early Fridays.'

'And if not?' said Bryan.

'We'll go somewhere else.'

Bryan looked at him. He was icy calm. 'All right.'

Phillip rang the bell. He rang again, insistently. Finally Rory appeared barefoot, his hair all over the place, clothes in a mess. Bryan noticed Maria, the au pair, peering down from the stairs, her chest covered by a towel.

'Phillip!' said Rory. 'Bryan? Kids?'

'Hi,' said Phillip, 'did you get my message? In any case, I've said the kids can stay with you tonight, I hope that's okay. Something urgent has come up.'

'I … well,' he looked at Phillip, Bryan, then back up

the stairs, although Maria had disappeared. 'Of course,' he said, making way. 'Nothing too serious, I hope?'

Phillip watched the kids go. 'Quite serious,' said Phillip, his voice dropping. 'Have you seen the news? Children are being seized from gay couples by the authorities and we've heard they're coming for us. We'll pick them up tomorrow morning and be on our way.'

'Fucking hell,' said Rory. 'Christ, guys ... I'm so sorry. Where will you go? What will you do?'

'Not sure right now,' said Phillip. 'Probably get out of the country.' He looked at Bryan. 'Norway?'

Bryan shrugged. 'Sure.'

'Anyway, we've no time to lose. So we'll come back tomorrow, okay?'

'No problem,' said Rory. He gave them both a hug.

'And not a word to the kids, okay? We need to think about how we're going to break the news.'

'Sure, no problem.'

'Norway, then,' said Bryan, as they drove to their house.

'Wherever,' said Phillip. 'I told you, Bry, I'm not going to let them take my babies.'

Bryan took his hand. 'And I said I won't let them, either.'

'For better or worse,' said Phillip, as he parked the car, 'richer or poorer.'

Bryan looked up at their beautiful old house, their tree-lined street. Well, he thought, certainly poorer.

Then he embraced Phillip. He held him tight, pressed his warm body against his and clung onto it like they did when they were making love. Love – he thought. Thank you, Phillip. Thank you, my husband, the love of my life – for reminding me what love really means.

They went into the house and started getting their things together. Bryan was going to suggest that they spend the night at a hotel, but, equally, neither did he feel in a tremendous rush to leave: it was *their house*, that they had saved for, furnished, paid the mortgage on. All these happy times, happy memories. It was the only stable home the kids had known. It was Hallie's palace, Ben's castle. Bryan remembered them kidding about as they cleared up after the barbecue. Such good times. He began to cry as he packed – packed to leave, perhaps forever, he realised. Just like that. This morning everything had been … well, almost ordinary. Now he was fleeing the country. And being completely impractical too. There were the photo albums, his late mum's stuff. The wedding gifts. Where to begin?

Phillip was being more organised. He had already made sure he had the passports and booked four tickets on the Eurostar to Brussels, one of the few capitals that had yet to fall under the populist spell. In fact, any spell, come to think of it: the Belgians hadn't actually had a functioning government for years. And then where? Norway? Or would they stay in Belgium? Holland? There were right-wingers there, too, but at least they were pro-gay. He shook his head. Too many questions. He got back to trying to remember the kids' favourite clothes, toys, books …

He crossed Phillip in the hall. 'We need more cases,' Bryan said. 'I've already filled them up.'

'I'll have another look in the loft,' said Phillip. 'There are a couple of old ones we've been keeping our CDs in. They'll be dusty, but should …'

The doorbell rang. They froze. It rang again, and again. Bryan took Phillip's hands, mouthed – I'll go. Phillip hesitated, then gave his fingers a final squeeze. He headed for the kitchen. Bryan heard the back door open, then close.

The bell rang again.

Bryan went to the front and looked through the peephole. It was as he feared: a social worker – Margery, herself – backed by police uniforms. Still, he felt his breath catch.

Margery was reaching up to try yet again when Bryan opened the door.

She looked at him. 'Bryan,' she said. There were a pair of female police officers flanking her while, partly obscured by the bushes, was a van.

'Margery,' he said, still having some difficulty breathing. 'Is there a problem?' She looked at the police officers either side of her.

'Can you give us a moment?' she said. The police officers backed off, pausing by the garden gate. 'I'm so sorry. We don't have a choice.'

'Everyone always has a choice, don't they?'

Margery nodded. 'That's fair, Bryan. I have to accept my role here, which is why I insisted on coming to you myself. But you must know what this is about. We were told ... we know you left early.'

'I was ill.'

'Of course,' said Margery. 'But you know what this is about.'

'Do you want to tell me?'

'There's no need to make this more difficult than it already is, for the sake of the children. You love the children, don't you, Bryan?'

'Fuck you, Margery.' The police officers heard and began to draw near.

'We don't want any trouble, sir,' said one of them.

'No trouble,' said Bryan.

'The children,' said Margery, 'Ben and Hallie. Where are they?'

Bryan shrugged. 'I've no idea. They're not home yet.'

'Phillip?'

Bryan shrugged.

'We have a warrant to enter your address,' said the police officer.

'I'm sure you do,' said Bryan.

Next door's front door opened and out stepped John Turner, carrying a large cardboard box. He took in the scene.

'Everything all right, Bryan?' he asked.

'Not really,' Bryan said.

'I'm sorry,' said John. 'Anything I can do?'

'It's all right, sir,' said one the police officers. 'Thank you.' John Turner looked at her and nodded, giving Bryan a sympathetic smile. He carried on down the path to his large white SUV, waggling his foot beneath the rear of the car. The trunk door rose upwards. He loaded the box.

'I'll have to ask you to step aside, sir,' the police officer said to Bryan.

'Is this necessary?' said Margery. Bryan thought she was saying it to the police officer, but then she added: 'Bryan?'

He shook his head. 'There's no one here,' he said. 'But go ahead.'

Bryan let them into the house. Meanwhile John Turner carried on going back and forth with boxes. 'Charity,' Bryan heard him explain to a policeman stood beside the van, then: 'And what do we have here? At bloody last!'

Bryan watched as John Turner strode past his front gate and headed up the street. Then he realised: he was walking toward Ben and Hallie coming toward the house accompanied by Maria, the au pair.

He watched John exchange some words with Maria who, looking fed up, spun around and began walking away. John stood with his back to Bryan, hands on his hips, talking to the kids, who glanced anxiously at the police van, before continuing with them toward the house. He was talking animatedly about something, although the children only had eyes for the police and Bryan.

John placed his arms around the pair as they passed and, almost bodily, guided them down his own front path. 'You two always arrive when the hard work's been done. Now get in there – your dinner's getting cold.' He shepherded them through the front door and slammed it behind him. Bryan looked at the police officers standing by the van, but none seemed to have batted an eyelid. Then Margery reappeared behind him, as pale as a ghost.

'This is very serious, Bryan,' she said.

'Packing to go somewhere?' said the police officer.

'I don't know what you're talking about.'

'Where are your passports?' said the police officer.

'I don't know what you're talking about.'

'Sure you do,' she said. 'I'm placing you under arrest for child abduction. You do not have to say anything, but it may harm your defence if you do not mention when questioned something which you may later rely on in court. Anything you do say may be given in evidence.'

'Abduction? You're fucking kidding.'

She turned him around and cuffed him.

'I'm so sorry,' said Margery. Bryan just looked at her, a police officer on either side of him, as he was led to the van.

24

Bryan sat in the police interview room and looked up at the CCTV. He had only seen these places on TV dramas, and had never imagined he might actually find himself in one. He wondered if he was being monitored at the moment, if in some gloomy room that nasty female constable was looking at his black and white image and discussing with another how they would 'play' him – good cop, bad cop, all that. He decided not to say a word until he had spoken to a lawyer. Until he had a lawyer sitting right here beside him, like on the TV, he would say nothing, do nothing at all that would place the kids at risk. They might try to 'play' him, but he wouldn't play their game.

The door opened. It was not the constable or any other junior cop. Bryan could tell, this was a chief inspector, or superintendent, or something like that. In any case, someone senior. The policeman laid down a cup of frothy coffee in front of him.

'Hello Bryan,' he said. 'I'm Superintendent Warwick, district operations lead. I put one sugar in,' he said. 'All right?'

Good cop, then.

'I want to speak to a lawyer,' Bryan said.

'You can,' said the Superintendent, a man about his own age, although plainly straight, Bryan thought. How could he tell? He had no idea, only that he screamed straight. 'But I'm hoping that won't be necessary.' Bryan didn't respond. He knew these games, he'd seen the shows. He glanced up at the camera. 'It's not on,' said the Superintendent. 'This is not a formal interview. Unless you'd like it to be, Bryan – *my* advice is to keep this informal, a casual chat.'

'I've been arrested.'

'You've been cautioned. You haven't been charged with anything, and as there's nothing recording this meeting there's nothing admissible in court. Even the fact that I've told you that would make it inadmissible if there *was* a recording. This will be as if it never happened.'

'Why?' said Bryan.

'Now, look,' said the Superintendent, 'I'd like you to know that we're … a lot of us here, are no happier about this than you are. We don't get a kick out of taking kids away from their families.'

'So you admit we're a family?'

The Superintendent sighed. 'Of course I do. But I'm not here for a debate. Look: it's my job to enforce the law, and I'll have to do that. But before we get to that, what I'm really interested in is the welfare of your children. Are they safe?' Bryan thought about Phillip disappearing, the Turners. 'Are they safe, Bryan?' Bryan nodded. 'All right, but you need to understand that this is not something that is going to go away – the order has come down from on high, like a ton of bloody bricks. We won't just be able to drop it. We will continue to look for them up until the point that we have established they are no longer within our jurisdiction. Do you understand?'

Bryan didn't react. He was still trying to process what the Superintendent was doing here, what he was trying to say, what kind of game was being played.

'Well,' said the Superintendent. 'Do you? Understand?'

Bryan nodded, although he was struggling. 'That you … have to enforce the law …'

'While we believe the children *remain within our jurisdiction*. After that, well, then it will be a matter for the courts … governments, and so on … and that could take … well … Don't you want your coffee?'

Bryan obediently reached for the cup and took a sip. It was too sweet. Of course it was too sweet – he didn't take sugar.

'All right?' asked the Superintendent. Bryan nodded. The Superintendent sat there, just looking at him. Bryan took another sip, *feeling* like a criminal, even if he wasn't one. Or was he? Actually, he supposed, he was. Sort of. The Superintendent let out a long sigh.

'You were packing your bags,' he said.

'I …' Bryan shook his head.

'Then you'd better get on with it.' The Superintendent got to his feet. He gestured for Bryan to do likewise. The Superintendent gave his hand a firm, man-to-man, shake. 'I can give you forty-eight hours,' he said. 'No more. Understood?'

Bryan nodded. 'All right then,' said the Superintendent. 'Come on.' He opened the door, stood by it. As Bryan went though he gave him a sad smile. 'Good luck,' he said softly.

Bryan left the police station in a daze. He found himself standing at the bus stop, then continued on toward the taxi rank after remembering he only had forty-eight hours, as the policeman had put it, to escape the country.

Was any of this real? He looked over his shoulder. Was he being 'played' after all? Was this simply a ploy to get him to lead them to his family? He couldn't see anyone but then, he wouldn't, would he? God, he thought, now I realise why I never went into a life of crime. I'm simply hopeless at it. A little laugh escaped that ended with a sob. Pull yourself together, man.

He got into a cab and took out his phone. But he didn't call Phillip – even if the police weren't following him, he was acutely aware how everything he did now had the potential to create a trail. Instead he called Rory. He wanted to ask him – *what happened?*

Rory's mobile was on its answerphone so he left a message, then he called his landline. Another long wait until, finally, it was picked up.

'Hello?' It was Emma.

'Emma,' said Bryan. 'I was calling …' He stopped. 'I wanted to find out …' There was silence. 'Emma?'

'*How could you,*' she whispered.

'I'm sorry?'

'*How could you be so selfish?*'

'I don't … understand?'

'Casually placing that burden on us. Breaking the law like that. They could have taken *our* children away.'

'I ...'

'And Rory's a *civil servant*, Bryan. *He could have lost his job.*' An intake of breath. 'We could have lost our house, children, everything. *So selfish.*'

'I'm sorry, I ...'

'You *should be* sorry,' she said. 'You should be *ashamed.*' She put the phone down.

Bryan looked at his phone, his mouth, literally, hanging open. He saw the driver looking at him in the rear mirror.

'All right, guv?' Bryan closed his mouth.

'Fine,' he said.

It was dark now. Bryan fumbled with the key in the lock and remembered he had promised Phillip during the summer he would fit a light. He opened the door. The house was silent, empty. It already felt abandoned. In any case, he called: 'I'm home!'

He went into the living room – the half-packed suitcase was still there. It certainly looked incriminating, he thought, no doubt about that. He went through to the kitchen where the computer was open on the table.

Where had Phillip gone, he wondered, although by now he had largely worked it out.

He opened the back door and stepped into the garden. The thing was, there was no exit – it simply backed onto another garden, so there was no way out, as such. He looked over the fence and into the Turner's kitchen.

There they all were. The kids sitting down, having something to eat, Phillip leaning against the kitchen worktop talking to Mrs Turner – Patricia?

Bryan stood watching them like Marley's Ghost. Finally, he went back into his own home and turned on the kitchen lights.

He went outside. Phillip immediately came out. They stood facing each other over the garden fence. At shoulder height, it was just low enough for them to reach across and hold each other.

'You made it,' said Phillip, 'you made it. Oh God, Bry.'

'The important thing is *you* made it,' said Bryan. 'All of you.'

'I'd just got out the back,' said Phillip. 'To be honest, I didn't know what the hell I was going to do. Then I saw John outside, getting some boxes. He helped me climb over.'

'He saved us,' said Bryan. He looked into the kitchen where everyone was watching them. The kids waved, as did the Turners. 'They saved us.'

'What happened?' asked Phillip. 'I've had the phone switched off in case they tried to use it to trace me. I haven't had a chance to speak to Rory.'

Bryan shook his head. 'I spoke on my way back, to Emma. She had a go at me. Said we were "a burden".'

'I don't believe it,' said Phillip.

'She said they could have taken Hamish and Isla from them …'

'What *crap*.'

'She was worried about Rory losing his job,' Bryan let out a bitter laugh, 'their house.'

'Jesus,' said Phillip.

'What do Ben and Hallie know?'

'Everything,' said Phillip. 'Well, not exactly everything. I've had to dress it up a bit. I've said we've got in a bit of trouble with the law, it's a huge mix up, but we have to leave the country for a few weeks until it's sorted out.'

'Do they believe you?'

Phillip shook his head. 'Honestly, I don't know. I've seen them whispering. In any case, I just couldn't tell them that the police had actually come for them, to take them away. We'll break it to them after, when we're safe.'

Bryan shook his head. 'Safe,' he said. 'I always thought we were safe here, at home. That this was the safest place in the world.' He closed his eyes. 'First Bill, now … us.'

'Come on, say hello to the kids.'

'How can I get over?' said Bryan. 'I'm not nimble like you.'

'That bucket, over there. You can stand on that.'

John Turner came out. 'Can I help?'

They didn't want to discuss too many details in front of the kids but the Playstation in the room of one of the Turner's sons dispensed with that issue. Bryan came upstairs with them to get it working. As they were fiddling with the settings, Ben said: 'We won't be away for long, will we Dad? I quite like the new school.'

'I hope not,' he said. 'And you'll like Belgium.'

'Why?' said Hallie.

'Well,' said Bryan, struggling to come up with an answer. 'Great food.'

'Will we be able to watch the football?' said Ben.

'Premier League is shown everywhere.'

'Have you told school?'

'We'll let them know ... Phillip explained to you ... the situation.'

'They're not going to put you in prison?'

'Oh no,' said Bryan, 'nothing like that.'

'So why do we have to escape then?'

'Good question,' said Bryan, wondering what on earth to say.

'We know, you know,' said Hallie. 'We heard Uncle Rory and Auntie Emma arguing.'

Bryan looked at them. In the gloom of the bedroom, Ben and Hallie were sitting beside each other upon the bed, Playstation paddles in hand, their eyes round, unblinking like owls. He wanted to weep, they were being so grown-up.

'I'm sorry, kids,' said Bryan.

'You've got nothing to be sorry for,' said Ben. 'It's like we read.'

'What was that?'

'Like the Jews,' said Ben. 'Like the Nazis.'

'They know,' said Bryan, coming back into the kitchen. Phillip looked surprised.

'You told them?'

'They heard Rory and Emma arguing.'

'I must say,' said John Turner, 'I didn't think they looked very convinced.'

'Thank you so much, for all your help,' said Bryan.

'Isn't that what neighbours are for?' said John.

They discussed their next move. They were booked on the Eurostar at nine o'clock the following morning. The kids would stay in one of the Turners' sons' bedrooms (they were on Duke of Edinburgh) while Bryan and Phillip would go back over the fence and finish packing up. They would sleep over there, although Bryan doubted how much sleep they would actually get. The big question was the departure – clearly the Superintendent was giving them time to get out of the country, but could he be trusted? Or was it just a way to trick them into breaking cover?

'I believe him,' said Patricia Turner, unconsciously rubbing the gold cross against her chest. 'He sounds sincere, otherwise I can't see him going to all that trouble. In fact, he was taking quite a risk in letting you go, and encouraging you to escape – if you *do* get caught and you say that he let you, even if they say they don't believe you, people won't forget.'

'Which is why it sounds so fishy,' said Phillip.

Patricia looked at John. They smiled. 'It's just my opinion,' said Patricia. 'I would say have faith in God, my atheist husband here would say "good". We usually agree to disagree.'

'It's God that's got us into this mess,' said Phillip.

Patricia shook her head. 'People use God,' she looked at her husband, 'or even "good", to excuse their bad behaviour.'

'I went to a Christian Brothers school,' said Phillip. 'There was plenty of bad behaviour there excused in the name of God.' Bryan gave him a censorious look – this was no time to get into a row.

But Patricia nodded. 'If we'd listened to the Church, we'd have rather more than two of our beautiful boys, and we're certainly not the only ones. But it's as flawed as everything else in this life. If it was that easy, then there really wouldn't be any need for religion. To suffer …'

'She's been suffering me for thirty years,' said John, doubtless making an effort to lighten the mood.

'And she hasn't converted you yet, apparently,' said Bryan.

'Oh, he converted, didn't you, love,' said Patricia, smiling. 'I wouldn't have married him, otherwise.'

John Turner grinned. 'Patricia was worth a Mass.'

25

With a foot up from John, Bryan and Phillip made it back over the garden fence. If anyone had been watching from the front, they wouldn't have seen any activity since Bryan had arrived home.

Now they started going systematically through the house, packing their cases with anything, basically, they were sentimentally attached to and wouldn't be able to buy abroad. A minimum of clothes, a maximum of heirlooms, souvenirs, photos – the really irreplaceable stuff.

Using the Turners' landline, they'd called Juno and organised the transfer of their savings into her account. Juno had agreed to meet them in Brussels with cash, and to send them the rest of the money when they had a bank account, or sooner if it looked as if the police were going into their financial affairs. Would they be able to sell the house if they were wanted criminals? Even as Phillip asked Bryan, they both had to smile at the sheer absurdity of it. They had no idea – once they'd got away, the first thing they would have to do was ask Sanjay.

It was the early hours by the time they'd got things sorted as best they could, then they prepared for a last night in bed – the bed they'd spent all that time choosing, along with the linen, the bedroom furniture … all the furniture, the lighting, decorations, they had carefully, painfully (there had been more than a few hissy fits) chosen for the house, their house, that had been created to contain, and embody, everything that they were. All of it about to be lost, overnight. 'Just things,' said Phillip as Bryan sat up in bed, looking around. He switched off the light and they lay facing each other. Phillip pulled him close, kissed him hard on the lips. 'Now, chuck,' he said. 'Try to get some sleep.' He closed his eyes, and tucked his legs up. He rolled over. In the space of a few minutes he was snoring.

Morning. Early – they had forgotten to draw the curtains. Phillip's side was empty. Bryan could hear him pottering around downstairs. He checked his watch. It was a quarter past six. They would be leaving in three quarters of an hour. He padded over to the bay window, the floorboards icy beneath his feet. Bryan felt every grain of the wood, suddenly conscious of committing these last feelings to memory. He looked out – he could see no sign of activity, no undercover cops slumped in a car. In the grey morning light it all seemed so normal – early Saturday morning in an ordinary North London street.

Ordinary for some.

He went downstairs. Phillip was already washed and dressed, had the bags closed and laid out, the passports piled up on the table, breakfast ready.

'You should have woken me,' said Bryan.

'One of us needed some sleep,' said Phillip. 'Sit.'

Bryan sat obediently at the table while Phillip made the tea. He looked out at their small garden, sprinkled with frost. He wanted to say to Phillip – do you think this is the last time we'll see it? The last time we'll see England, even? Is this our last glimpse of English frost? But as Phillip returned with the teapot, he kept his thoughts to himself and dished out their muesli.

The plan was for everybody to leave separately, and for everybody to leave from the front. There was no other way to go about it as they were blocked off from the back. Phillip would go first – on foot, walking to the tube. He would meet them at St Pancras station, outside the WH Smith near the Eurostar terminal. Bryan had ordered a cab, which he would travel in with the bags. The Turners would leave five minutes later in their car with the kids.

It seemed unlikely that if the police actually were watching they would have enough resources to track the lot of them, and perhaps they would go after Phillip first, but it would not be that easy to follow him on the

Underground, and he would be taking a roundabout route.

At the end of the day, it was a gamble that Patricia was right and the Superintendent had been trying to help them. They weren't criminals, although they may have been criminalised, and they couldn't be expected to have cunning escape plans in place.

Bryan and Phillip stood by the front door, holding each other tight.

A last deep, desperate kiss, a flurry of I love yous, then Phillip was gone.

Bryan was alone in the corridor … then dashed around to the living room, to see if he could catch Phillip through the window but he had passed by, if he hadn't already been bundled into a police car.

He rushed up the stairs, looked out from the bedroom bay. No – there Phillip was, safe, walking smartly to the end of the street, then turning the corner toward the tube station.

He walked back through the house, inspecting the rooms to make sure they hadn't missed anything. He couldn't stand to linger in the kids' rooms, it made him feel so sick. They had taken down most of their posters and packed them, along with their favourite books … in fact most of their luggage seemed to consist of the kids' crap, anything to make the transition less painful, in some way, perhaps, also to assuage their guilt – Bryan and Phillip's – for not being good parents, because at the end of the day, it *was* their fault that Ben and Hallie were being uprooted from everything they knew, because *they* had made the decision to adopt them, because *they* had believed society's lies, no, not lies; had placed their faith in the fickleness of human nature, had chosen to ignore the vicious streak they themselves had experienced growing up: their own parents' prejudices, their peers' sheer nastiness. Had permitted themselves to forget, consign it to the past; had made their offerings to the god Progress and told themselves that times had changed. Well, the times may have changed, but the people hadn't.

The bell rang. Was it time already? Bryan checked his watch. It was. He ran downstairs, opened the front door.

'Cab?' He didn't look like a police officer – an unshaven, dishevelled Kurd with tired eyes.

'Right,' said Bryan. He dashed back to the kitchen, scooped up the passports. The man was already hauling the suitcases into the back of his people carrier. He would have to tip him, thought Bryan, running around the house checking everything was switched off, then he snorted: Christ, he was acting as if they were going on holiday, which, I suppose, he added to himself, was at least the pretence until they got to Brussels.

The man was waiting in the people carrier. Bryan turned the lock and walked up the garden path. He glanced across to the Turners' and thought he could see, standing back from the window, John Turner and the kids watching him. Yes: Hallie waved. He was about to wave back but stopped himself. He closed the garden gate. He took one last look at his old life, then got into the cab.

26

Bryan checked behind as they pulled out, but no one appeared to be following. They drove toward St Pancras through the early morning traffic, Capital Radio playing. The driver didn't have anything to say – he just looked as if he was trying to keep his eyes open – and the radio was full of the usual imbecilic witter, at least until the news.

It was the third item, after an international incident and a royal baby: 'Gay rights groups are up in arms after raids across the capital saw dozens of children taken into care. A spokesman for Stonewall complained that no warning was given to families. "Children were wrenched from their parents. It's a disgrace." But the Minister for the Family hit back: "It is our duty to put the interests of the child first, and these lie with real, legally-constituted families, not pretend ones." The next item was unemployment figures.

Bryan looked out of the window at the world going by; the people waiting at the bus stop, walking with their heads over their phones, listening to music. The tragedy of his life may as well have been unfolding on the Moon.

They pulled into St Pancras. Bryan forgot to tip the driver. Laden with three suitcases and a couple of shoulder bags he made his way slowly to the appointed meeting place. Phillip wasn't there yet but Bryan wasn't about to panic – he knew he was going to take his time, and they had over an hour. Someone sat down at one of those old pianos on the concourse and started banging out chopsticks. His girlfriend laughed. Bryan looked up at the clock. One minute had passed. Stay calm, he thought. He realised he was dying for a coffee but he daren't move. He thought about buying a newspaper but knew he wouldn't read it. He would have loved to have called Phillip, but of course, they had the no phone rule. Was that wise, given all the other risks? Who knew? Who knew anything, anymore – that jolt as Bill was thrown over the side of the bridge, the crack of his neck. Bryan pushed it from his mind, looked up at the clock. Three minutes had passed.

Phillip appeared seven minutes later. 'What?' he said. 'You're white as a sheet.'

Bryan shook his head. 'Relieved.'

'And the kids?'

'They were supposed to leave five minutes after me. They should be here soon.' They looked up at the clock. Their conversation was sparse, staccato. Someone else sat down at the piano. A kind of musician this one, or at least he could play. An unknown composition. There was some beauty to it, they might have remarked upon it if they had been listening, but of course they weren't, not really, and nor was anyone else – everyone had somewhere else to be, something else on their mind. It was now fifteen minutes since Bryan had arrived.

'We agreed five minutes, didn't we?' Bryan said to Phillip. 'I'm sure we agreed they'd leave five minutes after.'

Phillip nodded. Bryan had always known his image as leader, or at least breadwinner, was somewhat fake – protected as he was by his guardian angel, the seemingly soft Saint Phillip. Yet even Phillip now looked on edge, glancing up and down the concourse.

'Should we call, after all?' said Bryan. Phillip shook his head:

'We don't have their number.'

Of course! They didn't have the Turners' number! How could they have been so stupid? And in that instant both were thinking the same thing – has the world tilted again?

Can we really trust these people?

The station clock conducted its own insidious torture as the time that had appeared to slow down, speeded up, yet still there was no sign.

'What will we do?' Bryan muttered, looking straight ahead.

'I don't know, love,' he heard Phillip reply, for the first time sounding defeated. 'I don't know.'

A group of police officers began to march purposefully

toward them. 'Stay calm,' Bryan heard Phillip say. 'Don't move, don't do a thing. There's nothing we could do anyway ...'

The police seemed to be heading straight for them but with a superhuman effort Bryan managed to remain statue-still. He fixed his eyes upon the pianist, while remaining deaf, blind to him; heard only the rubber-soled boots upon the concourse.

He finally dared to glance in their direction. The man at the front seemed fixed angrily upon him.

He dragged his eyes away, held his breath.

They passed by.

Breathed.

From somewhere distant he heard Phillip say: 'There.'

Ben and Hallie, carrying plastic bags, with the Turners behind them.

The men hugged the kids then quickly let go, looked nervously around.

'Sorry,' said John Turner. 'There was an accident, we got held up.'

'A woman had been knocked off her bike!' said Hallie.

'Frankly, it's a miracle we made it,' said John. 'We were going to call but ...'

'We made packed lunches,' said Patricia. She looked embarrassed. 'Does anyone do that anymore?'

Phillip looked at the clock. 'We'd really better get going,' he said.

They said their goodbyes to the Turners, with the promise of a proper thank you when they met again, and made their way to the Eurostar Terminal.

In a sense, Bryan and Phillip had reassured themselves, this part of the journey should not present too much of a problem – on this side of the Tunnel there were only the French police checking passports, and they shouldn't be looking for them. In fact, once they had made it through security, weren't they, technically, out of England? But either way, Phillip had said, he wouldn't really feel safe until they were sipping champagne in La Grand-Place.

They turned the corner, and that was when they saw them – the police from before.

Two men were pinned to the floor while a crowd stood watching. One of the men was writhing, screaming, the other passive. Both had their hands behind their backs, secured by plastic cuffs. Two young girls, little more than toddlers, were wriggling in the arms of a pair of female police officers.

'Keep walking,' said Phillip, 'to the exit, over there.' Phillip fell somewhat behind, as if they weren't together, while they passed the glass-fronted entrance to the Eurostar terminal. Bryan could now see other police officers positioned in front of the security personnel at the bag check.

The family kept walking, past an artisanal patisserie, Boots the Chemist, Burger King, all the way to the sliding doors and onto the outside concourse.

Phillip caught them up and led them straight to a black cab. They loaded their luggage and got in.

'Been anywhere nice?' said the driver.

'Belgium,' said Phillip.

'Nice,' said the cabbie. 'Where to, sir?'

'Russell Square,' said Phillip.

27

They booked themselves into a cheap hotel off the square – Bryan and the kids in one room while Phillip walked around the block, came in separately, and took a single.

They met again back outside, in a café in the square, one of those tastefully designed places with big windows and expensive coffee and cakes. It was then that Ben, who had remained almost somnambulistically quiet throughout their journey, said: 'What's happening? We thought we were going to Brussels? Were they arresting people like us?'

'What's happening?' said Hallie. Her eyes began to fill with tears. Bryan looked at Phillip who, glancing anxiously around, reached out and gave her hands a comforting squeeze before drawing back.

'Obviously kids,' he said, 'there was a problem at the railway station, but I promise you we're leaving. The sooner the better, I'd say. It's clearly going to be a bit trickier than we planned, but I promise we'll get there. We know they're not looking for us, personally, which is a good thing, but we ought to act quickly. We're going to have a think about it. There must be dozens of ways to get out. We just have to be clever.'

'You're clever,' said Hallie, looking at Bryan. There was silence, then Phillip looked at her.

'What about me, missy?'

'Well, yeah, you too, obviously.'

'Come here.' He hugged them both.

'My babies,' he murmured. 'My babies.'

The kids went off for a mosey around the square. Phillip looked at Bryan.

'Well,' he said. 'You're the clever one.'

Bryan smiled. 'We can't afford to be paranoid about phones and things now. We need to act quickly.'

'Shit,' said Phillip, opening his bag. 'I think Juno's booked on this afternoon's train.'

'Call her,' said Bryan. 'And Meena.'

They met later that afternoon, along with Sanjay and Aisha, at the café. They took a corner table and spoke quietly, although they were surrounded by tourists who wouldn't have the foggiest what they were discussing even if they had understood English. Bryan had suggested to the kids that they stay in their room but they were having none of it so sat with them.

'I can't believe Emma said that,' said Meena.

'It's done now,' said Bryan. 'It's just … one of those things.'

'A burden!' said Juno. 'Well, she's off my Christmas card list.'

'As if you ever sent them,' said Phillip.

'She *would* be.'

Meena turned to Sanjay. 'It's all legal, I suppose?'

Sanjay nodded. He opened his mouth to qualify it, but found he couldn't. 'It's legal,' was all he could say.

'You warned us,' said Bryan.

'But not even I really expected it to happen, at least not this … brutally. I thought if something did, at least there would be time to react. Appeal, draw the process out. But clearly,' he looked around the café, 'they anticipated that. They're very determined. It's easy to forget that a government can do what the hell it likes when it puts its mind to it.'

'It's that evil woman off the radio,' said Juno.

Sanjay shook his head. 'Oh, I'm sure she's one of them,' he said. 'She's a fanatic through and through, but she doesn't have the authority to drive something like this forward, to place all this pressure on social services and the police – that will be the Home Secretary, the Prime Minister. A pair of Patriots. Maybe just the Home Secretary – my point is, he pulls the strings. If he didn't want it to happen, it wouldn't.'

'So why, then?' said Meena. 'The Patriots aren't anti-gay are they?'

'Aren't they?' said Sanjay. 'They didn't have any problem waving the legislation through. You've got to think beyond what the parties claim to individually represent, it's the tendency they stand for. The desire to return to some imagined past, a Britain that's long gone, been replaced by something that scares the hell out of them. Gays just symbolise a part of that change, and are an easy target.' He smiled. 'It's probably not even personal. They're just working their way down the list.'

'Who's next then?' said Meena. Sanjay looked at her, then at Aisha sitting on her lap.

'Anyway, the thing is,' said Phillip. 'What are we going to do? Surely it's going to be too dodgy to use the ferry and airports and, if what our friendly cop was saying is true, we are going to be on the wanted list soon enough. I was thinking that maybe Juno and Meena could individually take the kids through… but they could be on the computers, on a watch list …'

'We need to stay together,' said Bryan, just the thought of the wait at the train station gave him chills.

'What concerns me,' said Sanjay, 'is your being booked into the hotel. They took your details, right?' Bryan nodded. 'You've got to get out of there while we think of a plan.'

'Go into hiding?' said Phillip. 'Here in the UK?'

While they pondered this, Ben whispered to Hallie: 'Like Anne Frank.'

'I've got an idea,' said Meena.

28

That evening Sanjay drove them back in the direction they had come. Bryan felt a growing sense of dread as they passed through the streets he had imagined he had bade farewell – now they seemed like the territory of an alien, hostile land. He would no longer miss these roads, this country. He felt like someone who had found their partner in bed with another person – nothing would ever be the same again, no matter what was said or done.

He felt a welling anger too, a rage that sprang from deep inside of him. It was all very well to tell oneself that London hadn't, on the whole, voted for this government. But his country had – it wasn't good enough to pretend the people who were doing this to him had just appeared out of nowhere. He remembered Bill making a similar observation years ago when Emma had corrected him in a conversation about the Second World War. 'It wasn't the Germans, it was the Nazis,' she said. 'Oh yes, I'm sorry,' he had replied. 'The Nazis. Space Nazis, right? The Nazis that came from outer space.' Bryan felt like that now, looking at the passers by. In years to come, if those years ever did come, they'd all be blaming it on 'the fascists' or 'the Patriots' or 'Shared Values' forgetting that they, the British people, had voted them in, endorsed their policies; that they had gone shopping, waited for the bus, toyed with their phones, while around them their neighbours were being arrested.

Meena met them at Trellis House. Of course, Bryan half-remembered this place – had been here himself more than a few times. God, it seemed like another life.

It was dark. They took the rickety, sour-smelling lift up, hauled their luggage along the walkway.

'There was a problem with the maintenance people,' Meena was saying as she searched for the right key. 'For some reason they didn't receive notification. It was on my list to re-file when…' She found the key that fit the steel door. 'Well, here we are.' The door creaked open, revealing another, standard, front door. Meena slotted the Yale in the lock and opened it. 'The utilities should still be on.' She reached for the light switch. The hallway was bathed in light, just as it had been left – the faded prints on the wall, knick-knacks on the shelf above the radiator. That musty, dusty smell. 'Anyway, let's hope it's not for too long.'

'Let's hope so,' said Bryan. He opened the door to the living room and found a man standing there with a carving knife.

29

Stuart had been there since it happened. That's not true. Not at all true. First he had begun to head north, home to Hetton, got half the way, pulled in at some services around Scotch Corner, got out for a McDonalds. That was when it really hit him. Or caught up with him. Or whatever. What he was doing – why it was *mad* for him to be heading up there. Where would he stay? With Jacky? With his mates? What mates? That would be the first place they would look and Vince ... and Mike ... they were smart, right quick like that: it wouldn't take them five minutes to track him down and then ... and then ...

He headed back the way he had come. At that point he didn't know what he was going to do, where he was going to go. One thing at a time – and at the minute that one thing was he had remembered that they were smarter than him. They were so much smarter than him, maybe smarter than all of them – the media, the government, everyone – so Stuart had to remember that – not to act like he wanted, instinctive, which they would expect. To act *unlike* himself, *unpredictable*. That would be the way to get through this.

Of course, he could go to the police. Of course, he couldn't go to the police. What would he tell them? That he had driven the car they'd put that bloke in, the journalist? That he hadn't known nowt about it until they'd come out during the attack by the Reds – Mike and Vince and a couple of other blokes – carrying that wriggling bloke with a hood over his head and thrown him into the back of the car. Stuart was surprised, but all right with that. For a start, it had happened so quickly. It was just chaos. It was war. It was a fucking war, and Stuart thought maybe they'd caught one of them. He didn't know what they would do with him, where they would take him, but he wasn't thinking that far ahead, he was just *looking* ahead, focusing on the road. Drive, is what Vince said, so he drove.

And that was all he was thinking about, the driving, until other stuff began to seep in, stuff he couldn't block out, stuff that seemed *off* ... wrong. The bloke in the back, for instance, he turned out to be that reporter, and Vince was holding his finger to his mouth at Stuart – like, say nothing – as the others were clearly pretending to be Reds. It was fucking weird, but he kept focusing on the road, doing his job. Was this some kind of joke, he wondered. Some kind of practical joke? Surely not, what with the Reds and the fire and all. We should be back there, fending them off, putting out the flames, not joking with this reporter. Unless it's not a joke ... but what the fuck? Just keep your eyes on the road Stu. Do what you're paid to do.

They ended up at the canals. Vince gave him this mask, said to stay by the car and then ... well, it was all over the news, the internet, wasn't it. And Stuart was just standing there, watching. Watching while the bloke ... well, one minute he was alive and the next he wasn't. Swinging there. But there wasn't a moment to lose – they were burning the car and making off down an alley. It had all been planned, see, at least they seemed to know what they were doing. They got in another car and Vince said, drive slowly, don't draw attention.

And then ... it could have only been half an hour and they were back at the Shoe Factory, joining the back of the crowd to watch the fire brigade, the ambulances. Vince had slapped him on the back, said: 'You did good today, Stu. You're one of us now.' And Mike had put his big arms around his shoulders and said: 'No going back.' And the Shoe Factory continued to burn, and there were the TV crews and Vince was already doing interviews and it was as if none of what had happened had happened.

But it had happened, hadn't it Stu. Even though they put him up at the house of a sympathiser who gave him their spare room, said he could stay for as long as he liked, and it was peaceful, with the garden and that, the birds and the foxes and Radio Two. He didn't get called into work, didn't have to do any driving – was on his own most of the day and couldn't help playing that video over and over again. Was any of it real? Were even the Reds real? He kept thinking back to some of the places he had taken Vince, some of the meetings where he had been asked to stay in the car, at pubs, lock-ups, parks. Was Vince a Red? Was that it? Was Vince, Mike – were they both really Reds? He didn't get it. But if they weren't Reds why would they want to burn the Factory down? Why would they have wanted to hurt their own people? Why kill that reporter?

Stuart felt a sense of being engulfed, of dirt falling on top of him, getting in his mouth, his nostrils, blackening his vision. It was as if he was at the bottom of the grave and the dirt was tumbling down, gradually blotting him out. He would wake, struggling for air.

He was afraid of death, he was afraid of dying. He was afraid they would find out he was afraid. He was afraid they would realise he wasn't one of them – whatever 'them' were – that he was scared, confused, unreliable. Worried they would decide he couldn't be trusted. And they would do to him what they did to that reporter.

So he ran.

30

'Don't hurt us,' said Bryan, holding up his hands, and also blocking Ben and Phillip from coming in behind him.

'You'll not take me,' said Stuart, waggling the blade toward them. 'Get away.' Bryan began to do just that.

'We're going,' he said. 'Just take it easy. We don't want any trouble.'

'Get away.'

They had already backed out of the living room, were half way down the narrow hall, when Meena appeared from one of the bedrooms. She plainly hadn't heard a thing, was saying, 'I'm afraid the bed linen is in a terrible state, I'll have to get you some from home,' when she passed between Bryan and Stuart, who had reached the doorway of the living room. It took her a moment to register what was happening – that this was not Bryan or Phillip, Ben or Sanjay. That this man was someone else, and this someone else was pointing a knife at her, looking as surprised as she probably did at the moment. She let out a yell of alarm.

The man – it was him, wasn't it, the man who had been here before in his underpants – jumped backwards, the knife falling from his hand. He looked down at it. Meena looked down at it. He picked it up.

'It's ... Stuart, isn't it?' said Meena.

Stuart was shaking his head. 'I ...' He didn't know what to say. He backed further into the room until he knocked into the TV. Bryan came up behind Meena. Suddenly, it clicked for Stuart.

'It's ... *you people*,' he said.

'The knife,' said Meena. 'Please, Stuart.'

Stuart followed her gaze to his hand, to the knife.

'Please, can you ...' He began to lower it.

'Thank you.' Meena felt the blood begin to return to her cheeks. She looked around. They were all crowding behind her. 'It's Meena, Stuart. Meena from Housing, remember? We came to see the flat, after your granny – your *auntie*, died.'

'I came too,' said Bryan softly.

Stuart looked at him. 'You're not with them, then?'

'Who are "them", Stuart?' said Meena.

'Reds,' said Stuart. 'Our ...' He stopped himself. Saw the little girl. The little boy. The Asian man. They weren't them. At least he didn't think they were.

'Please, Stuart,' said Meena. 'Please put the knife down.' Stuart looked at his hand again. He gave them another wary look then laid it on the top of the TV, but made sure it was within reach.

They stood looking at each other. Then Meena and Stuart said it at the same time:

'What are you doing here?'

31

Neither told the truth. Neither told even half the story. The first thing Stuart had them do was close the front door. He picked up the knife – all eyes fell on it – and went back out in the corridor, checking the doors were properly locked and turning off the hallway and kitchen lights. He came back into the living room where they were all gathered, laid the knife back down on top of the telly. He looked at them.

'It was empty,' he said accusingly to Meena. 'You'd left it empty.'

'I …'

'You said it was needed. You'd – the both of you,' he looked at Bryan. 'Kicked me out, said it was for urgent need. But for months … *months*, it was empty. Just as I'd left it.'

'I'm sorry Stuart,' said Meena. 'It was an oversight, an error …'

'It was *my fucking life*,' said Stuart. 'So you can't come … you can't just come now, barging in like this.' He looked at Ben and Hallie and Phillip. 'Are you giving it to them?'

Meena looked up. 'I guess …' But Stuart was shaking his head.

'Nah,' he said. 'Nah.' He tapped the side of his head. 'You think I can't see? The little girl – she's holding his hand. Your mate. Your work mate.' He meant Bryan. 'He's your boss. He works for the Housing, too. So you're giving it to him? To them? What's going on here? What racket is this? Do you think I'm thick or something? Do you all think I'm fucking thick?'

'It's just temporary,' said Bryan. 'We've had … an emergency. We're homeless. We've got nowhere to live.'

'Well boo-fucking-hoo,' said Stuart. 'Can't you go on the fucking *list*?'

Phillip spoke now. 'It's not … as simple as that.'

Stuart looked at him. Then at Bryan. At Meena, Sanjay.

'Your kind,' he said, 'posh folk, always find a way. You've got the money, the credit, the contacts. What are you doing here?' He shook his head. 'This isn't right. This is all wrong.' He crinkled his eyes, trying to figure it out. There was so much to figure out, so much just out of reach.

'Please, mister,' said Hallie. 'Don't throw us out.'

He looked at her, he looked at Hallie but he saw his Mary, saw his own. His Mary standing there with those tired, begging eyes, those pleading eyes (like his – everyone said they had his eyes) the last time he'd seen her. But would she even remember what he looked like? Would she even care? His face fell.

'Please.'

He couldn't do it – he couldn't let her down again.

Stuart let out a long sigh. 'Tonight. You can stay tonight. But no lights at the front, mind, and no opening up or hanging around.'

*

Bryan watched Phillip wedging the back of the chair beneath the door handle. He didn't think it would hold the angry man with the knife for more than a few seconds but it seemed to reassure Ben and Hallie perched at the end of the double bed. Although there were two bedrooms and the man – Stuart – had declared he would keep to the living room, none of the family wanted to be apart. Tonight they would sleep together, as best they could, fully clothed, on top of the dusty double bed with its pink quilted cover, both men ready to spring into action at the first sound of the door handle being tried.

Meena and Sanjay had left them with the promise to get something sorted out asap – if they had needed any encouragement, the presence of Stuart had certainly helped – of course, they could have stayed at theirs, but that would have seemed too risky, ditto Juno and Diane. Rory and Emma were out of the equation for obvious reasons.

CANARIES

Bryan hadn't expected for a moment to grab any sleep, but then he was waking up. He checked his watch. It was three. He looked left – the kids were, apparently, out cold. He looked right. Phillip was lying there with his eyes open. Bryan whispered. 'Hi.'

Phillip looked sideways. 'It's not right,' he said. Bryan didn't reply. Of course it wasn't right. Nothing was right. 'He seemed as frightened as we were,' Phillip continued. 'Turning off the lights, making sure the front door's closed.' Now he turned to Bryan. 'He's in hiding, too.'

'Him? Stuart?'

'He's on the run. It's obvious. It wasn't us he was expecting. It was someone … something far worse.'

'You're scaring me.'

'I'm scared.' Phillip shook his head. 'We shouldn't stay here, Bry. It's not safe.'

'Where can we go?'

'I …' Now Phillip's voice caught. 'I don't know.'

32

The next morning Bryan woke to find the chair removed. It wasn't Phillip – he was curled up, still. He looked sideways. Hallie was still there, asleep. But Ben ... Bryan sat up. Got to his feet, looked down. He was in his socks. That was right – that was the minimum they had all done, taken off their shoes. All right then, he trod softly toward the door.

He opened it onto the grey hallway. He could hear murmuring, a smell. Bacon. It was bacon. His stomach rumbled. Yes, he was hungry – when was the last time he had eaten? Then he heard laughter from the living room – the half open door. He paused, then prodded it ever so lightly. There he was – Ben, sitting with that man, Stuart, dressed in the same jeans and dark t-shirt, and another man, who grinned.

'Alreet, mite,' he said.

'Bloody hell, Bryan is it?' said Stuart. 'Was that your belly? We thought it was thunder.'

'Sit down Dad,' said Ben, gesturing to the space on the sofa. 'Havel has brought some bacon butties.' It was true. There was a blue and white striped plastic bag on the floor behind them, along with a few Styrofoam cups presumably containing tea or coffee. Bryan did as he was told.

'He's been feeding me, like I'm a chimpanzee at the zoo,' said Stuart proudly. 'There's electric but the gas don't work.' He patted the Pole on the shoulder. 'He's a good lad.' Then a thought passed across Stuart's face like a cloud. 'I pay and that.'

'Ah,' said Bryan, glad, if nothing else, to have some way to react to this strange scenario, 'we can give you some cash.' The Pole grinned. 'Alreet,' he said.

'Havel lives next door,' explained Ben. 'That's how Stu got in. He went over the balcony.'

'Ah,' said Bryan, surreptitiously looking around for the carving knife. He couldn't see it.

'Go on Dad, take one,' said Ben, holding up the bag. 'There's enough for everyone.' Bryan dipped into the bag, took out a roll. It was still warm. The fleeting memory of when he was a boy, the delicious bacon butty that had existed before the days of calorie counting, half-baked vegetarianism, biological whole foods and healthy eating ... he looked at Stuart and Havel nodding encouragingly. This was *still* their world, the only world they had ever known; a world that had, in truth, never gone away, that mocked his pretentions. He paused as the soft crust touched his lips. Then his stomach let out another rumble. Everybody laughed.

'What's this then?' Now it was Phillip. He caught Bryan in mid-mouthful. Bryan looked up at him almost guiltily, but Phillip had immediately grasped the situation. 'Breakfast?' he said. 'You're a star, Stuart.' He opened the bag as if it was the most natural thing in the world, even though he had been a Pescatarian for God knows how long. He bit into the butty without hesitation.

'Well, what a pretty pass this is,' said Phillip. 'I'm sorry about what happened last night.'

'That's all right,' said Stuart.

'We'll probably be on our way today.'

'Oh,' said Stuart. 'All right.'

'Where will we go Dad?' said Ben.

'Probably Auntie Juno's,' said Phillip.

'Hang on a mo',' said Stuart to Ben. 'Which one is it then, mate? Which one's your dad?'

'I'm sorry?' said Ben.

'Well,' said Stuart, 'earlier you called Bryan your dad, now you've called Phil here your dad. You can't have two dads, can you.' He grinned at Havel. 'That would be impossible.' Havel nodded enthusiastically. Ben looked at Bryan, then Phillip. He seemed about to burst into tears.

'Modern family,' said Phillip quickly. 'We adopted them, Stuart. We're gay.'

Stuart looked at the three of them, then at Havel. 'You're kidding,' he said.

Now Phillip smiled. Bryan didn't know how he did it, but he did. 'I'm afraid not,' he said.

'But, Ben,' said Stuart. 'You're not...'

'Not him,' said Phillip. 'Nor Hallie, neither. Us two.'

Stuart nodded slowly. 'All right, I get it,' he said in a way that made them wonder if he did. 'You mean like Elton John and his... wotshisface... '

'That's right,' said Phillip.

'But ... you don't seem ... you know, *gay*.' Bryan wondered if he had ever met, *knowingly* met, a gay man before.

'Well,' said Phillip, looking genuinely amused. 'We are. We both are.'

Stuart nodded at Havel, who seemed bemused by the conversation. 'We're not. You know ...'

'Yeah,' said Phillip. 'I get that.'

There was a knock at the door.

33

Out of nowhere the carving knife reappeared in Stuart's hand. 'Not a word,' he whispered. Then there was a sound from the hallway. Bryan realised – it was Hallie.

'Who is it?' she called.

'Juno,' they heard back. Stuart looked at them.

'Our friend,' said Bryan. 'Please, put the knife down.' Bryan watched him lay it behind the sofa. He got up and went into the hallway. Hallie was standing there, bleary-eyed. 'Is that bacon?' she said.

'In the living room.'

'But we aren't allowed to go in there.'

'We are now,' said Bryan. He found the keys and unlocked the two doors. Juno was leaning casually against the wall as if she attended secret meetings with fugitives every day. She smirked.

'I hear you've had a bit of an adventure.'

'You could say that,' said Bryan. He looked up and down the walkway and ushered her in.

'All right,' Juno nodded to Stuart and Havel. The men's eyes goggled. 'You're looking after my boys?' she laid a hand, almost like a blessing, on Phillip's shoulder.

They nodded like schoolboys. 'Good,' she said.

Juno helped herself to a butty – 'Delicious! Don't tell Diane!' – and said she had got it sorted: a friend of hers, well, a friend of a friend, was a keen yachtswoman and was prepared to take them to Ostend. 'What is it?' she asked Hallie.

'I can't swim.'

Phillip gave her a hug. 'You can swim, hon, remember those lessons.'

'Not very well.'

'You'll have life vests,' said Juno. She looked at Bryan. 'I'm sure. And anyway, why would you need to swim? It's a boat, isn't it. The point of boats is so you don't have to swim!' Hallie nodded, although she didn't look convinced.

The yachtswoman, Dawn, said they had to be ready to leave at a moment's notice.

'That won't be a problem,' said Phillip. He stood up, led her to the hallway. 'What is it about lesbians and yachting?' he said.

'I don't know. What is it about gay men and electro?'

Phillip's voice dropped: 'Depending on how long it takes,' he said, 'we may need somewhere else to stay.'

'What?' said Juno. 'Problem with those two? They look pretty harmless to me.'

Phillip shook his head. 'It's what he's hiding from that worries me.'

'I'll ask around. Of course you could stay with us, but,' she shrugged. 'Well, it probably wouldn't take long to make the link.'

'Could we stay at another "friend of a friend", though? There have a got to be a few more … sympathisers.'

Juno's hard smile softened. She took Phillip's hands. 'I'm sure there are lots.'

Bryan came into the corridor. 'It's Stuart,' he said. 'He's asked if he can come as well.'

Juno told Stuart she didn't know anything about yachts but would ask. In any case, she looked at Bryan and Phillip, she didn't see why not. What else could she say? They could hardly turn him down. Phillip thought Juno might ask him there and then what he was hiding from, but she didn't say a thing. Perhaps she thought it was better not to know – what good would it do them? Whatever he said, they were all in this together.

She left them with some papers and magazines for the kids, along with a burner phone. She had a bag of them. She would give another one to Dawn – when she was ready, she would message them. 'Otherwise, don't use it,' said Juno. 'And most of all don't use it to contact anybody you know. If they're monitoring it, they will be able find your location immediately.'

'Sounds like you've done this before,' said Bryan.

Juno grinned. 'I just watch a lot of TV.'

They closed the metal door, then the wooden one, and that was it – they were on their own again. In due course, Havel left to go to work (how much would he tell his workmates and friends they wondered, but Stuart said not to worry, he was a good lad) and then he and the kids watched television for the much of the rest of the day.

It was funny seeing Stuart with them, thought Bryan. He seemed perfectly at home with the kids, happy to be lectured about the intricacies of a teen vampire fantasy by Hallie or discuss Arsenal players' comparative strengths and weaknesses with Ben. He was neither the apparently unpredictable individual they had come across with the carving knife, nor the slightly pathetic man stinking of booze he had met that time at the front door, instead ... ordinary, respectable, grown-up, like a husband and a father. Bryan thought about asking him about that, about his background, what he was doing here, but then recalled Juno's reticence. Maybe it would be better not to get to know Stuart too well. Who knew what he had done, what he could do, what *they* might have to do if Dawn refused to let him on the boat. In a way Stuart the knife-wielding stranger, without the knife, obviously, seemed preferable to this Stuart – the human being.

Bryan found Phillip in the bedroom sitting by the window.

'Anything suspicious?'

'Everything around here's suspicious,' said Phillip. 'It's the unsuspicious things I'm looking out for.'

'Try not to get too stressed. We've not done badly. We should be all right here, for now. After all, we're hardly mass murderers. The police must have plenty of other people to look for.'

'Do you really think they're that bothered about mass murderers?' said Phillip. 'I think they're more interested in the ones it's easiest to catch, the ones that will please their political masters. We're the flavour of the month.' He shook his head. 'I never thought I would see ... what we saw at St Pancras. Not in my lifetime.'

'You were so cool, so quick-thinking. Thank God. I was so proud of you. So relieved to be with you.'

'You know,' said Phillip. 'When we're finally safe again, in Belgium, I mean, civilisation, I think I'm going to collapse.'

'You're stronger than all of us.'

Phillip shook his head. 'I'm not kidding, you big lunk.'

It got dark. They went into the living room to watch TV with the kids, along with Stuart, and Havel, who had turned up with some pizza. Stuart asked – have you heard from this lass, the one with the yacht? They said no, but repeated what Juno had said about seeing no reason why he couldn't join them … and really, when it came down to it, he was the least of their worries.

They watched the final ever episode of Channel 4 News before the station shut down and explained to Stuart (Ben did, actually) why it was so sad and everything. Clearly neither Stuart, nor Havel, had heard anything about it. Something about the BBC? Still, when Ben told Stuart why it was 'a disaster' he nodded. Yes, he could see that. Ben said it was important to have a 'plurality of viewpoints, like on Question Time' and Bryan felt tears prick his eyes to hear his son parroting one of his own phrases. Or was it one of Bill's? Either way, something had been passed on.

Stuart looked at him. 'He's right smart, your lad,' he said. 'My …' Then he stopped himself. He gave Ben a nudge. 'A right brainbox,' he said. 'Just like his father.' He grinned. 'Fathers!'

34

Meena saw Aisha off at the kindergarten, then walked down the red brick Victorian streets to the bus stop.

There was a light sprinkle of rain beneath the leaden London sky, but not enough for an umbrella. The gloom of the packed bus was illuminated by phone light, and she had to stand most of the way. She walked across the courtyard at work, returning acknowledgements from colleagues. Only, one colleague would be absent – Bryan – and Meena knew where he was: hiding in another part of the borough.

Bryan, Phillip, Ben and Hallie – *in hiding*. It was surreal.

'Morning,' Nathan was there uncharacteristically early.

'Hi,' said Meena.

'Nice evening?'

She paused. 'Fine, thanks. You?'

'Oh,' said Nathan. 'Good … you know … I was just thinking. It's terrible, isn't it … about what happened – to the gay parents, I mean.'

Meena nodded. She switched on her computer.

'I was just wondering,' he said. He nodded toward Bryan's desk. 'Have you heard anything? Is Bryan coming in today?'

Meena shook her head. 'I've no idea, Nathan. I haven't heard a thing.'

'Right,' said Nathan, and looked back at his computer.

The day carried on as normal, albeit without their boss, although at one point the Deputy Chief Executive did look in. 'Bryan?' he asked. They shook their heads. 'Right,' he said, and was on his way. Otherwise, it was as if nothing had changed. Certainly Meena didn't feel inclined to discuss it with Nathan, who was back to his usual routine, going loudly through the lists and disappearing for long coffee breaks.

She headed down to the Seminar on the Compliance Certificate for Public Sector Employees, grabbing a few biscuits from a side table and sitting at the back, two rows behind Abidoyah, who had studiously ignored her since their bathroom rendezvous. She switched her phone to silent and looked up as the HR person came into the room. It was Sasha, she noticed. She found herself wondering what was going on – if anything – between her and Nathan. Then her mind wandered back to her discussion with Sanjay that morning, all right, *argument*, about who should take them – Bryan's family and Stuart – to the boat. Sanj of course had said he should, being the man, but she had said no. Bryan was her friend.

'What's that got to do with it?' he replied.

'I want to say goodbye.'

'Don't be silly, it's not like forever, we'll see them in Belgium.'

'This is important to me.'

'It's dangerous.'

'It's not dangerous,' she countered.

'It's illegal.'

'But doesn't that make it even more important?' Meena said. 'You're a lawyer, you can't be found breaking the law. You'll lose your job.'

'And you don't think you would?'

''You earn four times as much as me, Sanj.

He couldn't argue with that.

'You've got to be joking.' Up front, Sasha's sunshiny smile had frozen. Meena tuned in. '*You've got to be bloody joking*.' It was Abidoyah.

'I'm sorry,' said Sasha. 'I don't understand.' It was clear from her blank blue eyes that she really didn't.

Abidoyah was shaking her head. 'Why isn't your boss doing this, love?'

'I'm sorry?' Sasha said robotically.

Abidoyah turned to the colleague next to her, another Nigerian woman. 'Grace should have been here. Typical.'

Now a middle-aged Indian woman (most of them were woman, and most middle-aged – it was for middle managers, after all) spoke up. 'The requirement,' she said. 'To include our religion.'

'And not only that,' said Abidoyah. 'Our parents' birthplace.'

'Yes,' Sasha nodded, still sounding like a chatbot. 'That is a requirement. It's for statistical purposes.'

'But it's not anonymous,' said Abidoyah, 'and neither is it voluntary.'

'I'm sure,' said Sasha, 'all of your data will be protected.'

'Outrageous!' said Abidoyah.

'I'm sorry,' said Sasha, looking crestfallen. 'It's only a pilot.'

'The fact that the government,' said the Indian lady, 'requires the religion and ethnic background of every public sector employee doesn't strike you as sinister, young lady?'

'And sexuality,' said another voice from the front.

'That's millions of people,' said another.

'Half the workforce,' said another.

'I'm sorry,' said Sasha, her white skin looking almost translucently pale. 'It's ... a pilot.'

Sat perfectly still and silent during the hubbub that followed, seven rows back and barely visible behind the larger women, her handbag resting against her chair, Meena Hussain, Senior Housing Officer, wife of Sanjay, mother of Aisha, carefully laid the plate of biscuits upon the floor, picked up her bag and slipped out of the room. She made her way slowly along the corridor. If someone had passed her by they would have asked if everything was all right.

No one passed. She made it back to the office. It was empty. She sat carefully down at her desk, which was opposite Bryan's. Clean and tidy as ever. The bare in-tray, a couple of bits in the 'out'. The computer mouse sitting dead centre of the mat. The back of his framed family photo. She wondered if she should take it. She looked at her own – of her and Sanjay and Aisha. She wondered if she should take that. Her phone buzzed. She took it out.

'Hel-hello?'

'Everything okay?' It was Juno.

'Yes. Yes, fine.'

'It's on,' she said. 'We need to pick them up at three.'

'So soon?' Meena had expected it to take longer.

'Something to do with tides,' said Juno.

'All right.'

'You're sure you're okay?'

'Sure.' She turned off her computer. She put on her coat then went over to Bryan's desk. Hesitated, and picked up the photo and popped it in her bag. That was when she saw Nathan standing at the door.

'Off out?' he said.

'Case meeting.'

Nathan Drake stood aside to let her go. After he had watched her disappear down the corridor, he went to sit at his desk.

He clicked onto Outlook, checked Meena's calendar. She had no appointments scheduled for that afternoon, certainly no case meetings.

He went onto his email and opened a message tagged 'Confidential'. He pressed reply.

35

Juno arrived first. She knocked on the steel door and cupped her hands against the opening.

'It's me, Juno,' she called. There was the sound of movement and first one door, then the other, opened. It was Bryan, looking grave.

'Everything's okay?'

He stepped aside. 'Fine.'

'You're sure?'

'Didn't sleep too well,' he said, following her down the hall to the bedroom where Phillip was sitting with the luggage. 'Nerves.'

'Kids?' said Juno.

'Next door,' said Phillip. She opened the door to the living room. They were sitting on the sofa next to Stuart, some quiz show on the TV.

'Is it time, Auntie Juno?' said Ben.

'Almost,' said Juno. 'We have to wait for Auntie Meena. You're all set, Stuart?' He gave her a thumbs-up.

'There won't be much space for extra luggage,' she said. Stuart nodded. He understood.

Her phone rang three times. It was Meena. Juno went to the window. There was the car.

She went back into the bedroom. 'Okay guys,' she said. 'We're on.' She took a shoulder bag. 'I'll go first, check the coast is clear.' She opened the front doors and stepped onto the walkway just as one of the neighbours was going in next door. She waited for him to close the door then headed to the lift and called it. She looked down the stairwell, leant over the wall. She couldn't see anyone. She went back to the flat. Bryan and Phillip were standing there with their cases. They wouldn't get them all in the lift in one go, so she said: 'Bryan – you go with your cases and the kids. Phillip, we'll come back for you.' She saw Stuart, standing behind him like a phantom. 'And you,' she added.

She and Bryan loaded up the lift and squeezed in

together with the kids. They began to descend. Juno, for one, held her breath as the lift door opened onto an empty atrium – just beyond it, Auntie Meena standing by the open boot of the SUV, which dwarfed her.

They loaded it up and Bryan and the kids climbed in while Juno went back up. She set off down the walkway to the open door, grabbed one of the suitcases beside Phillip and he followed her with the other. But when they got there the lift had already descended. She called it. 'Where's your mate?' she said.

Phillip looked around. 'I've ... no idea.'

'For fuck's sake,' said Juno. The door opened. A man was standing there. He wasn't tall but filled the lift from side-to-side. They got out of his way. He walked past them as if they weren't even there. Phillip slid the first case in, the second, third, then got into the lift himself. He looked at Juno.

'Coming?' She was looking back toward the flat.

'Hold it,' she said. Phillip sighed.

'If the idiot's decided to bottle out ...'

'Just a moment,' said Juno, and pulled a case forward so it blocked the door.

She went back along the walkway. The flat door was pulled to, but not locked. She gently pushed it open. There was Stuart's bag in the hallway, but no Stuart.

Just then there was the sound of a toilet flushing and, almost immediately, the bathroom door opened. She was looking straight at – not the big guy, but the skinny one she had seen going in next door. There was something about him she recognised but couldn't place. He smiled. 'You must be the lesbo,' he said.

She heard Stuart's voice from the living room: '*Run.*'

Juno stepped back, slamming first one door then the next. She ran down the walkway, shoved the case into the lift and pressed the Ground button over and over again.

The door finally closed and they began to descend.

'What happened?' said Phillip.

She watched the numbers descend. 'Ready?' she said.

'Did you see Stuart?'

'He's not coming,' she said. 'Like you said. Bottled it.'

The doors opened. There was no one there – only Meena visible through the grubby glass doors. For a second time Juno uttered a little secular prayer of thanks.

She glanced up at the stairwell. 'Come on,' she said. 'No hanging about.' She grabbed two cases and trotted to the car.

36

'Leave it,' Vince held Mike back. 'You'll never catch her, and what if you did? Do we really want a bunch of howling homos on our hands? This one here's enough.'

He looked down at Stuart sitting upright on the sofa. 'What happened mate? Get the willies?'

'Just let me go, all right? I swear I won't say a thing.'

Vince shook his head. 'I thought you were *sound*, mate. Didn't we do all right by you? What did we do for you to treat us like this?'

'Look,' said Stuart. 'I don't want any trouble. I just want to go. I'll leave ... leave the country.'

'But it's *your* country, mate,' said Vince. 'Why would you want to do that?'

'Just let me go, all right?'

Vince shook his head. 'Sorry, mate. Doesn't work like that. You're going to have to be re-educated, so you see things our way. So you understand our point-of-view.'

'I swear I won't tell a soul. Our England – I'll never see them again.'

Vince looked at Mike, then back at Stuart. 'But we are Our England,' he said. 'Who do you think we are?'

'I ... you're. You're whoever you say you are.'

'What?' Vince said. 'You don't think we're really Reds, do you, Stu? Blimey.' He shook his head. 'He thinks we're Reds, Mike.'

'Not the brightest button in the box,' said Mike.

'Makes you wonder if he *can* be educated, let alone re-educated.'

'Please ...' said Stuart.

'Let me make this simple, Stu. We dressed up as Reds so they would get the blame, *capisce*? And so it came to pass – the emergency legislation, all that. They're now terrorists next to the Islamics, so we've done – *you've done* – the country a huge favour. Give yourself a slap on the back, mate.'

'The attack,' said Stuart. 'The people, burning ...'

'Tragic,' Vince nodded. 'Casualties of war. But for the sake of the many, the few ... what was it Spock said, Mike?'

'We owe so much, to so few.'

Vince shook his head. 'That's Winston, mate. In any case: martyrs to the cause. We've learned that from the Islamics. Speaking of which,' he looked out of the window. 'I see your friends have buggered off. They didn't hang about. See? A Mozzie bitch and pack of queers. You chose the wrong side, mate. See what happens?' He nodded. 'Mike.'

Mike moved forward to grab him but Stuart started forward, toward the balcony. Vince moved to block him and the pair rammed the glass doors. They popped open and the pair of them crashed onto the concrete floor between the flowerpots. They hit the ground with an audible thump.

As they lay there, Vince looked momentarily surprised, amused even, to find himself on his back with Stuart looking down on him. But then alarm swept across his face.

Stuart felt Vince's body harden as if he had been shot through by a bolt of electricity but Mike saw, as he grabbed hold of Stuart, swept him up and hurled him across the living room, that it wasn't electricity that had caused Vince's body to jig, blood begin to froth from his mouth, his blue eyes boggle. It was a carving knife stuck into his chest, up to the hilt.

37

'I don't understand,' Ben was saying. 'He seemed like he really wanted to come.'

'Me neither,' said Bryan, looking at Juno sitting in the front, programming the navigator. He turned back to Ben in the seat behind them. 'But people are sometimes odd like that. Grown-ups. Adults. Maybe he just had a change of heart.'

'What did he say, Auntie Juno?' said Hallie.

'Only that he'd changed his mind,' she said, distractedly. 'Last minute.' She looked at Meena. 'It's a little bay. It's not got an address, but we can just aim for the town and follow the signs.'

'All right,' said Meena.

'Is that all?' said Ben. 'He'd changed his mind?'

Juno swivelled around. 'What can I say, buster? Like your dad said – us adults are strange un's. Excited kids? This time tomorrow, it'll be moules and frites!'

'Mules, Auntie Juno?' said Hallie. 'Donkeys?'

'Mussels!' said Juno. 'Although,' her voice took a confidential tone, 'they probably eat donkeys too.'

They were heading for a small former fishing village near Hastings, on the Sussex coast. The navigator said it would take them three hours.

Bryan wondered what had really happened to Stuart – surely Juno and Phillip hadn't actually abandoned him? – but he couldn't ask now, and in any case, whatever had transpired, that was one thing at least that was, blessedly, out of his hands, and for someone else's conscience to contend with.

He allowed himself to relax a little, looked out at the busy city.

In the space of a few days he had gone from being an ordinary middle-class parent to a 'fugitive from justice', and now an actual refugee – Sanjay had already been in contact with a leading lawyer in Brussels who was certain they would be granted asylum.

He had lost his home, career, friends … was in the same position as the kinds of people he had devoted so much of his life trying to help. Now he would be on the receiving end. But how would *he* be received? Where would *they* live? How, for that matter, would they earn a living? Would their relationship withstand the strain? Would Ben and Hallie grow to hate them once reality set in – being stranded abroad, having to learn a new language, not having the cash for all those gadgets they loved? Would they ever forgive them?

Bryan woke up. They were pulling into a motorway service station.

'Sweet dreams?' said Phillip.

'I was sleeping.'

'You were.'

'Where are we?'

'About half way.'

'Hurry up, Dad,' said Ben, 'I need the loo.'

'There's a Burger King!' said Hallie. 'Can we, Dad?'

'We can,' said Phillip.

Ben led the way with the others following behind. They spread out, Phillip thinking to pick up some magazines and pop and other trashy stuff for the trip, although Bryan warned him not to overdo it or they'd all get seasick, then they regrouped outside the Burger King.

Juno checked her watch. 'We'd better get takeaways,' she said. 'We're a bit behind schedule.' Meena thought: actually, I'd rather you didn't get takeaways, think about the mess in the car. But then she had to laugh. Despite their ordinary surroundings there was nothing at all ordinary about their circumstances: they were on the run and here she was worrying about tomato ketchup!

They were heading back to the car when she spotted him, behind the wheel of a Ford Mondeo, sitting beside a

CANARIES

woman she didn't recognise. He was on the phone, although looking straight in their direction.

Meena didn't know his name but she recognised his face – she had seen him often enough in the Child Services unit. A police officer. Not a senior one, but a cop nonetheless. And way outside his area.

Somehow Meena managed to carry on toward the car as if nothing had happened. It wasn't until they were all inside, unwrapping their burgers, that she told them. They sat there in silence.

Then Phillip said:

'It could just be a coincidence.'

'It could,' agreed Meena.

'Don't all look around,' said Juno, 'but, Meena, check the mirror. Have they moved yet?' Meena looked. She shook her head.

'Okay,' said Juno. 'Let's pull out. See if they move when we do.'

'Can't we finish our burgers?' said Hallie.

'Not now, darling,' said Phillip.

Meena started the engine and began to drive slowly toward the exit.

'Are they moving too?' asked Juno.

Meena checked the mirror. 'Yes,' she said.

'It's the blue Mondeo, right?' said Juno.

'Yes,' said Meena.

Juno placed her half-eaten burger on the dash and unstrapped her seat belt. An alarm began to ping. Well, folks,' Juno turned around to face them. Bryan noticed her eyes were shining. 'This is where I love you and leave you. Stop, Meena.'

'What?'

She turned toward her. 'Stop. The car, Meena.' Meena braked sharply and the car shuddered to a halt.

'What are you doing Juno?' said Bryan.

'You lot,' said Juno. 'Drive on. First chance you can, get off the motorway, take the back roads.' She began to open the door.

'Juno,' said Phillip, '*no.*'

'Just don't bloody waste this, you hear – drive the hell on. And don't look back.'

'*Juno.*' But Juno was already out of the door. She ducked her head back in.

'Don't worry kids,' she said. 'I've got my steel toe caps!' She slammed the door and began running toward the Mondeo.

38

'*Drive*, just drive!' It was Phillip in her ear. Meena put the car in first and it lurched forward. Hardly a speeding getaway – that would be asking too much – but Meena pulled off while in the rear mirror she could see that Juno had dragged the female cop out of the car, was holding her by her hair as the man came around from the driver's side. Juno swung the screeching woman in front of him before the three of them were on the ground in a tangle of arms and legs.

Meena came on to the motorway but, as Juno had told her, took the first available exit. She pulled into a pub car park, ostensibly to change the navigator so it didn't keep telling them to turn around, but in reality to check what was happening behind her. Hallie had been in hysterics since Juno had jumped out, and Bryan, Phillip and Ben were having trouble comforting her. Meena got out of the car and opened the rear doors.

She told Bryan and Phillip to get out and climbed in, pulling down the seat separating her from Ben and Hallie.

Hallie looked at her desperately: 'Auntie Juno! We left Auntie Juno!'

'We had to, darling.'

'She'll go to prison!'

'She'll be fine. I promise…'

'They're going to catch us, Auntie Meena.'

'Of course they won't. Look – we're getting away.'

'But I don't want dads to go to prison!'

'They won't, I promise you. Come on, come here,' said Meena. Even though Hallie pushed her back, she persevered, and finally took her into her arms.

'It's going to be all right, my darling,' she said. 'I promise you everything's going to be all right.' As she pressed Hallie to her, she looked at the men and the boy, their stricken faces, and she prayed she was right.

Meena took Hallie into the front seat with her and gave her the task of looking out for signs, even though she had adjusted the navigator accordingly. In any case, it seemed to distract her.

They continued down the back roads. It lengthened the journey, but they managed to keep on schedule ... *just*, thank God.

The dark began to draw in. A kind of expectant silence settled upon them. All eyes were drawn to the luminous green blob with its chequered flag – their destination – as it grew larger against the electric blue coastline on the screen.

Hedgerows were interrupted by villages, villages by hedgerows. The few glimpsed shops were closing for the day, the handful of people were wrapped against the cold. Fruit machines flashed in gloomy pubs. TVs glowed in living room windows.

They pulled off the main road and, after a winding drive along a narrow lane, turned onto a wide untarmacked track, bordered by trees.

'There it is,' said Hallie, pointing at the sign caught in the headlights. 'Marina!'

At the end of the track was some kind of wooden house – a boathouse, they realised – then a small, decked, dimly lit jetty lined by modest, family-sized yachts and a few rusty fishing boats. The place seemed deserted. They stopped the car and got out. Nothing, except for the sound of boats bumping against the jetty and, in the air, the smell of the sea.

'Maybe it's not the right place,' said Hallie.

'I knew we should have carried on,' said Ben.

Bryan looked at Phillip, as if to say: what now? Phillip reached out and took his hand. They peered into the darkness together.

A shadow stepped out from behind the boathouse.

'Where's Juno?' she said.

They followed Dawn, silhouetted by their headlights, to the end of the jetty where her boat was moored. 'It's tiny!' said Hallie.

'I'm sure it's big enough,' said Meena, although she did wonder as they began to load the suitcases on board.

She looked up at the starry sky. Did that mean calm weather?

She switched her phone on. There were half-a-dozen missed calls. A couple from work and the rest from Sanjay. She called him, explained what was happening, and what had happened to Juno. He let out a long sigh.

'That's serious,' he said, 'what Juno did. And you're implicated. It'll aggravate the offence. If you're arrested, say nothing, absolutely nothing until I get there, okay?'

'Okay,' said Meena. There was silence.

'But you did well,' he said. 'No matter what happens, you did the right thing. I'm proud of you. So proud.'

Meena passed the phone to Bryan, Phillip and the kids, watched them saying their goodbyes, braced herself as she realised that this was it – they were actually leaving.

'Is everything all right?' asked Bryan.

'Fine,' said Meena.

'I hope you won't get into trouble.'

'That's the advantage of having a lawyer in the family.'

'I'm sorry to have dragged you into this.'

She shook her head. 'Don't be silly.'

Dawn turned on the yacht's motor then leaned out. 'We shouldn't hang about.'

Now it was their turn to say goodbye. They hugged but as they let go, found themselves bathed in grey light. At first Meena thought it was from the cabin of the yacht, but then she realised – headlights were tracking the marina.

Headlights topped by winking blue lights.

'Go,' said Meena. Phillip was already ushering the kids on board. Then he crouched down and began trying to untie a mooring line.

Bryan seemed mesmerised by the approaching police van and just stood there.

'Go,' Meena shoved him toward the yacht. This

seemed to wake him up. He ran over to the other mooring line while Meena set off in the opposite direction – to her car.

39

The rear end of the SUV coming precariously close to the edge of the dock and letting out a battery of warnings, Meena managed to turn it around so it was facing the exit of the marina, and the oncoming police van. She began driving toward it.

In her rear-view mirror, she could see Phillip coming over to help Bryan as the kids stood watching anxiously by the yacht's rail, the contrast with their orange life vests bleaching their already pale faces. She focused on the road – the narrow dirt track – ahead, her car beginning to flood with light from the police van.

It pulled up in front of her. Meena hit the brakes, too, and the pair of vehicles faced-off along the narrow strip in a blaze of headlights. Meena looked across the pair of bonnets at the two police officers – a man and a woman – and they looked back at her, as if unaccustomed to not being permitted to pass. The police officers began talking to each other, then the driver – the man – reached for something and there was the blast of a siren, the blue lights changing from a lazy flash to a rather irritable flicker. Meena kept sitting, bolt upright. She checked the rear mirror. She was too far away to see all the details now, but the yacht didn't appear to have moved. Dawn – yes, it looked like Dawn – was with the two men, crouched by Bryan's mooring line.

Meena pressed the central locking button and her doors let out a reassuring clunk. Then she thought better of it and pressed the button again. As the police van flickered and whooped again, she opened the car door and stepped onto the track. The police officers conferred, then the man opened his own door, looking more perplexed than wary. 'Miss?'

Meena turned to face the marina and, with all her might, hurled the key into the dock.

'Now, what did you do that for?'

The female police officer got out of her side.

'It's come through,' she called. 'It's the one.' The man, raising a hand to shield his eyes from the glare, peered into the darkness. Meena turned around. The yacht was beginning to move off.

'Fuck.' He began to make toward it. But first he would have to get past Meena. There was a comedy moment as he stepped first one way, then another, trying to get around her, and then it clicked that this tiny woman intended to block him. He pressed ahead, holding out a hand to push her aside like a rugby player, but she grabbed hold first of his arm and then, when he shook her off and she fell onto the ground, grabbed his ankles, was half-dragged behind him as he tried to move forward.

'Fuck.' He tried to peel her off. 'For fuck's sake. Sheila!'

Meena felt herself being wrenched backwards, then flung forwards, as the man got free and she was face-first on the dirt. Her arms were yanked behind her, her wrists snapped together with plastic cuffs. She looked up, the female officer pressing a knee into her back, as the man ran along the marina. But the yacht was slipping into the darkness, the family lined along the rail, looking on.

'Come back!' the policeman yelled. 'Come back here, right now!' Then: 'Shit.'

*

The van doors slammed closed. Meena remained lying on the floor as it began to set off. Exhaustion overcame her and, her wrists still secured behind her back, she rested her head flat against the cold, hard rubber surface. She remained like that, listening to the groans of the van, her heartbeat pounding in her ears until finally, as the van reached a smoother surface and began to pick up speed, she realised there was someone else there, too.

Uncertainly, as if at sea, she began to lift herself into a sitting position. She blinked into the gloom, tried to make sense of the shape sat crooked upon the bench.

She got onto her knees, began shuffling toward it.

CANARIES

It was Juno.

Her hands were cuffed behind her back like Meena, and her head was hanging down. She could see now, blood smeared across her jeans, t-shirt.

Meena propelled herself onto the bench beside her.

'Hey,' she said. Juno lifted her head. Her face was ballooned and bloody, one eye closed entirely.

Juno gave her a crooked smile. 'Hey.' She winced with the pain of something.

'Made it?'

'Made it,' said Meena.

Juno rested her head against Meena's shoulder. The van rumbled on.

CANARIES

The airport seemed almost deserted, as if they had arrived at the end of the world, which, in a way, they had. Certainly after Frankfurt (Meena had refused to connect at Heathrow, even though it was cheaper) it seemed like an oasis of calm, which she supposed was the whole point. This was a place of escape, one way or another.

They had no problems getting through with their Canadian passports and were in the arrivals hall within half an hour. They stood uncertainly as the glass doors slid behind them and they searched the waiting faces. Then he was standing there.

'Auntie Meena?' She looked up. It was him, she realised now – Ben. She stopped herself from saying it (how he had grown) and instead gave him a hug. She came up to his chest. Sanjay did the same, although Aisha, now fourteen, hung back and gave him a sort of bashful wave.

'Look at you,' said Meena. 'Like a real Norwegian.' And it was true, there was something indefinably Scandinavian about Ben, despite being neither blond nor blue-eyed. He had filled outwards as well as upwards and with his dark bristles and wild hair he was ... well-built, rugged, outdoorsy. No wonder Aisha was blushing.

'The others are on the ferry up from Trondheim,' said Ben, taking Aisha's suitcase. 'Except Hallie – she's getting the train from Oslo. Arrives tomorrow.'

'How are her studies going?'

'Studies?' Ben grinned. 'I suppose she must.' They stepped through one set of double doors and then another into the brittle, breath-catching cold of the Norwegian winter. Ben chuckled. 'I guess you must be used to this?'

'Next year, the Caribbean,' said Sanjay.

'Then we'll come to you,' said Ben.

'But you're happy here?' said Meena. 'Bryan told me you couldn't get enough of it.'

'The nature, Auntie,' he said – it was as if they had

only been apart ten weeks, not years, Meena thought, 'the night sky.' She followed the sweep of his arm across the twinkling constellations, the glittering dust of galaxies.

'That's something you don't get in Toronto,' said Sanjay. 'Light pollution.'

'It's beautiful,' said Aisha. Ben grinned:

'Listen to you with your American accent.'

'*Canadian.*'

They began loading their luggage into the car. 'Did you find the language difficult?' asked Meena.

Ben shook his head. 'Not really. When we came here, the kids were,' he shrugged, 'really nice. And all my degree stuff was in English anyway. Work too – it's an international project.'

'Bit nippy this time of the year, though,' said Sanjay. 'Forestry.'

Ben grinned. 'This is the holiday period – if we're not in the office, or somewhere nice and warm, we're chasing the lights.'

As Ben put the car into Drive, Meena placed her hand upon his. 'It's so nice of you to have us, Ben. I hope you haven't got somewhere else you'd rather be.'

'Are you joking?' said Ben. 'It's my pleasure.'

*

They were standing in the arrivals area at the port the next day during the short time between sunrise and sunset, watching the people come off the ferry.

Meena spotted Bryan soon enough, looming above the others, although she probably wouldn't have if she hadn't got used to seeing that big bushy grey beard of his every time they Zoomed, but wrapped up in their bright new winter wear, the rest of them looked much the same as any of the other passengers – it was only at the last minute she realised *here* were Juno and Diane, for example, in their lime green and orange ski suits. Juno threw her arms around her. 'You didn't recognise me!' she said. 'Surely I haven't aged that much!'

CANARIES

And here was Phillip, whose once dark hair *had* turned grey and been shorn short, hugging Sanjay. But Meena wasn't going to say anything – what with Sanj's belly and her, well her own, she could hardly speak. 'It's the context,' she said. 'The clothes!' She was engulfed by Bryan's bulk, then a space opened up in front of her – there were a couple she didn't recognise.

'This is John Turner,' said Bryan. The bald man grinned, held out his hand. 'And Patricia.' His wife did likewise.

'It's getting dark already!' said Patricia.

'That's right,' said Ben. 'An hour if we're lucky this time of year, but before it was even worse – full on 24 hours.'

'How do you cope?' said John.

'Look forward to the summer and 24-hour sunshine!'

'Is it true what they say about the suicides?' asked Patricia.

'Myth,' said Ben. 'Made up by the Americans when people mentioned Scandinavian social democracy – they said, ah, but they all kill themselves in those long winters. Complete fiction.'

'No surprise there, then,' said John.

'What?' said Bryan. 'Criticising your favourite nation, John?'

'Nice place to go on holiday,' said John. 'Happy to leave it at that.'

Ben had borrowed one of the Centre's monster SUVs to carry everyone, and he punched in the destination. The car pulled off on its own, the steering wheel in front of Ben guiding itself out of the port car park and onto the main road. Ben turned around, looking a bit embarrassed. 'They insist we use self-drive if we take the car for non-official use. Trouble is, in the past people have gone a bit crazy off-road and ended up wrecking them or whatever. This way at least they know their property will stay in one piece.'

'Very sensible,' said Patricia. 'It's nice of them to let you use it.'

'Yeah,' said Ben, echoing the old teenage Ben, Meena thought. 'I suppose.' He looked at Juno. 'No luck, then?'

She shook her head. 'I'm sorry, love, did my best.' Ben nodded.

'What's that?' said Bryan.

'I thought it would be nice ...' Ben looked at Juno. 'Well, I didn't think he would be able to come or anything, but I thought it wouldn't do any harm asking him – *Stuart* – if we could find him.'

'I'm sorry,' said Juno. 'I went to the flat, but there was no trace. Asked about ... but it was a long time ago. And of course, we didn't even have his surname.'

Phillip was shaking his head. 'Stuart ... You wanted to invite Stuart, Ben?'

'I don't know,' said Ben, looking uncomfortable. 'I just thought it would be nice. If only to thank him. To tell him how well we're doing.'

'Come here,' Phillip reached over the seat and gave him a hug. 'My boy,' he said. 'My good boy.' The car, meanwhile, carried on smoothly through Tromsø's snow-crusted streets.

The hotel was far enough into the countryside to eliminate even the minimal light pollution from the city and although it was only three in the afternoon, it might as well have been midnight. Ben explained that the northern lights could be an elusive phenomenon, moving from place to place, time to time, but with luck they should see them at some point during their visit.

'Don't worry,' said Meena. 'We're here to see you, that's all that matters.'

'It's just wonderful we're all together,' said Bryan. 'Finally.' He looked around the group gathered by the huge log fire in the reception. He raised his glass.

'Skål!' he said.

'Skål!'

CANARIES

As Bryan was emptying the remains of the second bottle of Prosecco into Patricia's glass, he noticed movement around them, people drifting toward the hotel entrance, stopping to pull on their jackets and snowshoes. He heard someone say: 'Don't forget your camera.' He looked at Ben.

His son wandered over to the windows and returned, grinning.

They followed Ben between the pines and up the icy slope – ahead of them, over the crest, through the trees, was a kind of distant flicker like a laser show. As the slope became steeper and more slippery, Bryan took Phillip's hand, Phillip took Juno's and Juno Diane's. The Turners, Meena, Sanjay and Aisha were bunched behind, variously holding onto each other, slipping, sliding and, in the case of the Turners, who had been imbibing, rather than the Husseins, who had not, giggling tipsily. They finally joined the others on the crest where, above and below them, the universe was washed by silent emerald and violet waves.

There may not be a God, thought Bryan, but standing here ant-like among the trees – and he could now see the tiny shapes of dozens of other people dwarfed by the pines, let alone the vastness of the Northern Lights – then Man certainly amounts to very little in this scheme of things. He felt a sudden rush of fear, but then looked at Ben and Phillip together, gazing upwards, their faces full of joy and wonder. No, there may not be a God, but Bryan undoubtedly felt blessed.

Meena held onto Aisha while Sanjay stood behind her, fiddling with his camera. 'Are you getting this, Dad?' said Aisha.

'Give me a chance.'

Meena began to recite a prayer. Her mouth moved, although no words came out. It was a prayer to infinity – to infinite wonder, this magnificent gift of Creation. In those wavering lights, against that endless backdrop, Meena Hussain was overcome by the majesty of the universal soul.

Phillip thought, as he often found himself doing, of Bill. I wish you were here, old friend, he thought, you'd love this – you might even get a column out of it – and Juno was thinking, and it surprised her because she didn't dwell upon it much, about what she had actually found out about Stuart. But that was best left unsaid – it wouldn't do Ben any good to know the truth. Still, this one's for you, Stu, she thought, even though I barely knew you. She placed her arm around Diane, who placed hers around Patricia Turner, who supressed her initial surprise and put her arm around her husband, who looked along the line and grinned. He reached out for Bryan, who reached out for Phillip, and so on. Arm-in-arm, brothers-, and sisters-in-arms, the friends gazed at the Northern Lights.

In a little clearing not far removed from their own, Nathan Drake, Housing Adviser to London's Mayor, taking a well-earned break from his exhausting schedule, removed the phone from in front of his face. It was then he saw them standing there, their shining, smiling faces illuminated by almost-Christmas colours. At first he could barely believe his eyes. And then he stepped back into the dark.

AFTERWORD

Canaries was not published overnight. It was completed before the US Supreme Court ruled against Roe v Wade, ending the constitutional right of American women to abortion, and the government of my home country Italy banned gay adoption and removed non-biological parents from birth certificates. I did not foresee either when I set out to write *Canaries*. Other developments, including what were widely reported as 'the English riots' of 2024, and the precipitous decline of Britain's public health service, also overtook publication, but such are the risks of speculative fiction.

Writing in 2025, my publisher suggested I cite even more recent global developments, but *Canaries* was never really about predicting the future, rather it set out to provide a warning from the past, inspired as it was by my own experience as one of the 'losers' of Britain's referendum on membership of the European Union: a Briton living in Italy, I was one of millions shocked to realise that the foundations upon which I had constructed my life were built upon sand. A right I had literally grown up with and heretofore considered 'inalienable' vanished overnight. *Canaries* is not a story 'about' Brexit, but it would not exist without it.

It couldn't happen here?

The British Parliament wields extraordinary power, cleaving more jealously to its authority than almost any other legislature in the world. The reference to *ex post facto* law, its function and practice in the UK, is correct.

Members of Parliament are elected according to a system in which parties compete in each of the UK's 650 constituencies in a 'winner takes all' contest, which tends to guarantee the dominance of the established political order.

According to the BBC, in the 2024 general election, Reform – a party that would not look out of place in the coalition government formed in Bryan and Phillip's Britain – won roughly four million votes, which translated into a 14% share of the total votes cast in the election, but only 1% of all the seats in the House of Commons. The Liberal Democrats won 12% of total votes cast and 11% of seats in Parliament. Labour won 34% of total votes cast, but about 64% of the 650 seats.

Although the first-past-the-post system has existed for as long as anyone can remember, it is increasingly coming under question: when the Liberal Democrats held the balance of power following the 2010 election, they forced a referendum on electoral reform which they lost, although this may have had as much to do with the unpopularity of the Lib Dems as the merits of their proposal.

In 2014 no party held an absolute majority in Parliament – the Conservatives were kept in power thanks to an alliance with Northern Ireland's Democratic Unionist Party, fervently homophobic evangelical Christians who campaigned against gay marriage ('Peter will not marry Paul in Northern Ireland'), abortion, and for the return of the death penalty, along with being fiercely anti-Catholic.

But what if the DUP had been a national rather than a regional party? Certainly, no religious group can be expected to vote as a bloc, but in 2017, *The Spectator* magazine published an article by the Centre for Theology & Community exploring the possibility of Britain's two million evangelicals doing just that.

As democracy is placed under increasing strain, the electoral system that served to produce decades of stable government risks becoming a pressure cooker. It is not for this author to prescribe solutions, but I was struck by the almost indefinable quality (although we know it when we see it) that united the supporters of Bryan and his family, regardless of their identity – what George Orwell termed 'common decency'. It is a typically modest, undemonstrative term, one that Orwell, writing in his essay *The Lion and The Unicorn*, said distinguished many ordinary people from those who had thrown in their lot with the prevailing credo. In a certain sense, it seems like the antithesis of modern times, but I believe it is overdue rediscovery – one day it may be all that stands between us and the knock at the door.

ACKNOWLEDGEMENTS

My agent Bill Goodall first submitted *Canaries* around 2020, and after the first flurry of rejections, I worked with him to rejig it, sadly to no avail. Editors were kind but typically responded that readers were tired of politics and they would struggle to sell it. In the meantime, my debut novel – *A Quiet Death in Italy* – had been published as Tom Benjamin (I chose the pseudonym Alex Makepeace solely to avoid confounding readers of different genres) and I ran *Canaries* past colleagues in my D20 group of authors. They came back to me with enthusiasm and useful suggestions, so in addition to Bill, I would also like to thank Trevor Wood, Nikki Smith, Victoria Dowd, and Philippa East.

By now we were in the depths of Covid and I had a sequel to *A Quiet Death* to write, so while I concentrated on *The Hunting Season* and others, I put *Canaries* on the back burner. But I never forgot it because I was convinced it had an enduring message that would continue to capture the imagination of readers. I am therefore tremendously grateful to Peter Buck, Editorial Director at Elsewhen Press, for sharing this vision. It has been a pleasure to work with him, and a huge thanks to editor Sofia.

I would also like to thank my wife Lea for tolerating my obsession with this book (or perhaps by now she has just learned how to feign interest) and other 'Beta' readers including Nick Lawrence, Nino Giuffrida, and Nick Cobban (who I only wish had lived to see it published). It is dedicated to Prue Crane, who 'read it in one session' and hasn't stopped asking me about it since.

Alex Makepeace, Bologna, 2025

Elsewhen Press
delivering outstanding new talents in speculative fiction

Visit the Elsewhen Press website at elsewhen.press for the latest information on all of our titles, authors and events; to read our blog; find out where to buy our books and ebooks; or to place an order.

Sign up for the Elsewhen Press InFlight Newsletter at elsewhen.press/newsletter

Other Elsewhen Press titles you might like

TOMORROW WAS BEAUTIFUL ONCE

AMY ORRELL

Jack can only choose one future…

2150 – time travel has accelerated climate change and set humanity on the brink of destruction. As a Person of Mixed Era Origin with the ability to recall parallel versions of time, British historian, Jack Elliot, seems the perfect candidate to travel to the past and prevent the advent of time travel.

The catch? Success means Jack will cease to exist.

Critically injured when he arrives in the past, Jack's life is saved by Maddie, a second-generation immigrant and resistance fighter, who mistakenly believes he's connected to the disappearance of her sister, Suraya.

Jack's denial soon unravels with the discovery that Suraya can lead him to his father – the man who robbed him of his mother – and that they are all searching for the inventor of time technology.

What begins as a fragile alliance soon puts their feelings and their missions to the test. Jack's won't be the only life affected by his sacrifice, but does he have the right to decide who should live and who should die – and will it be worth it for the futures he and Maddie hope to create?

ISBN: 9781915304759 (epub, kindle) / 9781915304650 (396pp paperback)

Visit bit.ly/TomorrowWasBeautifulOnce

Other Elsewhen Press titles you might like

RINK
Chris Matravers

The world is a nursery in which selves mature after multiple incarnations

What if some souls are not bound to a body but can exist in a 'between place' for years after death before 'shifting' into a new body.

Most people live as ephemeral humans, 'Phems', oblivious of any previous life. But a few become 'Rinks': fully aware of previous incarnations as selves of different genders and race and in diverse civilisations. Continuously re-incarnating they are unaware that eventually they could mature enough to evolve onto another plane of existence. Or, at least, that is what is supposed to happen but renegade Rinks are failing to mature. Running rampant as crime and war lords, they are intent on exploiting the Phems.

When Jay re-incarnates in London in 2026, he is shocked by their activities. He has endured too many lives: he's seen and done everything. Previously he's searched for a way to stop the seemingly endless cycle of life and death but now he finds himself compelled to try to restore order and so Jay enlists the help of like-minded Rinks to defeat the renegades.

But what will he do when he's forced to choose between the love of his life, and death…

ISBN: 9781915304735 (epub, kindle) / 9781915304636 (280pp paperback)

Visit bit.ly/Rink-Matravers

ABOUT ALEX MAKEPEACE

Alex Makepeace was raised in London and began his career as a journalist before moving into international aid and public health, where he learned that what might seem like a catastrophe to some is just another day at the office for others. That got him thinking, and that got him writing. He also publishes Italy-set fiction as Tom Benjamin.